welcome
to the
abyss

Steve Nahaj

ISBN-13: 978-0-692-38329-2
ISBN-10: 0692383298

For anyone who's been.

winter

1

I KISSED HER GOODBYE and gave her a big hug.

Somehow I knew it would be the last.

Five years sealed with a kiss and off I went into LAX, ready to blaze across the country to Maryland where I would meet with family and be whisked away for bottles of beer and good times. Francine just smiled and I tried not to look back as I turned toward the cold terminal.

I swallowed hard and the lump eventually disappeared.

All the way to the gate her smile faded.

I was exhausted. The past year had been tumultuous, filled with busy phone calls and pleading for money—funding for a feature film. Left without success, I had already begun to sink into depression, spending nearly twenty grand in investment with little bite on the other end. This frustration bled into my relationship with Francine, a charming beauty with a dangerous smile. She beamed with energy and yet I had been draining it from her quip by quip. When the money stopped flowing, I stopped caring.

So there it began in the December sky, my eventual slip into the period of my life I call the Abyss—a term that I would define and redefine over the coming months. All I knew at the time was that I generally felt like shit.

Next to me on the plane sat two twentysomethings about my age. One named Bobby who rocked his head to techno beats, eyes closed, lost in a neon dream. Beside Bobby sat a seductive blond who also happened to be a bookworm.

"What's your name, dude?" asked Bobby.

"Johan."

"Ah, rad name! You're the only Johan I've ever met."

"I'm honored."

He noticed my lusting for the bookworm and offered to switch seats.

"Get her number, man."

Normally I wouldn't—I'm loyal—but something tapped me on the shoulder: She's gorgeous. Go for it. I certainly tried and not much came of it. She was younger than I thought, fresh from college and bashful. I don't remember why she was living in LA—working for a producer I believe. Anyhow, I turned back to Bobby who was jabbing credit cards at the stewardess, ordering whiskey shooters.

"I manage a night club," he said. "Been up all night. Might as well keep at it!"

We drank four of them each and by the time the plane landed I was feeling high and mighty. In the terminal I saw the blond across the carousel, staring at me with a kind of longing. I wanted her badly but only waved as I walked away. This sense of emptiness would haunt me for the next year, infecting my heart with eyelashes and soft skin.

—

THE NEXT FEW DAYS were relaxing and I made sure to update Francine on the trip and musings from my life, which was routine for us to do. She had just touched down in New Orleans to spend time with family. I imagined her enjoying a humid holiday with barbecues and flip-flops—something foreign to our frigid east coast winters. And it was certainly a cold night when I journeyed into the local pub—Moonshine Tavern—with my younger sister, Kelsey, who just arrived from Virginia. She was my only sibling, and we had grown estranged. The only relative who understood my anxieties and restlessness. And the immediate cure was directly in front of us: two glasses of whiskey and whatever.

Scanning the room, I saw no one familiar.

We planned to meet Jarrett Jones, a mischievous black guy with a surplus of smiles. He was quite the player and always spoke about women as some sort of game. Sure enough Jarrett showed along with two of Kelsey's friends, Morgan and Lynette. Pale, short-haired girls with too much eye makeup contrasting their milky complexions.

We stayed at the bar long enough to generate a good buzz and then everyone wanted to hit the next dive. I was tired and mainly searching for women. I told myself to stop, but could only think of the girl from the plane. 'Maybe there's another like her. Someone else. Something more. Something better.'

Yes, there had to be.

What about your beloved Francine?
But I couldn't picture her face.

And then I saw the one I had been waiting for.

She parted the drunks with the presence of a queen and our eyes met for a very slow second. Dressed in all black, a light-skinned black woman with short hair that cut across her face like the end of the world. Curves, confidence, gravity.

I lost her somewhere in the mass of bodies.

"C'mon man, ain't no dimes in here," Jarrett interrupted, ushering me out the door.

We left, cruising a long stretch of highway to a pub with a much better beer and supposedly female selection. Kelsey drove. Jarrett was hyper, bouncing to bass and laughing at everything. Morgan was wild and couldn't stop repeating the word ratchet.

"You're all *crazy!*" Kelsey shouted.

"You see any broads at Moonshine, Johan?" asked Jarrett.

"One in particular," I said.

"Light-skinned? Like me, but lighter?"

"Yep."

"Look like she used to be a stoner?"

"I guess."

"Yeahhhh man, she's dope. Got a kid though."

Normally I'd be running for the hills upon hearing this, but surprisingly I didn't care. Details didn't concern me. I had been infected with the longing, the seeking. I didn't want to know anything besides my own fantasy.

Lo and behold there were tables of girls at the next bar—blond-haired county girls chatting over sweet cocktails. Jarrett walked a bee line towards them. I went to the bar for a drink, antsy and daydreaming. Swirling cubes.

Reality seemed a joke, I thought. One big ongoing performance with a permanently opened curtain. Everyone running around to the next thing, caught up in the running as I'd been over the past year, and now that I had stopped I saw the show for what it was.

Before long, Jarrett finished flirting and Kelsey and Morgan were anxious to leave. It was nearly two in the morning and I didn't think there was much chance of my mystery woman still being at Moonshine; but we stopped in anyway for a final drink.

Upon entering I was pleasantly surprised to see that she was still there, sitting with her sister, a tall chick with an unruly afro and sprawling tribal tattoo below her neck. "People think it's chest hair," she would come to tell me.

I was double-fisting beers, fumbling around when I approached my crush.

"Do I know you?" I asked.

"Don't think so."

But we had attended the same high school. I spent a couple of minutes jogging her memory, describing old habits.

"Wanna dance?"

I would later learn that she hates to dance but clearly made an exception that night, tearing up the floor of the small town bar. I managed to get her number and we agreed to rendezvous at a later time.

I liked her name.

I stared at it on my phone.

Sage.

—

THE REST OF THE WEEK was spent with Kelsey and my father, which is when I first noticed a growing trend of depression in my family. When we weren't drinking, we were somber and negative and nothing was right. We sat around the sad living room watching the sad TV, hoping for a message that would lift us from the sad couches.

My eyes jumped from person to person.

There was Kelsey typing away, completing the online college courses she hated.

And Dad, awash in flickering fiction.

And next to everyone was Bella, my niece, staring back at me with her squinty six-year-old eyes.

"What are you looking at, Uncle Johan?"

The realization that I was no different started to eat away at my soul, further nudging me toward the Abyss.

—

JUST BEFORE CHRISTMAS I agreed to meet Sage for dinner and drinks—a date. I had to know how it felt to be with someone else.

Was Francine the one?

I purchased an engagement ring earlier in the year but couldn't muster the courage to propose.

And so Sage and I sat on our stools at the bar, chatting about this and that. She told me about her son and how she hadn't been in a relationship in years and wasn't prone to starting them. But there we were, sifting through small talk to find commonalities, creating bonds and smiling at each other.

She was beautiful.

But more than that, I felt at peace with her.

I excused myself to use the bathroom and, nearly wasted, stumbled upon a urinal and pissed all over my underwear. Apparently I wasn't holding my dick properly—or wasn't holding it at all—and that was that. I trashed them and went commando for the rest of the night.

We left the bar and I started to feel uncomfortable about the whole ordeal, so I rushed Sage back to her car and left her without a kiss, certain it would be the last time I saw her. On the way home I parked behind the old brick school building I attended as a child and sat there.

Why was I being unfair to Francine?

Why was I resisting Sage?

It's as though I wanted and denied them both at the same time. None of it made any sense. I went home to put on a fresh pair of boxers and let my dreams do the dirty work.

—

A FEW DAYS LATER I met Sage at Moonshine again and played darts with her tall, tattooed sister who I learned was a philosophy major. She spoke with a dry haughtiness I could only expect, and I tried to humor her, suggesting that she take up meditation and call it a day.

Sage and I snuck outside for cigarettes, huddled on cold benches, learning more about one another. I began to see that the Abyss was familiar territory between us. She spoke in low tones, uncertain, with that beautiful aura of hers that I wanted to bolster because I knew she was capable of so much more. I sat spewing my guts out about film and music and travel, and Sage just nodded her head. A powerful woman indeed, but I shuddered at her resistance. I wanted to tell her I loved her simply because I didn't think she heard it enough.

"So, just to let you know," I started, "I'll be leaving town tomorrow for Pittsburgh to see my mother."

"When will I see you again?" she asked.

It was the beginning of many questions like this.

"When I return next week, of course."

Inches away, her arms around me, I knew what I had to do.

I wanted to end everything right there, make a clean exit—I hadn't done much damage yet. But we kissed again and I walked away tasting her lips.

2

THE APPALACHIANS WERE a winter wonderland and my brain was a blizzard, warmed only by Mom's home-cooked food and the innocence of Bella. It was an unusually warm winter, but there was enough powder for sledding and huddling by the fire with hot chocolate.

My mother's house was my retreat, a sanctuary from life's impending questions, a solid home with solid foundation. Brick and oak. Decked with country knick-knacks; abundant with aromas.

And of course there was lasagna and we all sat around the table discussing our lives—stories from the past year. This was the small talk and the heavy talk would come later after cocktails.

My mother couldn't sit still. She got up every few minutes to run to the oven or refrigerator or sink, shooing me away when I tried to help. A resilient woman who had weathered a slew of bad relationships, I witnessed her struggle to find *the one* following the divorce of my parents as a child. The abusive men she attracted over and over—men who were no good—yet she braved the bastards with a hopeful heart.

"I just want everyone to be happy."

—

FAMILY AND FESTIVITIES. But all I could think about was Sage—getting back to her and continuing our affair. One night Francine called in a bitter state of mind, blabbering about her pregnant friends, picking a fight.

"Do they make you jealous?" I blurted.

"A little," she said.

"Don't you think we'll have a kid some day?"

"Not at the rate we're going."

It was ammo for argument, exactly what I was looking for. A reason to push for a split. We bitched for a half hour and I mentioned breaking up, anxious to sever the ties and pursue sweet Sage. Francine backed off but I was persistent. The next day I would resurrect the topic and continue pushing away.

It was endless drama.

One afternoon I came across a photo of us on the mantle and thought it might start fading backwards like a possessed Polaroid.

My mother had little to say about the situation.

"Follow your heart."

Yeah, good luck.

But I loved my mother and the comfort she provided. I always felt her advice more than I heard it. Everything was simple and in your heart—anything and everything you ever wanted to do or know about life. Somehow she couldn't help me now.

—

ON A THURSDAY, Kelsey and I went to visit my grandfather at a local retirement home. Despite his good physical health, our once jovial "Pap-Pap" had become afflicted with debilitating Alzheimer's.

The place was a somber sanitarium, chock-full of shriveled faces hooked to machines, gazing up as though I were some sort of god or death himself, there to finally set them free. They sat and blinked. Most were beyond ninety and my grandfather looked especially fit and handsome for his age, but had to exist in this cage due to his ailing memory. I thought of pictures I'd seen of him when he was younger—one in particular where he was lying on a grassy knoll near an air force base; a candid photo where he stared off into space. It was boggling to compare the images of now and then.

Yet I knew the memory problems weren't the start of his withdrawal from life. When my grandmother died fifteen years earlier, he crumbled. Ceased working, slept all day. It was a startling transformation and I wondered about the nature of human relationships and the importance of our strength as individuals. Who would I become without Francine? Who was I before? I couldn't remember just as my grandfather couldn't.

And so I just watched him, a stranger I once knew, staring up at me and smiling the uncertain smile. Breathing machines. Jeopardy. Spoons clinking in the kitchen.

—

DAYS PASSED.

Bottles of beer and delectable dinners. Nervous laughter and the portly beagle called Tootsie—child to my mother and stepdad, Arthur.

Art had lost hair and mobility since he first met Mom, but his eyes glowed increasingly vibrant. He had lived one hell of a life. From Oklahoma farms to airplanes caught in hurricanes, years spent overseas, political involvements, and finally his work as a lawyer. Three bachelor degrees and a doctorate hung framed in the basement, which appeared to be a shrine to himself. Now, tired of the hustle, he'd resigned to reading, napping, and watching Fox News.

Mom's rhythm clashed with his.

Brimful of energy, she'd wake up at five in the morning to cut grass—the same lawn she'd cut days prior. If she wasn't cutting grass, she'd bake. She'd repaint a room or create her own version of a board game. She needed outlets and found them in her own ways.

Art shook his head while my mother ran circles around him. "It's exhausting just watching her," he'd often say, lighting or stamping out a cigarette.

—

IN THE WEE HOURS of the night after Art went to bed, Mom, Kelsey and I sat around talking. I spoke of Francine and

Sage—the dilemma between new and old love. I was angry, thinking of all the things I hated about Francine.

"She won't exercise! She's gained weight and I didn't want to tell her, so I bought us a pass to the gym, yet she won't go unless I do! She won't even read the nutrition labels on the food she buys. I can't do it."

For months, surely I bickered with Francine, pining for argument material. Mostly it was about the small stuff, and in one case I remember complaining about her breath, sarcastically suggesting mouthwash.

The whole thing was brutal.

We had been through a torturous summer living in an old apartment, burning in LA heat waves, fighting over a portable air conditioner. Francine ran a small pie-baking business, heating up the hundred-degree apartment while I sat in my bedroom making calls to marketing departments, attempting to secure funding for my film. It was lousy. I despised the drudgery of churning profit from my art and despised myself for it. All I wanted to do was write. I had lost touch with creativity, and my compassion fell by the wayside.

And so I described all this to my family as they told me about their trials. Kelsey was toggling between two lovers named Chad, and explained how she couldn't decide who she wanted to be with more. If nothing else, it was because of this shared dilemma that she and I connected more than ever.

My mother sat and nodded, and occasionally ran to her bedroom, returning with a photo album. She had closets full of albums, and thousands of stories to describe them.

"Here's the time we went to the water park," she said, pointing at a picture. "Shortly after I broke up with Darren. You remember dysfunctional Darren? Oh, but he had his good moments. And look at those big ice cream cones! How did you ever eat all that?"

—

New Year's Eve I was back in Maryland ready to celebrate. Jarrett was waiting at Moonshine and I hoped Sage was, too. I was still fighting with Francine on a daily basis and wanted nothing more than to drink it all away.

I was happy to see my favorite bartender, Lorenzo, smiling at me, already pouring Jack into a highball.

"On the house," he said, walking away.

I stood there toasting Kelsey and Jarrett and looking for Sage. And she appeared as always, parting the crowds with her queen-like presence.

Look at her go! I thought.

The drinks kept coming, and I kept sweating and dancing and shouting. Francine kept texting and I hardly felt the vibration tickle my thigh. Jarrett watched me and Sage from across the bar and raised his glass in approval.

Eventually, Sage and I made our way back to her apartment and I followed her hips into the bedroom. In the moonlight I watched her step backwards toward the bed, beckoning with her finger—"Come here."

And I fell into her as I fell into the Abyss, drunk and wrapped in her body. It was clear there was no turning back. This would be more than an innocent lip-locking; a mere meeting of minds or connection of kindred spirits. We stripped and I kissed her all over, delirious with passion. I wanted to carry her off to a distant land and never return, and for the night it was so. Our king-sized island.

Then she stopped me.
"We can't. Not tonight."

The next morning I awoke to a clawing at my arms—Sage's two dogs. Abnormally large puppies that hopped onto the bed and scratched the hell out of me. Six o'clock and they were relentless. Months earlier she found the sibling shepherds at a shelter and decided it was a good idea to raise both of them in her humble apartment. I didn't understand it, but loved them as much as I loved everything else. I hugged 'em and took 'em for walks. We sauntered along a snow-covered beach and watched the rascals dig holes and roll around in the frigid wonderland. The beach was magnificent in winter. My boots crunched and carved prints, and I thought about the vastness of the ocean and all the horizons yet unexplored in my life. What have I wrought; what direction was I to turn now? Everything was both beautiful and uncertain, and I thought to myself on the newest day of the year, 'Maybe that's the nature of life.'

—

I SAT IN MY CAR for hours.

The night weighed on my conscience and so I called a woman I'd been working with—my career coach, Natalie. She helped with my professional endeavors and occasionally acted as a therapist even though she repeatedly proclaimed "I am *not* a therapist!"

Ah well. I needed one.

I confessed as I would to a priest all that I had done and felt. And the phone went silent, as Natalie also worked with Francine and cared deeply for us both.

"You have to reside in integrity with her," she finally said.

No. I couldn't tell Francine what I had done. A wave of guilt came rushing over me. I wanted out. Wanted to end it with without saying anything. Just end it and she'll never have to know.

3

"DID YOU SHUCK THE RUCK?" asked Jarrett.

I had no clue what he was talking about. I assumed it had something to do with sex and Sage.

"No, dude. No."

I was still drunk.

Jarrett had slept at my father's house, too hammered to drive after the celebrating, and now at eight a.m. wanted to keep drinking, shoving beers into my hand and egging me on. As I'd come to learn, Jarrett was constantly seeking entertainment and I *was* his entertainment. Kelsey. Anyone past their limit.

Our constant audience, he'd hang around our house all day, long after we sobered up. Watching movies, playing video games—it was endless. I'd take a shower, come out, and he was still there on the couch waiting for the next thing. O aren't we all though? Jarrett was no different. I went to bed and he eventually left. I dreamt of distant lands.

—

BUT I SHOWED UP at that bar—good ol' Moonshine—time and time again. Cold glasses poured by the hand of Lorenzo, the smiling Cuban bartender that could charm the world to its knees. And the liquid coating my esophagus, trickling its way to my stomach, merging with my blood and spirit and screaming its way into my soul—and oh man what nights!

Nights when I'd walk outside with Sage into a wall of chilly air and blaze cigarettes and huddle together and kiss and smile and gaze and live moments as if they were gemstones never to wither. At least not for a very, very long time.

No, this seemed pure as crystal, this love. A fusion of kindred spirits. I hugged her and smelled her neck and body, and everything entered my nose, went straight to my brain and I thought 'This is it, I can't leave.' I loathed my hometown for being my hometown, and I'll be damned if Sage hadn't given me an exceptional reason to stay.

Sure enough, one night after plenty of wine and movie-watching in Sage's vortex of a bed, we got to making out and more than making out, and I found myself lost between worlds in the sheets of a better existence.

I'd never met a more passionate woman.

She dug her nails into my arms, clawed my back.

Her skin was soft and I wanted to dissolve straight into it. To savor the feeling of the moment and forever remain in our lotus land of floral fabrics and Blu-ray glow.

—

IN THE MORNING we had breakfast at the local diner.

It was foggy outside and people were slumped in their Sunday seats and all I could think about was the night and days to come. It seemed that at the greatest pinnacles of life the horizons receded as quickly as they'd arrived. The waitress approached with a steaming steel pot and affirmed my sentiments by rushing off.

Sage just sat there, dark eyes questioning me as I reached across the table and held her hand.

"Like your coffee black?" she asked.

"Certainly do."

I felt as though I'd never be able to leave her. I couldn't bring myself to tell her that I wasn't planning on staying. I wanted to prolong the moments; pretend that I was ready to quit the whole seeking-and-voyaging lifestyle I'd been living. She was a golden goddess with her golden pancakes and sweet smile.

I was hungover and nauseous.

It was the best breakfast I'd ever had.

—

FRANCINE WAS WAITING back in LA.

At this point we had broken up over the phone, but proper closure was necessary to move forward, and besides, I had an apartment full of belongings to recover.

Before taking flight, Sage and I made final plans to meet in New York. There, we would hang out with my old pal Ricky Spiegel, a newly-minted New Yorker who had been working in the film industry for quite some time.

The night I arrived in the big gray city, I met Ricky at a warehouse where he was working on a production. He invited me on set and allowed me to sit in the director's chair.

I fell asleep in it.

—

AS PLANNED, I met up with Sage at Penn Station in the morning, and as always she parted the pedestrians with her queen-like presence. I adored her. She was wearing all black with her suitcase in hand, weary from traveling. I hugged her and smelled her coat. I never thought I would leave her, and knew that if I did I would come back and hug her the same. We checked into our hotel and watched TV for hours, cuddling and joking and doing nothing.

Afterwards we hit the streets to meet up with Ricky, and so began one of the greatest nights of my life—wandering the city corridors, the best of the bars Ricky had discovered. The hippest of enclaves and slickest of safe havens for those with spiritual bones.

Sage and I held hands. She noticed how cold mine were.

"Cold hands, warm heart!" Ricky chimed.

I looked at Sage. "And warm hands?"

"Don't even!"

We laughed and kept walking.

One bar resembled a speakeasy and we had to be put on a waiting list. Upon entering, our coats and jackets were taken and we were directed to a curtained off area like veritable VIPs. Following a round of specialty cocktails we returned to the streets, smoking our way down alleys and into Brooklyn-bound cabs. Inside the next pub: a long-haired Japanese pianist sweating over hard white keys, playing his heart out as we listened and bobbed our heads—loving our youth and barely worrying if it would ever end.

And it was one hell of a night, save for an argument in the cab back to the hotel where I spewed my guts to Sage about all that I wanted from life. She challenged me. Something about "big dreams" and "gotta be realistic." I was drunk and fired back about her being realistically negative.

The bickering continued into the hotel room and we tried to screw it all away, but alas the mood wasn't right and she pushed me off of her. I laid there and rubbed her back and told her that regardless of what happened I wanted her to know that she was beautiful. It was a tearful moment and I somehow knew that we wouldn't last and that I had to tell her something that would.

—

WE WERE LOOKING for a psychic.

I don't remember how Sage and I came up with the idea, but we both felt a soulful connection and sought a semblance of clarity in strange times. Lying in bed earlier that morning, we surfed the internet seeking our great guru. A bistro appeared in the listings and we mused at the unlikely combination—"Vicky's Vietnamese Sandwiches & Psychic Services."

We finally began walking with a place in mind only to get sidetracked by the spontaneous possibility of a neon PSYCHIC sign, following a narrow staircase to a purple door. We nearly turned the knob when Sage spotted a rusty saw blade on the floor.

Back downstairs we went, five more blocks to Samsara Bookshop where we sniffed our way through exotic incense ("Smells like spirituality") and passed the Buddha figurines, smiling like Hotei himself. Behind a curtain we found two chairs and one Tabitha Meer, a dreadlocked black woman who was already getting high off our energy. We sat down before she smoked us away and I soon learned of a most strange history.

Apparently I'd met Sage in a past life and had scheduled to meet her again—our coming together was planned and destined. Tabitha dissected our spirits and opened pathways, unknotting little pieces of our souls and tying them to new foundations. Tying us to each other perhaps.

I walked away holding hands with my queen, ready to dig into the asphalt and rip it apart, exposing the dark underbelly for what it was. I sized up the Empire State, wanting to climb it like a skinny, shaven King Kong.

Sage and I descended into a basement pizza joint and stared at each other as we had over pancakes that one morning. It was the same feeling as before. Her eyes, ripping apart the asphalt of my soul.

"You're not coming back from LA, are you?" she asked abruptly.

"I'm coming back."

"Oh yeah? What about that girlfriend of yours?"

"She's not my girlfriend anymore."

"We'll see about that."

"Why don't you come with me? Start a new life on the west coast?"

"Aren't you forgetting that I have a son?"

"He can come, too. We'll make a road trip out of it."

She made a little smirk with her mouth and I shrugged a little shrug.

4

"CALLING ALL PASSENGERS traveling from Baltimore to the Abyss."

Could've sworn I heard it, shuffling and swearing down the walkway onto the plane, cushioned next to a frumpy fellow—an old man who worked in advertising on Madison Avenue back in the day. An original Mad Man, I thought! Being a fan of the TV show I picked his brain for hours, doing my best to bury the fear of landing. Not so much the landing of our steel entrapment, but of my foot to California concrete and Hollywood linoleum.

But of course it landed and off went my mad old friend. I wanted to tag along and present a clever pitch that he purchase me a room in his towering hotel. Martini at the bar. Anything to stay in the sky.

Soon I found myself heaving luggage from the depths of my cab. The warm, dry Southern California night. Its glowing moon mocking me from behind a smoggy sheath.

"Fuck you!" I yelled.

I stepped inside the quiet apartment and watched as the demons came to help with my bags, directing me to the sad bedroom where I found my possessions packed and stacked in boxes. My poor rolled up rug. I'd come to joke with Jarrett over the phone—"She even packed my spices, dawg!" Indeed, there was my Morton Salt and Old Bay.

Bold. Bold she was!

I didn't want to stew in the echoey chamber, so I kicked my suitcase into a corner and left to find a bar.

—

WANDERING SUNSET BOULEVARD, cigarette in mouth, a bum reached out and I reached back. I had lived in this city for years and saw it for the first time as it really was. Not from the perspective of a bushy tailed twenty-year-old enthralled by buzzing signs and spaced out palms, but as a wounded spirit silenced from the quest and all its questions in queue. Bulbs shattered before me, palms toppled behind. There were no cars. Billboards advertised nothing. I existed with the bums and the bars, and as with previous weeks that's where I found my light.

I slumped on a stool and wondered about the notion of the Abyss. The term originated weeks earlier when I described to Jarrett the lure of utter intoxication. A darkness in which time passes on its own, undetected, while you're off floating in a dream or not even dreaming at all; rather, numb for the moment. I wondered if we get drunk in order to commit temporary suicide, only to be reborn in fresher daylight, waiting once again for five p.m. when we can justify our poisoning all over. Again, again, again. We show up at the bar like flocks of geese—gathering, hunching, swigging and lunging. But why ground ourselves in this sickening way? It seemed there was someplace darker than binge blackouts. The influence of a true unknown.

I sat there at my Hollywood haunt talking to an older lady across the bar. She looked like Mrs. Robinson, but with a surgeon-sculpted face and breasts. I tried to picture what she looked like before the plastic, fantasizing about her removing the costume of herself and lying down across the bar with me. But nothing came from our exchange and I threw a tip on the counter, walking outside to light a Marlboro—a lost cowboy looking for his hat.

Or horse, was it?

I was solo and solitary and searching for something other than the key to my apartment. But before long I walked back and passed out on the futon.

—

SOMETIME AROUND TWO A.M. I awoke to the soft touch of fingertips and opened my sticky eyes to Francine. The fish tank gurgled behind us. She smiled.

I didn't want to open my mouth.

I knew there would be plenty of time for talking in the days to come.

I don't remember but there may have been a kiss.

—

AT DAWN I hit the streets again and stumbled into a corner donut shop, ordering a dozen. I smoked and carried them back to the apartment where Francine was pleased, as we loved our breakfasts together. I remained tight-lipped about Sage and the whole east coast experience—this was never part of our phone conversations. And although we were officially broken up, Francine and I continued on as before. My stuff was packed, but it was plainly a move on her behalf.

We went to dinner that night to discuss our relationship and what could be done to save it. I couldn't tell her about Sage. I wouldn't. I digressed, beating around the bush, chewing my way to an agreeable end.

"You know my co-worker, Gina?" Francine asked.

I squeezed a potato into my mouth. "Uh-huh."

"Well, she mentioned that you could be putting on this act because of another woman. You didn't meet another woman while you were in Maryland, did you?"

"I mean, I met women. Sure."

"But one that you really liked?"

"They were cool, yeah."

"But *one* that you really liked?"

Everything about the moment annoyed me. The servers too slow, patrons too loud, silverware too shiny, and why the hell was the AC on? And why were we sitting directly under the vent?

—

IT WENT ON like that for a while. Each day I milled about the city, unemployed, while Francine worked at her downtown office. Car-less, I didn't mind. I embraced my shoes and their ability to cushion me for miles. For the first time since moving to LA, I allowed myself to really explore, to vanish, and was subsequently reminded of a conversation I once had with a hair stylist.

"You know," she said, "LA has been called the City of Babylon."

I thought I was dreaming when I heard her because I tended to fall asleep during haircuts.

"Oh yeah?"

"You can either find yourself here or wind up completely lost."

And now it seemed that the city had truly morphed into Babylon—the Babylon of today—with its ruins directing shiny cars in circular motions.

I didn't recognize any of it.

—

FRANCINE AND I enjoyed a few more dinners together, and one night we danced on those Hollywood floors, drunk from a bottle of cabernet, and I wondered how I would ever tell her the truth—how I would look into those sparkling brown eyes and stick forks in them.

I couldn't bear to stay any longer.

One night she complained about something and I booked the first flight out, three days away. And three days later she touched me and we kissed and the flight was canceled.

Another time—gloomy afternoon—Francine and I were sitting on the futon together, staring at each other as we tended to do. She was already late for work, but remained sitting, staring, like nothing else mattered, like we had all the time in the world.

"Hey babe," I started, "there's something I have to tell you."

"Yeah?" she quivered.

"You know those women I met back east?"

"Yeah?"

"Well, it really was one woman."

"Gina was right."

"Forget Gina."

"But she was right."

"Sure, okay."

"You went on dates with this woman? What's her name?"

"It's not important."

"I want to know everything about her."

"It's not important. Just listen."

"Did you fuck her?"

"I—what?"

"Did you fuck her?"

"Yes. But you have to understand—"

"Asshole!!"

She stormed out of the apartment, swinging her handbag, nearly knocking over the poor fish tank.

"Asshole! Asshole!!"

I booked a flight.

—

IN THE MORNING I made breakfast and apologized best I could. I told Francine that I'd be leaving in a few days, and again to my astonishment she worked with me. She fought vehemently, valiantly, determined to keep us alive. I cancelled the flight.

Madness, I thought.

—

BY NOW family and friends were poking me, asking when I'd return home, and truly I only planned on being in LA a few days—I never thought I'd find myself waking up on the futon with naked Francine.

Sage stopped messaging days earlier and we were no longer talking.

"Are you trying to patch things up?" she asked.

"No, but it's not easy. I'm a guy with a conscience, what can I say?"

"Didn't seem to have one when you were with me."

And now with sweet Sage upset at me and my hometown two thousand miles away, I was presented with the perfect opportunity to hide from the world, under the covers with Francine in a place where spring had already arrived.

We laid on that futon morning after morning into the late afternoon hours, absorbing the California rays. She'd go to close the blinds and I'd tell her to leave them open.

I sought the sun—its warmth comforted me. It was not judging, but nourishing. And what I needed most in that moment was nourishment. I hated myself for what I had done. As much as we continued to try, I couldn't convince myself to reconnect with Francine because I could barely look into her eyes. Furthermore, she owned the cutest animal in the world—Kiwi, a small parrot—another pair of eyes I had to stare into usually one at a time. The bird was our proverbial child and had been part of our lives for three years.

Kiwi was basically a miniature human, exhibiting the intelligence of an actual three year old. His chirps effectively conveyed emotions—valiant attempts at linguistics—and his mannerisms alone were enough to get his point across. Not to mention he was one hell of a dancer. I sat on the couch while Francine caressed Kiwi in the palm of her hand, petting his head with her finger; jealously watching as he tended to bite me.

Cute Kiwi we called him.

A tiny knife in my heart.

—

THE LONGER I STAYED in LA, the more acidic the guilt. And I mean this most literally as I had been experiencing bouts of gastritis, the walls of my stomach ablaze between meals. I knew it flared up due to stress and rather than renew my pill prescription I let it burn. As with the sun, I sought comfort in feeling something other than emotional pain.

Despite the burning, I stumbled out of bed each morning and wandered cracked sidewalks to the corner shop for boxes of dough and cups of oil.

It was surreal.

Cars honked at me, bums mocked me. The city laughed and tried to tip me into the Pacific. But I clung to a lamp post until the ground leveled out; until my head fell back into place between bony shoulders.

One day I bumped into an old colleague at the donut shop. We'd worked together months earlier on a TV show. He stared at me like a concerned doctor. I barely said a word. I was over words. I found solace in the face of a short Asian woman behind the counter—always smiling.

The donut shop was practically a halfway house for pimps, prostitutes, and the various tramps of Tinseltown. Open 24 hours, its glowing neons served as a beacon for the distressed. Vagrants gawking. Faces stained and creased as the streets. And although I avoided eye contact I felt instant connection—the connection of lost souls in the city of angels—a place where winged creatures flock in search of higher ground, only to fall gracefully and occasionally straight down. It was sad, and I always thought LA was a true test of belief, for once you arrived you were quickly mixed in like a salt grain fighting against your own dissolution.

I remembered first arriving after the long cross-country drive. Warm desert air kissing my skin; lips pressed to a palm tree in celebration. Everything was pristine and I felt princely, finally transported to my throne in the land I was to conquer. The palms would bow, not bend or break, and studio doors would fling open upon my approach like the automated gates of Walmart. It was a wild time of wonder, and I wanted to keep driving past the Santa Monica Pier, straight into the waves, as I was certain they'd pave if only I believed enough. I would end up somewhere in Japan— China maybe—and the freshness would continue from country to country. The world would stay polished and I would keep my sunglasses on.

5

"Moving?"

"Kind of."

"Won't you miss the beautiful weather?"

"Yes . . . yes I will."

"Well, you can always come back."

And with this exchange I handed the postal worker four cardboard boxes containing everything I owned, to be shipped back east.

It took me a week of visiting post offices every day, only to hesitate and drive away each time. There was a finality that came with the shipment. So long as I had the boxes, Francine and I had a chance. We could always buy new furniture, revamp the apartment, or start over in a new place. My stomach churned on the morning that I pushed the squeaky cart into the office for the last time. Strangely, no one stood in line and I rolled right up to the window, anxious to get it over with. The lady clerk stamped everything and within minutes it was over, like an injection. I thought of her advice about being able to come back.

After all, it's not the first time I'd left LA.

Bitten by the travel bug two years earlier, I went through the same process—selling my car and emptying closets in order to fulfill dreams of driving a big rig across America. And it was the same test of courage: leaving Francine behind at the bus station, backpacking into blistering heat to the training academy. Adventure on the horizon, regret in the rearview. The only exception then is that we had decided to stay together, maintaining the relationship via phone calls and such.

Now it was all over. There would be no Johnny Cash or highway through God's country; no hissing of airbrakes and charming roadside diners.

—

ON THE NIGHT before I left, Francine and I laid down on the futon for the last time. It felt like death. I slept two hours before the cab arrived at five a.m.

No lamp. Everything dark.

I dragged my luggage out the door and wrapped myself in the poor girl, leaving her with the final chunk of my heart. Driving away, I caught a glimpse of her peeking through the blinds.

I told the Nigerian driver everything—why I was leaving and where I was going. He was one of the most compassionate people I'd ever met (certainly the most compassionate cabbie) and I wondered if there was a reason he came to pick me up that morning.

We sped down the 10, void of traffic in the wee hours, and the man choked up while talking about his wife and daughters he left behind in his homeland. He mentioned something about God and not knowing how the pieces fit together, yet taking comfort in the hand that's helping to construct the puzzle.

At LAX, I pulled my luggage from the trunk and shook his hand.

I wanted to give him a hug.

I'd probably never see him again and it saddened me. I thought of all the great people I'd met in my life that I would never see again, and how for moments, a mere fifteen minute cab ride, we share this crazy life together.

The stark white terminal slapped me in the face and I lost memory after that. I awoke in Baltimore, jet lagged and waiting on a curb, tail tucked uncomfortably between legs.

My dad picked me up and tried to make conversation. He wanted to eat at the Silver Diner—a lighted beacon between the airport and home. It was our tradition and we never missed stopping off for a cozy seat and conversation.

"Just take me home."

Winter had found me again. Forehead pressed against cold window—crooked, bare branches reaching out as we whipped past in the nick of time. The sky dimmed as we dipped south and the silence deadened all, leaving only the droning engine; my moaning conscience.

"How 'bout McDonald's?" he said. "Can eat McDonald's!"

—

THE BED BECAME my best friend. My childhood room, a coffin. Soul-less body blanketed, bucket nearby for vomiting as I had contracted a nasty virus somewhere between coasts. I found myself staring at the ceiling—plastered with glow-in-the-dark star stickers. It was a fond memory, watching my mother stand atop a ladder, adhering them for my enjoyment. Must've been four or five years old.

I coughed myself into mind-bending migraines and Nyquil-induced nightmares. The star stickers morphed before my eyes and the ceiling blew off the house, revealing actual stars, quickly covered by clouds that dripped acid droplets.

I laid still and listened to ancient flute melodies, drank OJ, and thought about Sage. I felt her presence nearby, but it would be a couple more weeks before attempting contact.

—

"TRYN'A GO TO THE ABYSS TONIGHT?" asked Jarrett with a grin.

By now I realized that I was already there in my sense of the words and, still recovering from the flu, only sat with him over a couple of drinks.

I glanced around the bar looking for Sage, hearing that I just missed her by a half hour. I imagined seeing her walk through the door just as I had originally—dressed in black, everyone stepping out of her way as if a trail of fire preceded her.

Instead, another girl approached—one who I met on the same night as Sage but never called because, frankly, she was young and uninteresting.

"Heeeeyyyyyyyy it's you!" she spouted. "Aren't you s'posed to be in LA producing a show or something?"

"I'm taking a break."

"Uh-huh."

—

I COULDN'T WAIT any longer to call Sage. Had to know if she would take me back. Regret stood by as I picked up the phone and dialed. There was no answer, so I left a message, only to hear the phone ring ten minutes later.

It was her. She invited me to her new house.

Eager to see it—eager to see her—I raced over with a bottle of pinot and found her at the door smiling her smile. The crazy dogs jumped on me, scratched and sniffed the shit out of me, and after she caged the beasts we sat down in an empty living room, opposite one another.

I was happy to be there.

She grounded me and I both loved and hated her for it.

We talked for hours mostly about the past month, offering mutual apologies for tactless texts and misconstrued messages. She took me upstairs to see her bedroom which was immediately my favorite room of the house, and we laid down together as we had always done before.

In due time we were making out which is when I felt that something was off—I needed more time to adjust. Visions of LA danced in my head and I tried to shake them, but alas it was too soon.

—

WORD GOT 'ROUND that I was back in town and before long my phone was ringing—good ol' county friends wanting to hang out like the good ol' days.

One afternoon, I agreed to meet my buddy Fred Mattingly for an adventure at the outdoor shooting range. I had only fired a pistol once in my life and wasn't prone to playing with guns, but having worked in law enforcement, it was a requirement for Fred.

Before going to the range he showed me his collection, pristinely cleaned and kept, boxes of bullets, scopes and other assorted arsenal. He was proud of it all. Apparently his wife, Larissa, bought him the AK-47 as a Christmas gift. I watched her grin her sheepish grin, and then their two dogs slid around the corner and dug into my skin. By now I appeared to have been in a brawl with Edward Scissorhands.

Anyhow, I didn't understand their obsession with guns and it seemed that a certain amount of paranoia accompanied it. Fred suspiciously watched neighbors and presented scenarios of them breaking in and how unlucky they'd be for doing so. There was a pit of lava boiling beneath the surface of this otherwise calm man and I wasn't sure whether to worry.

And so we ended up at the shooting range, waiting our turn to blast away invisible enemies. Fred had paper targets, some with graphics of zombies on them. I watched the faces of other gunmen—narrowed in concentration, snarling, then gleefully high-fiving each other.

When it was our turn to shoot, Fred contained his giddiness, remaining professional about the whole thing. I watched while he unloaded clips and revolvers from the AK-47 and .357, respectively. After a few clumsy attempts I did the same, releasing triggers and frustration—shell casings tumbling through the air and snot oozing from my nostrils.

I understood why people like guns.
I understood because I felt it. Felt the power.
Guns speak for us. Speak for our souls and the protection of all we believe in. When we cock the hammer, we poise ourselves to be released as the bronze bullet; to soar at high speed and inflict damage.

Power, yes!

As with the firing of pistons propelling us down pavement, we fire our guns and let our spirits fly through contraptions—a symbolization of our wants and desires—the temporary highs of mankind.

And then you pack it all away, park the car, pocket the keys, and swallow your soul. Grab the remote and fire up the tube. *CSI* is on.

—

HAVING BEEN STAGNANT for weeks and not finding the clarity I was seeking, I decided to take another trip to Pennsylvania to see my mother. Along the way I was to meet with my aunt and uncle to pick up a car they no longer needed. They wouldn't divulge the type of vehicle; only said that I would enjoy it.

I jumped at the opportunity.

Surprisingly, the bus driver dropped me off just outside my aunt's house, located in the desolate farm valley of Salemville. When I stepped down I was greeted by the bunch: Aunt Nancy, Uncle Jed, and yes, their peppy little pup.

Still fighting off the flu and stomach acid, I felt like shit the first night and only sat on the couch wondering what beautiful machine awaited me in the shed.

I looked around at my aunt and uncle—their double-wide trailer—and framed a portrait of them in my mind. The place was quite nice as Jed was a skilled handyman. He worked at a lumberyard and traded penny stocks in his spare time, and one of his favorite things to do was explain the tricks of the trade. Usually I only traded expressions, furrowing my brows, nodding a series of "Uh-huhs" and "Ahhhs." He was proud of saving money, making money, and knowing about money. I'd pull a box of crackers from the cupboard and he'd comment on their deliciousness, followed by "And only a buck!"

They were good crackers, I thought, and swallowed the savings.

Then Jed pulled something that looked like a body bag onto the floor and unzipped it. Inside, everything needed to survive the impending apocalypse, including brand new, unfired sniper rifle. He let me hold it, and as with Fred I wondered about his infatuation with such things. If this was indeed reality, then why was I not adequately prepared? Why didn't I feel the need to rush out and buy a rifle of my own?

My aunt stood by and yawned as Jed pulled out his last toy: a vacuum cleaner. It looked like something from Kubrick's *Space Odyssey* and I patiently waited for it to begin talking to me. Jed described how a salesman came knocking on their door one day and pitched the machine as being the most powerful vacuum cleaner on the planet.

And it was one hell of an instrument, romping across the carpet and couches, purifying the earth of the house. I thought maybe it would suck the germs and turmoil straight from my body if I got close enough.

But no. The plug was pulled and I went to bed.

THE NEXT MORNING Jed found a dead deer on the side of the road and I watched him drag it up past the house, staring at the shed as if it were a giant, wrapped gift.

Somehow I felt that I didn't deserve whatever sat behind those doors.

And when they were finally opened, there was actual unwrapping to do, as the car was covered beneath a blue tarp. Jed handed me the keys and told me to start it up before the unveiling. I already knew from the contours of the body that she was a beast. I sat down in the black interior, cushioned in a bucket seat, and turned the ignition. The engine growled to life straightaway, bellowing the throaty tone one can only expect from a 5.7-liter V8.

"Give 'er a rev!" Jed shouted.

It was music.

A behemoth screaming in defiance, rumbling for all the right reasons. I felt the power I had felt holding the handgun, the power of the vicious vacuum cleaner. The car screamed for me so that I didn't have to (although it might've been better that I did). I ripped off the tarp and admired the burgundy 1987 Chevy Camaro Z28, immediately falling in love as I did with everything else.

Jed took me for a ride, roaring down country roads while roaring Mennonites shook fists. I imagined them hollering, "You damn kids!!" Jed was indeed a kid, and I watched his wild eyes locked on the windshield just as I'd watched Fred's eyes locked on targets. We all go wild for something, and I knew this car would take me on my wildest adventure yet.

6

GRATEFUL AND GRINNING, I waved goodbye to Nancy and Jed and drove away in the Camaro, caressing the dash, acquainting with my monstrous mistress.

What a beaut.

O she bellowed through the Appalachians as I careened across the state to see my mother. And I spoke to the car as I had all my vehicles, asking her to be kind and not break down, wooing with promises of timely oil changes and hot waxings. I cranked the volume on hair metal bands and it felt right as rain.

When I finally reached my mother's house, I was greeted, as always, with open arms and buckets of love. Within minutes a cold beer was in my hand and we were telling stories on the cold porch. The portly Tootsie moseyed over and I was thankful to finally be in the presence of such a benign dog.

Toots was a walking miracle.

Her story rivaled most humans', having been abused half her life, evidenced by the buckshot bullets revealed upon x-ray. She once accidentally drank a bottle of rat poisoning, has fallen out of a moving truck onto the highway, and now in her old age found paradise in my mother's home—a princess deserving of such a palace.

"She just keeps on loving."

—

SOON IT WAS SNOWING and I sought comfort in knowing winter was still around. It had been the longest winter of my life and I didn't want it to end. It was comfortable to look outside the window and see everything dead.

My mother left me alone most of the time.

34

I sat around writing, rattling my keyboard throughout the night while Toots laid by my feet. I noticed that the picture of Francine and I was still on the mantle and didn't bother to take it down.

In the mornings I'd wake up and sometimes remain under the covers for a long time, hiding from the world. It's a coping device that continued for months. I hid under covers with Francine before leaving LA—the sun would brighten and lighten them, creating a warm sanctuary. Now the sun was gone, but the covers continued to be a place of peace and I breathed the smell of linens and wished my conscience to be just as clean.

—

ANOTHER UNCLE of mine, Wallace, lived in the area, and one afternoon I stopped by to pay him a visit. He opened the door to his apartment and I walked into what appeared to be a newly minted hotel room.

A middle-aged bachelor, Wallace had undiagnosed OCD, and one gander at his abode offered enough diagnosis for the average Joseph. Everything immaculate, lined parallel or at ninety-degree angles. Cupboards of canned goods with front-facing labels; emboldened dates of purchased meats and vegetables. Order and organization was priority. Furthermore, this was a man seeking perfection. Not a hair out of place, not a smudge on the Buick. He had always been this way. I recalled opening his closet as a kid and seeing shoes spaced so evenly apart that it must have been done with a ruler.

We had lunch at a sandwich joint and Wallace complained about the temperature of the room for the first few bites. Then he noticed an old friend from high school and hoped they wouldn't see him. Started gossiping. The gossip morphed into regret.

"I almost made it to the pros, you know. Football. Should've seen me—I was fast. Just wasn't tall enough. Gotta be tall. Gotta be born with it. Yeah."

He quizzed me about LA.

"I watch that show *The Hills*. What's Hollywood like? Ever drive the 101? Meet anyone famous?"

He spoke about acting.

"Think I could act?"

And teaching.

"Think I could teach?"

And all the things he wanted to do but wasn't ready for.

With medication, Wallace was a healthy, intelligent man and could do just about anything. Yet he placed the biggest hurdle he could find in his path: himself. No matter what piece of advice I imparted—famous stories of success and inspiring quotes—he only nodded, "Yeah."

I began to wonder if any of my family members believed in themselves. Wondered if there was a positive bone in our bodies. Was the gene pool corrupted along the way or was it cultural? Did someone, generations prior, beat everyone into pulps of lost potential?

You can't do that. You're not good enough. Why would you go and do that? You'll never make it.

—

WHEN HIDING under covers failed to suffice, I sought refuge at the local library, spending my days reading and gathering books, CDs, and DVDs to take home and devour. Sometimes I stayed in my bedroom from dawn 'til dusk and Dad would come home from work, peek his head through the door and ask, "What did you accomplish today?"

To which I replied, "Nothing."

I was certain it made him cringe—a man of constant unrest who felt he didn't live a day he didn't work. At any given moment he was doing something, and in that sense wasn't so different from my mother. Rather than cut grass, he went and had his hair cut every few days.

"I'm going to get a haircut," he'd announce. Even though it was already of acceptable military standards.

Grocery shopping. Cleaning the bathrooms. Laundry.
Laundry was huge. My father did laundry before the hamper was half full.
Fixing appliances for other people.
Computers and cars. VCRs.

Go, go, go.

Once during dinner, Kelsey and I asked him, "What do you do for leisure? Not to accomplish anything—just for pure enjoyment. Besides watch TV."

A long pause.

"Watch TV."

Of course he loved sports as well, but saw it as exercise—a productive kind of activity.

He was lonely and I felt compassion. I observed as he came home each night, popped a plastic tray into the microwave and plopped onto the couch. No pets to greet him. Even the fish tank was empty, yet he kept cleaning it and changing the filter ("It looks nice. Completes the room").
Never remarried and hardly dated anymore, although at one point he had been quite the debonair. Friends would joke—"Your dad's a pimp." But he didn't seem to care anymore. Wasn't enthusiastic about anything. And that's when I realized that he too was at the Abyss.

My father and I connected through two mediums: sports and cars. Days not spent at the gym were spent in the garage, musty and oily, hovered over the engine bay of the Camaro with bright lights and tiny mirrors, trying our best to pinpoint leaks.

Dad came alive in these moments. An engineer by profession, he thrived on rescuing old radios, computer hard drives, and other busted gear abandoned by original owners. He adopted things, took them into his care and inspected them like a dutiful dentist and patient. I thought about how this was his unique way of showing love. He provided hope in bringing things back to life—'Your computer's not dead, see? I fixed it.'

Our bond was subtle. We worked quietly on the car, but there were good moments and he loved to teach most of all.

"See how this tube is connected? It draws suction from the reservoir."

"Uh-huh."

"Everything is powered here. Take a look."

And I looked and listened, and that was our way.

—

SAGE AND I continued to see each other, and by now it was routine for me to drop by the liquor store on the way to her house, picking up a bottle of wine and box of condoms if need be.

One night after making a run to grab a second bottle (one was never enough), we passed by a road leading to a nearby beach—a cute little beach at the shore of the Chesapeake. We returned with a blanket and glasses and sat in the sand, awash in moonlight, hearing the subtle crash of waves that filled the air with salt. We poured wine and huddled under the stars and listened to music emanate from tiny cell phone speakers.

Old Muddy Waters and Billie Holiday.

It was the perfect night—a moment to remember on my death bed, and they were the only moments I sought. We kissed and commented on how there should be a bonfire for such chilly opportunities. I found a pit of wet logs and made an attempt at sparking them to no avail. In the distance, another group had gotten one started and, envious, we could only mock them—"But they don't have Billie! They've got fire, we've got Billie!"

We went back to her place, so on and so forth.

I never stayed the night at Sage's because she always woke up for work at five in the morning. Sometimes I forgot that she had so much responsibility, complete with a full time job and child. I was still bumming around as I had in LA and started to loathe myself for it. Everyone seemed to dance around me, locked into a circle while I stood in the middle, an outcast. A drifter peeking into the windows of a house I once lived in, seeing people that I recognized but preferring to stand outside, simultaneously feeling as though something were wrong with it.

I had to do something. I was now living solely off money made from selling the engagement ring and it was diminishing fast.

Sage wanted me to stick around, suggesting opportunities, this and that. I ignored her and it pained me to do so. I knew that leaving again, even a few hours away, would mean the end of our relationship.

But the east coast was not for me. My soul was much more at peace in the vast expanse of the west, where spirits wandered freely and dreams seemed to carry through the wind. And as such, the land began calling to me again.

Go west, young man.
"I've been west."
Go again.
"Why?"

spring

7

TREES WERE BUDDING, blue jays clung to cold rails, and similarly I clenched the last shreds of winter not wanting it to end. It had become obvious that I missed everything in life because I loved everything. Regardless of how painful or tumultuous a time, I cherished every last pebble of experience. It was all part of the greater picture, the journey, the unfolding film that would one day project onto the back of my eyes while I sat and stared out the window.

Easter was upon us and Kelsey was back in town with Bella, who showed off her skills on the scooter as I ran alongside the morning they arrived. We were about to leave for Pennsylvania again with my father—a good ol' fashioned family road trip. I couldn't wait to get back to my mother's where I knew she'd be waiting with smiles and good food.

I was an obsessive reader by now and brought a stack of books along, one based on the subject of Buddhism and mindfulness. I was trying to transition into healthier coping methods and ultimately failed, for at last Kelsey was in town! At this point it was clear that we both resided at the Abyss, and for the first time ever swam alongside each other, downstream toward the waterfall. And this is how I viewed all relationships in the ocean of life. We're minuscule fish swimming around on our lonesome, trying our best to blend with other schools.

Anyhow, it was the same as any trip save for the air of anxiety. My mother was always on edge during the holidays. An immense pressure bestowed upon her—everything had to be perfect and complete. Tablecloths and placemats, fresh unlit candles, and a full schedule of activities, unlisted but hinted at. Kelsey and I shook our heads and speculated as to whether we were the continuation of this chain of restlessness.

Was it in our blood?

The answer would come in the form of our grandmother, a small-but-spunky lady with hair like an electric cloud. She joked and laughed with the rest of us and brought boxes of wool-knit hats and blankets, hand sewn to perfection.

I followed one of the hats as it was passed around the table.

There was Uncle Charlie, thumbing over the fabric and nodding approvingly.

"Very nice."

And Aunt Samantha, who held one with both hands as though it were breakable.

"So much detail in the stitching."

And Art, who put down his cigarette before touching it.

"Think it'll fit me?"

Their laughter went straight through my skull.

This was quite the contrast to earlier in the morning, watching my mother fret over which dress she should wear on the day we celebrate a man who wore rags. Listening to the weigh scale beep on and off. Tasting the sting of strong cocktails, everyone drunk and drinking to survive Easter.

But it wasn't Easter we were surviving, it was the falsehood that I soon came to witness. Inquisitive stares from across the table, questioning motives. 'You think you're better than me?' Wondering how everyone else is getting along in the game of life, and me wondering what the point of the game is.

It's cultural, I concluded.

Society has taught us that life is a fight! Which tricks us into silently killing those we love only to die ourselves, as everyone dies. It makes zero sense and yet we seem conditioned to continue this way.

I couldn't take it any longer. Kelsey felt the same—neither of us wanted to be part of the act. We practically swallowed our ham whole, tasting only half its goodness, itching to get back to Moonshine. I wanted to wrangle the entire table and jettison them down with us.

—

NESTLED ON STOOLS, Kelsey and I strapped ourselves in for the ultimate trip down liquid lane. Lorenzo sauntered over with his permanent smile and two glasses of bliss. We toasted to nothing and off we went.

Drunken ideas spilled onto the table.

"We should do a five-day Moonshine challenge! Spend every night at the bar!"

We solidified the plan with more liquid.

I hadn't seen Sage for a week nor spoke to Francine, and similarly Kelsey had ceased communication with the Chads. Truly we lived in a world of our own, surrounded by a force field, and wherever we went we were whole—one with God, smaller gods, gods of the bar. Curtains lifted upon our approach, a red carpet rolled out, stale yellow bulbs brightening. The music became louder and drinks stronger. The audience watched us through the slits of their eyes, the haze of highs, and laughed from behind stained teeth and smoky mustaches.

I imagined all the sounds muted—focusing on one person at a time, hearing the inherent loneliness and all their yearnings behind the laughter. Let sleeping dogs lie! Chuckles, music, and the clinking of glasses meant that everything was all right.

One night Kelsey and I looked up to see a legend of a man who seemed to go unnoticed by everyone save for the bartender.

"He comes in every night and orders the same thing," she said. "Water with lime."

Pushing seventy, thin frame and thinning hair, Ronald was an enigma of soggy Southern Maryland—a soaring spirit in the guise of a disgruntled drunk.

But drunk he was not!

I was thankful to learn of his water secret; to know that this man was at the bar for other reasons. He was a lover of life and all the happenings—a die-hard spirit—one who had driven past the horizon and back again.

I sensed this before we approached Ronald.

His face read like a book. Lines leading to places and people which had shaped his skin into folds of stories, unfolding before Kelsey and I as he spoke openly about his many near death experiences. From almost drowning as a toddler (which he claimed to vividly remember) to catapulting off a motorcycle at sixty miles per hour. He spoke of his travels to Asia, divulging details as we indulged, astounded, reveling in the opportunity of meeting this celestial celebrity.

"There are no rules!" he cried. "In life, there are no rules!"

On the surface it seemed ludicrous, but we contemplated it for days.

Could it be? No rules?

Ol' Ronald, Ol' Ronald, where are you now?
Where do you go when you leave the bar?
What will you do when the limes stop growing?

—

WE CONTINUED our five-day challenge, skipping one or two, as I would black out each night and wake up with a hellacious hangover in much need of recovery. But after a day of recharging we stretched our limbs and were back at it again, slamming drinks into our brains; absorbing toxicities while releasing others.

So long as Kelsey was in town, Sage stayed away.

Everyone did.

We were dripping fireballs bouncing wall to wall.

46

I never stopped to think about why we were doing it. Drinking brought us together, but it was more than a means of bonding. It was the need to escape the bullshit and its subliminal roots.

—

THERE WAS A NASTY RAIN on the final night of our challenge when we arrived thirsty at Moonshine. It was a wild night. Jarrett was there, and somehow I ended up wrestling him outside in the mud. Kneeling in a pool of water, I latched him in a headlock while he scratched the shit out of my arm. We pulled away from each other only to look down at pairs of sodden shoes.

"Look at my Chucks!" I yelled.

"Look at my Stacy Adams!"

He wore his best clothes and I felt bad.

Kelsey and I went home with insatiable appetites and wiped the cupboards clean. I hardly remembered eating and woke up astonished to find a trashcan full of packaging.

"We ate all that?"

My father just shook his head.

He'd be working in the yard only to come in and find us lying on the couch. Again, I was sure it drove him nuts and pictured his bite-scarred tongue. It was a form of therapy that I knew he understood on some level—that we had to go through this phase of rebuilding—the destruction of faulty foundations.

—

SOON KELSEY RETURNED to Virginia along with Bella who had been staying with her father, a man Kelsey divorced years earlier. I was somber and found myself back at the library, scouring shelves and cozying in corners.

Even when the library closed I sat in the parking lot, reading while the breeze blew through the ol' Camaro. I was comfortable sitting in my car and, along with hiding under bed sheets, it became a haven of sorts. A place where no one could find me. It reminded me of my trucking days—lying behind the curtains of the sleeper berth, listening to diesel engines, meditating to the cacophony of strange lands.

I never wanted to go home.

By now I was tired of being there and my father's negative energy was leeching any spirit gained from literary legends. I'd enter the house on a high only to hear "What'd you do today?"

I could do nothing for the man.

But I loved him and wanted to see him uplifted, sometimes asking that he accompany me to church.

"I don't want to go," he'd say. "They've changed all the response patterns. I don't like the new rules."

I mentioned that I'd never known the rules and simply sought peace there as I did everywhere.

Eventually he slipped out of his work gloves and into a pew. He was uncomfortable, and although I likewise hadn't found home with organized religion, his going was a step towards hope.

—

AT THIS POINT Sage was coming around, or maybe I was showing up. In any case we were back to our old antics, meeting for wine at her place and stumbling onto the little beach.

The first night back I came prepared with firewood and kindling, and after fumbling around got the damn thing going. It was a healthy fire that threw heat in our direction and I was proud of myself for building it. Now all I had to do was wander off into the woods and hunt dinner. 'Me bring food, woman!' Alas I only wandered to piss, shattering a wine glass along the way, splattering my poor Chucks. By now they had become a canvas for life; I liked them better for it. The fire was great and we kissed and drank until it reduced to embers, and even then I kicked it around just to keep the night alive.

Unforgettable as our evenings were, I loathed waking up at my father's house, disgruntled over my dependence on him.

I didn't know where to go.

But my subconscious was speaking.

Although I didn't know the specifics of what I wanted, I knew what my soul desired—the things that made me tick. I didn't know *where* I wanted to travel, but knew that I had to travel. I didn't know the *concept* of my next film, but knew that I had to shoot. Had to write.

And there was something about new experiences that fueled all this. I had to move, keep going, and the voice inside was merciless—'Get off your ass!'

I ignored the voice, afraid, even though I knew there was truth to it. And to alleviate the feelings I yapped at Sage—blabbering about my ideas, showing off my creativity.

"Look at this shot! Tell me that couldn't be an opening sequence for a film!"

Then I'd go on about traveling.

"Let's take a road trip."

"Where?" she'd ask.

"Somewhere."

"I can't really leave. I've got a child and job."

And so I'd become somber and bury the desires under a pretty flower patch. And it never quite worked, for the dirt always cracked, oozing dreams all over and I'd have to go back and clean it up. It was a nightmare job and I was too broke to hire a dreamscaper. So they just kept oozing, and every night they would overflow as Sage played janitor. Much as I loved her, everything about the situation served to bring me down.

8

"WE WERE NEVER TOGETHER in the first place."

I took a swig from my cocktail and swallowed her words, scanning for hints of emotion.

Sage remained Sage.

"Might as well enjoy our last night together," she said.

And so we did, drinking in the cheesy lounge bar with sour pop tunes playing overhead. We smoked and joked and the tension wore off—so much that I second-guessed whether I told her anything at all. But we both knew that I had.

We stopped at the beach on the way back to her place—bottle of wine but no fire. It was a cold night.

"Just go."

She turned her back and that was that.

—

THE REMAINDER of the week consisted of pacing around the house, a terrible waste of time. I lost all gusto. The walls were slick and slippery and climbing seemed impossible. Easier to stay down.

I wound up at Moonshine night after night raising glasses atop my demons. And of course Jarrett was there having reclaimed his throne as King of Moonshine. So long as Kelsey was away it didn't matter. The only reason I loved the little pub was because of Kelsey and our good times.

I showed up one evening to a crowded room and noticed Sage across the way, draped over some meathead. It was the old game and I knew it well having grown up in households of drama.

I sat in the Camaro with Jarrett, watching Schwarzenegger hop into her car.

"Welcome to the game!" Jarrett teased, "You're in it now!!"

"I don't want to be in it. I want out."

"She's playin' you, dawg. You're too sensitive. Let me hear you rev that engine."

BRAWWWWWWWWRRAAWWRRRR

"Need some of that in your veins."

—

THE ONLY FIRE I felt in coming days existed in my stomach, gastritis prevailing meal after meal. Eventually I scheduled an endoscopy—a procedure in which a miniature camera is snaked through the esophagus.

I didn't want to go.

I was terrified of hospitals.

The stark white walls and sterility, the seriousness of it all. Blanks and empty checkboxes. Patients passing by with passive eyes. It reeked brightly of death and I'd always feared death. But I laid down in my gown preparing for the pinch, and then it came and went, and I remained plugged in staring at ceiling tiles, counting the tiny holes in each of them and failing to do so.

Soon I was in the company of doctors stretching latex; staring down at their specimen. The old ten count and suddenly I was in a different kind of abyss.

—

"YOU GUYS NEED some artwork on these walls."

"Good luck gettin' 'em to pay for that," the nurse quipped.

I was being wheeled somewhere.

—

WHEN I CAME TO, the doctor showed me images of an inflamed esophagus. I cringed and thought about rivers of alcohol gushing through the soft channel. They let me keep a printout and I buried it under the front seat of the Camaro. Later in the year I'd dig it up only to cringe again.

Any idiot could tell me it was due to drinking. Any idiot could tell me to stop. Any idiot but me. I was frightened of death, yet there was clearly something scarier.

———

I CONTINUED TO READ and did my best to avoid liquor. Sometimes I wandered about, rediscovering my hometown like some kind of vagabond. It was hard to believe I'd spent half of my life there. The land was the same, but I was not. My experiences as a traveler had revealed that a place is never the same upon returning. Places are mostly memories. Mostly people.

I drove small distances, cruising to the southernmost tip of Maryland, ending up at the mouth of the Chesapeake.

Standing at shorelines with all the sandy white houses nearby.

Barbecue grills on backdoor decks.

Adjusting my seared eyeballs to seagulls,

wishing the water would pave across to Africa

Somewhere

Anywhere!

Despite these excursions, I was lost without women in my life. An ugly sight of a man circling around an empty house. And with each pace it became smaller and smaller. Iron bars dropped down across windows, door frames shrunk. Sometimes I'd lie in the living room (hardly a place of life), inhaling stale air and exhaling decaying soul. My father was away at work, but still I heard his nagging voice—'What'd you do today?'

I was doing nothing.

I was watching a ceiling fan oscillate, trying to follow a single blade with my eyes.

I stared at the backyard, searching for signs of life.

Blue jay. Stray black cat. Where's it going? How does it feel to be a cat?

Bird?

Caterpillar?

I slipped into their skin, squirming and flying, sensing my twiggy legs catching ground on the way down. Prowling the woods with wet paws, batting at slimy worms and continuing in search of food, smelling everything along the way. What a simple existence, I thought. I wondered which of us creatures was more envious. Sometimes I'd spend hours lying on the carpet thinking crazy thoughts—thoughts I typically didn't have time for—and was subsequently reminded of childhood. These were the thoughts of childhood! Observing, wondering, imagining. When it was an adventure just opening your eyes.

"What did you do today?"

I knew it.

I wanted to tell him that I transported, meditated, pondered the mysteries of the universe.

"Nothing."

We ate a quiet dinner, occasionally coughing to break silence and maintain rhythm.

It was Friday. Pizza night.

It was also the night that Kelsey came back.

—

"SALTWATER AND CIGARETTES, the smells of Southern Maryland!"

There we were again, me and my sis, dancing arm in arm toward the boardwalk on Salamander Island, just over the county line. A local tourist town replete with all the seafood you'd expect. And on this cool April afternoon, the seasonal re-opening of the Tahiti Bar was the main attraction. My father joined for the occasion and I was intrigued as to how the event would unfold.

The scene was tacky, drinks sticky, the patrons a little of both. Mai Tais filled to the brim with ice and umbrellas. Dad threw money at scantly clad bartenders and off Kelsey and I went like rockets into the sandy skies, pushing our way through crowds. We paused to observe my father from afar. He was red-faced and gleefully chatting with work buddies—a man we didn't know. He seemed happy and we wondered if it was the alcohol or sheer connection with others. A sense of belonging perhaps. I bought another round and soon Kelsey and I were spinning, reeling, creating familiar faces if we didn't find any.

But O they showed!

Sage arrived with her brother—a few years older and few inches taller than me. He was the quintessential overprotective brother and I couldn't blame him. I was out of my mind. We played the glance-and-glare game for awhile, but soon I approached Sage and even sooner we were kissing.

Whenever I lost Kelsey I would simply listen for her. Then we'd find each other, drunker than before, dancing and chumming with strangers while the totems stood bewildered. The skies darkened and grumbled as bloated cumulous clouds descended upon our party. I bought Kelsey another drink which she fumbled and spilled on some guy's jeans, and a large shiny-headed man grabbed her by the arm—apparently a bouncer and quite barbarous at that. He escorted her out of the pub while I walked alongside.

"Hey man, that's my sister! Lay the fuck off!"

My dad met Kelsey at the entrance and warned about the impending storm, but I had a full drink in my hand and surely could not waste the taste.

The rain came suddenly, strongly, perceivably to wash away the whole mess. Hoards of people slopping through streets in search of vehicles. I walked next to a younger girl and laughed with her—"Don't ever forget this moment! This is life!" She agreed and we soaked it all up.

Lightning sliced the sky.

I reveled in moments like these. What was this feeling? I wanted to capture it in a jar and store it away for monotonous days. Drenched, I bent over and screamed at the top of my lungs.

9

IT WAS AROUND this time that I began seriously planning my escape from Maryland, scouring the web for opportunities—anything and everything that gave me reason to hit the road.

I was trying to find my place.

Manhattan media jobs did not appeal to me, yet I spent hours crafting clever cover letters, all while my gut was telling me no, no, no.

I felt flat, the letters fell flat. It was all unbearably flat.

I needed something with shape.

Browsing Craigslist postings one night, I caught my opportunity:

PHOTOGRAPHER NEEDED – ROCKY MOUNTAINS

A position that called for someone to shoot photos of tourists riding horseback in the small town of Zephyr Heights, Colorado.

Yes, yes, yes! my gut nudged.

A chance to make lots of money over the summer—their busiest season—as well as to live in one of the most scenic regions of America. I applied right away with a snazzy letter littered with confidence, for I had nothing to lose. I falsified my address, inventing a story about how my aunt owned vacation property in the area.

"Oh what tangled webs we weave," Dad would later say.

Truly, I was venomous.

—

FOR THE NEXT FEW DAYS all I could think about was Colorado. I'd wanted to live there ever since crossing through in my trucking days—hooked by its high altitude beauty, progressive culture, and microbrews. I did little research on the town of Zephyr. Panoramas of snow-capped peaks offered more than enough bait. My imagination ran wild; I saw the summer of my dreams.

Mountains! They would surely ground me.

And indeed my stomach sprouted butterflies on the night I received invitation for an interview. I sat on the couch, silently jumping up and down while my father watched TV. John Denver's "Rocky Mountain High" played in my head and I was practically already on the road.

"Yes, I'll be there!" I responded.

Then a strange thing happened. . .

Shit, now I have to go. I wonder if this is the best choice.

I started looking around the room.

Aw, dad. Look at dad watching TV. He's such a good dad and he's lonely. He needs me.

I became overly sentimental about everything.

Aw, the library and *Aw, Moonshine.*

The comforts I sought to escape became my protection when suddenly invited into the unknown.

—

AS IF MY OWN fear weren't enough of an obstacle, other people began offering opinions—"This is what I'd do if I were you."

And options!

Before telling anyone my plans, I found myself amidst a plethora of opportunity.

One evening I met Fred and Larissa for dinner at a steakhouse.

"Looking for local work?" asked Larissa.

"Sure," I lied.

"There's an opening at the summer camp where I teach. Low stress, pays well. Give you some capital to go back to LA with."

She described the job while I nodded and chewed my food, noticing her freckles and bright blue eyes. Quite European, I thought, and wondered about her heritage. I thought about the mountains waiting, calling across Kansas and the plains—faint whispers by the time they reached the coast and gently sat next to me.

Fred took the baton.

"'Course, you could always get a job working at the jailhouse. Six month training period, but the pay is fantastic once you're in."

Mountains.

"If experience is what you're after, you'll sure as hell have it by the end of training."

He was right—experience was what I was after. But this was not it. My stomach twisted at the utter thought of abandoning my Colorado dream for anything else. I literally became sick, sweating over my steak.

"I'll think about it and get back to you."

I rushed home and hit the commode.

—

WEEKS BEFORE I was to leave for Colorado, I started reaching for the booze. Afraid to go. Afraid to start all over. Afraid to leave Sage. Afraid because I had no money.

And with this fear I fell deep into the Abyss.

The closer the departure date, the more I drank.

One night I bought a bottle of Crown and sat in my room alone, drinking and writing. I wrote my heart out, laughing at myself and the myriad of possibilities ahead—a god within the walls of my bedroom. In these moments I was fearless, king of my destiny. The warrior I couldn't summon in sobriety.

Colorado, I don't know by day.
Colorado, here I come! by night.
Wrestle a lion? Bring him in!

—

MORNING CAME and I stumbled out of bed fully clothed, still drunk.

Bottle on my desk nearly empty.

I opened my laptop and read pages I didn't remember writing, emails I didn't remember sending, and yes, found empty containers of food I didn't remember eating.

I thrust my body into the sunlight and strapped myself to the Camaro, barreling down the highway in search of smokes. Much as I despised myself for binge drinking, I enjoyed the certainty that came with it. I immediately knew what I had to do.

Had to keep writing.

I lit a cigarette and hit Gina's Cafe, my favorite breakfast spot. I was ugly and unkempt but smiled my way through the meal and all the waitresses winked back. I was comfortable in my skin; happy being me. Everything was right in my world—I was eating, writing, smiling. What was this feeling? I thought I'd bottle it alongside my stormy night. Despite being drunk on both occasions, surely there was truth to be found. Are we simply screaming to be brave? To be ourselves?

—

LATER IN THE DAY, still buzzing, I picked up Sage and we took a spontaneous trip to Annapolis—a plan birthed by my drunkenness ("Let's go somewhere!").

During the trip she asked about my job search and, meekly, I mentioned Colorado.

"Why would you go all the way to Colorado for a three month gig?" she asked.

It's good money," I said. "Besides, you can come visit. It'll be an adventure."

She was quiet for a long time. Not until we arrived in the city did she finally loosen up.

A chilly afternoon, we stepped in and out of Old Town shops for warmth. Antique book attic. Carefully cracked bindings. Creaking through and smirking at each other, knowing that everything was outside our price range.

Eventually we ended up at a seafood joint with live music, seated next to a large speaker. Sage seemed not to mind. She loved music and it's one of the things I loved about her.

I admired her beauty.

She was golden as ever in the low light, and I loved the restaurant for it.

The music was on par with our style—guitarist exposing his soul to us—Hendrix covers and blues tunes we could only expect from such a passionate person. I clapped until my palms throbbed.

Our food arrived and I suddenly became sick—the same feeling I had while eating with Fred and Larissa. It wasn't the scrumptious crab cakes. No. This was anxiety. Welled up anxiety triggered by Sage's presence and the knowledge that I was about to walk away from my queen. The knowledge that this feeling would not last as with everything in life.

How can I bottle this? How can I bottle it!?!

Alas, I did not manage to bottle it, but the good times rolled as we hailed a rickshaw driver to taxi us back to our car.

It was cold. Sage and I huddled together and watched the ambiance swirl around us as we jarred over stony streets. My stomachache disappeared and I temporarily forgot about Colorado, infected by Sage's awesomeness. Everything was perfect and I speculated as to why I couldn't let it be.

—

UPON TELLING MY PLANS to my father he was surprisingly supportive, convinced that it could be a good move. I sensed that he didn't want me sticking around my hometown.

Shortly after, he made attempts to reconnect with me, as is always the case. When you realize how little time is left, you savor the moments. It's unfortunate because we always have the chance to live and love this way.

And so we had fun playing frisbee, watching movies, working on the Camaro. We took a trip to D.C. and browsed museums, and I remembered being there as a child with him on a school field trip (he was the chaperone of our group).

And it was not the exhibits I remembered most, nor my father's intellect. It was watching him tuck a pencil firmly beneath his pointer and pinky fingers, snapping it with a slap on the knee. My friends gasped. I was proud—*This is a powerful man!* Billions of years of history surrounded us and we were awed by pencil-snapping.

There would be no pencil-snapping today, but we soaked up the displays and exchanged words like a couple of chummy colleagues. After we finished with the museums we walked along the National Mall together, next to the Reflecting Pool, which is when I grew impatient with my father's hurried pace. He bounced from sight to sight, never once stopping to breathe.

Kelsey and I noticed this in previous weeks and I finally decided to test him.

"Can we sit down for a minute, Dad? Kind of tired."

"Oh, okay."

We sat there in silence, people watching and breathing. Doing absolutely nothing. It was the first time in my life that

I observed my father simply sitting and was once again proud of his strength.

We eventually left and hit a nearby restaurant. Dinner was uncomfortable. I could sense a strange talk on the horizon—inquiries that had been brewing for weeks and sure enough they started pouring out:

"So, how much money do you have saved for Colorado?"

"Not much."

"What's 'not much'?"

"Couple hundred bucks."

"Ugh," he rolled his eyes. "How much would you say you need?"

"Few grand."

"How about five thousand? Would that do it for you?"

"That'd be plenty, thanks."

"No problem," he said. "Now this is a loan. You get the special Bank of Dad interest rate of 0%. Don't waste it. Now, tell me, what's your plan for a job?"

"Work this photography gig. Use the money to return to LA."

"And what about in LA?"

"I don't know," I said looking around. "Wait tables?"

"What experience do *you* have waiting tables?"

"I could learn."

"I think you should get a job at one of those catering companies. 'Hello, Mr. Clooney, would you like your asparagus raw or steamed?'"

I shrugged off his quip, too grateful to care.

"Whatever it takes, Dad."

10

I STRUGGLED to leave town.

I passed by Sage's, our pretty beach, and pictured her pretty eyes. I mashed the throttle and flew past the Kingdom of Moonshine—glancing, hearing the laughter. And then came the high bridge to Salamander. Water shimmering, stretching vast as if to ask why I'd abandon its glory.

Kept driving.

I drove until I saw towns I didn't know—towns with strange faces—and even then I chose the back roads, for the highway was too connected to the love I left. I yearned for solitude. Take me someplace dark; someplace where people spit and kick.

Found myself inside a porta pottie riddled with sharpie writing:

WE ARE HOME DUMB FUCKS!

I kept driving.

Kept the windows down and music up to create a symphony of noise. The trees were lustrous and leaning in, hunched over the road, and I couldn't wait to hit the state line where they'd back off into the hills. Ah, I wanted love and the trees came in for hugs and I rejected them in lieu of vastness, however cold and distant. Do we reject love for a reason? Is there a part of us that desires isolation? Maybe it's a realization that, essentially, we're all alone in the world. And while there is an urge to attach ourselves to others, it's sometimes necessary to walk away and fall for ourselves again.

—

I SOON HIT THE APPALACHIANS and knew it would only be another hour before seeing my mother, where I planned a one-day stopover on the way to Colorado. Maryland was behind me and I was breathing freely through a cigarette filter, blowing off steam. I hammered through the hills and blared upwards into the old neighborhood, pulling into the quiet driveway. I expected Toots to come trotting over, but was instead greeted by my mother with tearful eyes. "We've had a death in the family," she said, closing in for a big hug.

"What?! Who?"

We walked to the porch where she had set up a memorial to Tootsie—a little table complete with framed photos and doggie treats and flowers. Apparently the big-hearted beagle had been quickly losing weight, which my mother attributed to a new diet. Full of energy until the last week, Toots withdrew from the house, hobbling off into the woods to lie in ditches, free from the shame of her condition: brain cancer. The story was crushing. My mother carried Toots from the ditches repeatedly, back to the house, laying her on a cushy bed, blanketing love as only a mother can.

—

I FELT COMPELLED to stay.

For days we weathered the gloom, sitting on the porch, beers in hand, coffees in hand, cigarettes in hand, and we drank and smoked and talked and walked. And the front yard was covered in lavender petals, bunched neatly around a tree that had somehow died despite the spectacular spring. It was an early, purple autumn, and one day my mother decided to clean up the leaves, and in doing so fashioned a smiley face that spanned the yard.

"So that Toots can see it in heaven. This yard was hers."

—

LEAVING LITTLE TIME to make Colorado, I said my final goodbyes and hit the road. It was a particularly warm day, rendering the ol' Camaro a veritable oven. Saturated with sweat and emotion, the road that had always invigorated me with promise now seemed too long for the cause. Why was I leaving? Why Colorado? What the hell were mountains going to do for me?

I writhed in my seat as I approached an automated tollbooth. I wished for human contact—someone to be inside, someone who would question me for leaving or present a better option. Alas, the road opened up and invited me to make the decision for myself.

—

THE HIGHWAY was void of all traffic. A barren spread of hot grey that seemed to melt me into its surface. I felt like I was trudging through tar, getting nowhere, as if Colorado were rejecting me from beyond the plains—*No! You are to stay in Pennsylvania! I am jagged and mean. I will defeat you.*

Fuck.

I fell into panic and missed my exit, only to turn around and wind up at the same tollbooth having to pay all over again.

Fuck!

I was a mess and nearly out of gas.

—

I PULLED INTO a truck stop to fuel-up, then parked and sat. The parking lot would provide comfort, yes! Moreover, this was a truck stop parking lot, which transported me to my great trucking adventure. The hissing of brakes, salty smells of shitty food, and diesel fumes infecting my brain, stealing a few cells to numb subconscious pains. I welcomed it all. I ate the shitty food and wandered the lot as if I were a trucker all over again, and sure enough a trucker approached me.

"Like milk?" he asked.

"Huh?"

"Got a half pallet of almond milk that was refused by the warehouse. Not really damaged, just dented cartons. Want it?"

"Not the whole pallet, but I'll take a couple gallons."

I don't know why I accepted. How was I going to keep it fresh on the long journey? But there I was, sweating in the hot sun with two gallons of almond milk. O how sentimental I was! Now I've got almond milk.

I can't leave Pennsylvania, I've got *almond milk*!

And so I sat in the parking lot with my milk, watching the drooping sun do its thing while I did nothing until I couldn't take it anymore and went for a walk, winding up at a grocery store. And thus began another strange ritual. Along with sitting in parking lots and hiding under sheets, I was now accustomed to wandering the aisles of grocery stores. For nothing. I was there to buy nothing, yet I found solace walking each aisle, absorbing the colors and people, pretending to be a local—sometimes holding a basket just to fool them into smiling at me.

'Who's that?' I imagined them thinking.

Yeah, I live here. I belong.

By now the sun was gone, the moon illuminated the cloudy sky, and I drove around the little truck stop town checking for vacancies at shabby, overpriced motels. A rusty pickup blared past with teenagers hanging over its edges screaming profanity, and I could smell their Marlboro jackets long after they were gone. Chafed faces, wiry goatees. Cantankerous construction workers clonking boots over the pavement and I thought to myself, 'Fuck this. I need a bed.' Back east I drove, half an hour from where my mother lived, yet I didn't want to see her. I needed neutral space.

I ended up outside my grandparent's old two-story home that sat perched on the top of a sloping street in a run down neighborhood. It loomed over me as if to ask *Why are you here?* I remembered visiting as a child, the warmth emanating from its shingles and glass, spilling into my youthful mind as the image of Grandma's House. Watching people spill out its front door to greet and hug and kiss me.

It was strangely cold in the house.

I creaked through the basement to turn on the gas and warm its wooden bones. I promptly refrigerated my sad little milks and then sat in the kitchen, ruminating on the day and why I couldn't seem to leave town.

Tiny jukebox in front of me on the table.

I turned it on, listening to Johnny Cash, Patsy Cline, old Pennsylvania Polkas. Stink bugs collected on the ceiling and I watched them lick the light or whatever fluorescent fun they were having. Then I saw one climb atop another. Jealousy kicked in and I turned off the lights.

I walked upstairs to my grandmother's room wondering if I'd feel a shred of her presence. A gust of wind, a faint whisper that shouldn't have been.

Nothing. I slept.

—

CRACCKKKOOWWWWW

I jolted forward just in time to catch a powerful flash outside the window. The walls split open and a hand reached down, yanking me into the clouds.

"WHY ARE YOU STILL HERE?"

I was speechless.

"You're supposed to be on your great adventure. MOUNTAINS! GOOOOO!!!"

The hand opened and I dropped miles through the sky, slowly, past the clouds until a bolt caught me and blasted me back into bed.

I hid under the covers.

—

THE NEXT MORNING I moseyed around the house, admiring it for the museum that it was.

Framed pictures

Smelly perfume bottles

Scribbled shopping lists of '96

At this point I was definitely going to miss my interview. I wasn't sure what to do besides be patient and let things play out.

I was getting ready for the day, searching for a pair of socks when I heard the front door jiggling—someone trying to get in. I looked for a weapon but could only find my socks, and by the time I had the ball of soft fury in my hand, the door swung open.

Nancy and Jed came barging in.

"Heeeyyyyyyy!!!"

Hugs and kisses and all that.

Apparently they had made an impromptu trip to clean up the house—cut grass, dust, etc. At one point, Jed approached me with a proposal to stay in Pennsylvania and live at the house for free, so long as I helped fix it up. His eyes were wild and this seemed a dream more suited to him, not I. My gut churned.

We all went to pick up my grandfather from the retirement home, ushering him over to his sister's house for a visit—Aunt Priscilla. As with Sage, I loved her name. Priscilla was in her seventies and lived in a tiny little house that reminded me of a dollhouse. She had stark black hair and I couldn't tell if she dyed it or not because it had always been black, and I remembered her smoking profusely. She no longer smoked but still had the voice.

I pulled beers from the fridge and we sipped them like whiskey, and all I thought about was what the hell I was going to do next.

Priscilla looked at me and frowned. "So sad, isn't it?"

She was referring to my grandfather. The fact that he sat there gulping his beer and shifting his eyes and actually wanting to go back to his cell simply because he didn't know anyone. I sat there watching them—my aunt and uncle, grandfather and Priscilla, and was struck by the sadness of it all. I wanted to get up and shake the house.

—

BEFORE LONG I was headed back to my mother's, and of course she waited with heaping hugs, piping plates and pastries.

How could I leave this place? How could I ever walk away from such love?

I cracked a beer with Art and he pummeled me with politics, and I listened to it all because it was all he had to offer. I sat on the porch late into the night, writing and job hunting, wishing Toots were still around to warm my feet. And upon daybreak, my mother and Art treated me to all that was tantalizing, from barbecue cook-offs to microbrews at the bar, pointing out blonds on stools—"What about that one?"

No. No más.

Couple days later, I was sitting in the kitchen being treated to some kingly meal when my phone rang. It was the job recruiter from Colorado, Bill. Or Colorado Bill as he called himself.

"We're low staffed and no one seems to have the experience you have. Still interested in the job?"

He was begrudging about it and I didn't care.

"Sure. I'll be there in a few days."

By God, Colorado was going to happen after all!

"You don't have to go," my mother insisted, fighting for me to stay. "You have a place to live here. I'm making blueberry cobbler."

Cobbler sounded good. Yet I had to leave the next morning and she was baking it in the morning. It was cobbler or Colorado.

11

I AWOKE the next day and threw myself out of bed and into the shower. This is it, I thought. Rich aromas swirled throughout the kitchen and I plugged my nose. I endured loving smiles, robust cups of coffee. The house closed in around me.

Cobbler is on the way, I'm staying.

NO! I was pulled into the clouds. I'm going.

But I would be tested one last time.

My father called to tell me about a trucking job in the oil fields, good money to be made in Pennsylvania, and suddenly I was jotting down notes and calculating salaries. As usual it all sounded good to my brain, but my gut calculated otherwise. Home was comfortable, money was comfortable, but my soul sought new experiences, which are never comfortable.

"You know you have a place here," my mother reminded.

"I know."

"So are you leaving?"

"I don't know."

Art butted in—"You don't know!?"

"I don't know."

"Well you have to decide. You've got two days to get across the country for Christ's sake!"

"I know."

"Might as well stay now. Not gonna make it at this rate."

He was right. I wouldn't. But I sure as hell wasn't staying. I was simply paralyzed by indecision, and the longer the cobbler cooked the more guilt I felt for leaving. I imagined the cobbler going to waste, heaved into a trashcan after days of crusting and molding. I gave it a face—a cute little cobbler face made of blueberries—and indeed such creative presentation was possible; the immeasurable love my mother poured into her craft. Guilt and indecision were two ways that my fear manifested, and most of the time I didn't recognize it as fear. I simply thought I was making a bad decision or being a shitty person.

Art had been all over the world.

"How did you make decisions when you were younger?" I asked.

"Just walked through doors when they opened," he said.

And that was that. I knew that a door had opened for me in Colorado, so I lugged my luggage downstairs and backed out of the driveway for the last time, pointing the nose of the Camaro west. Past the tollbooth, past the truck stop, past the state line, and suddenly I was in Ohio.

Calls poured in.

"You know you can turn around."

"I know, Mom."

And I knew the cobbler was already baked and waiting, but I hammered down as I had leaving Maryland.

It was another blazing hot day, and because the Camaro's AC was busted I took my shirt off and rolled down the windows. Not even the sun would stop me this time. I was going to watch it set from my windshield, pavement rolling beneath my feet.

It was total freedom.

I breathed easy, the sun washed over me—blinded me— and all I could see was white light and tiny taillights. The car had no visors and sometimes I had to guess where I was on the road, steadying the wheel as much as possible. I waited for a feeling of weightlessness, the road to break from underneath, a sudden cliff leading back into the Abyss—the comfortable place I just left. For this was not the Abyss. This was courage and it was certainly uncomfortable. So uncomfortable that I continued looking for reasons to cease the whole adventure. And when we're afraid, we become experts at finding excuses.

Cobbler. Weather. People. Money.

A rattle under the hood of my car.

Yes, a rattle! The car is probably going to blow up. I should pull over to take a look.

—

SO THERE I WAS back at a truck stop, peering under the hood knowing damn well there was nothing wrong. Kelsey called and, similar to my mother, only encouraged my fear, saying things like "Maybe it's not meant to be."

And no wonder!

It was a reflection of what I was projecting—crying for help without realizing it. My quivering voice, hesitance in taking action, asking her opinion. She told me what she *thought* I wanted to hear, not what I *needed* to hear, which was "Keep driving, damn you!"

I'd hear that from my 'therapist', Natalie.

But even Natalie's words slipped through the cracks as I meandered around the convenience store, my bright little Abyss filled with racks of snacks and romance novels and a blinking arcade, which I was promptly drawn to.

I passed time shooting terrorists, winning virtual victories to erase real life losses. I made my way into the food court, seeking grease, digesting a salad that tasted like toenails while peering out the window at the sunset.

No rolling pavement tonight.

I watched another guy about my age order an equally greasy meal. Shaggy-haired. Face of an intellectual, spine of a hitchhiker. In my travels, I'd often met people on the same journey as me, wandering the world in search of answers. I could always pick them out of a crowd.

When I first began my adventure as a trucker I met a twentysomething with distinguished looks—bookish and keenly aware of me. One day we ate lunch at the same table, sitting across from each other, masks securely fastened around faces until he removed his.

"You have a college degree, don't you?" he asked.

I looked around at my trucker buddies who were listening close.

"Well," I started, "I went to film school."

"Yeah, but you have a degree."

"I do."

"So what are you doing here?"

"Experience."

Turns out he was a philosophy graduate trucking for all the same reasons—looking to forge a new identity, discover the underbelly of life, seek truth in the unlikeliest of places. I was both drawn and repelled to him, as we were too similar and our paths collided like midnight trains.

Anyhow, the guy in the grease line reminded me of him. Could have very well been him and I could have approached and asked, but I preferred to keep the mystery.

I trashed my toenail salad, checked into a hotel and listened to chugging diesel engines outside, wondering where my courage went.

—

ONE DAY to reach the Rockies was impossible.

I called Colorado Bill to let him know about my car situation—or more accurately, car excuse—and only caught his voicemail. Not knowing whether or not to continue onward, I moseyed in the parking lot of a McDonald's.

A couple of old folks passed by and I smiled when our eyes met. I'll never see them again, I thought. They'll go back to their Ohio home, eat a few thousand more breakfasts and dinners, watch game shows, walk the dog, water the azaleas. They'll probably attend church on Sundays, eventful evenings congregating with the community, and then someday they'll die. But today, for one second—one blink of their epic lives—we shared a smile.

73

Hours passed. My stomach grumbled and soul growled. I crammed my face with jerky and stomped the pedal, back on the road, straight through Ohio into Indiana—oceans of farmland offering the west on a green platter.

The flat invited the rocky.

It was a veil of sorts, like a low cut dress on a beautiful woman. Tiny rises in elevation, wild deer roaming through roadside woodlands and all the foliage I hoped to find in the sky.

I hit the Illinois state line and yet another "you can turn around" speech from mom. Thought about it. I wasn't too far out, plus I still hadn't heard from Bill. With no lodging and possibly no job, home sounded pretty sweet. But my foot would not let up. I was cruising steadily despite the tug of the coast. Highway 70 connected all the way back to Maryland and I saw it as one long conveyor belt I raced against.

The sky dimmed to blue and I felt blue, and when the horizon no longer appealed to me, I stopped for fast food. While standing in line for toenail salad take two, I met a man from Quebec who mused with stories of his filmmaking dreams, as did most upon telling them my own. It seemed dreams were infectious and I planned to infect the entire country. I ate dinner, bought a six-pack, and hoofed it across the street to a hotel.

—

MORNING CAME. Halfway to Colorado and the plan was to drive fourteen hours straight.

I wouldn't sleep, I thought.

Knowing that such a drive required energy, I proceeded across the street to a shining diner, just as you'd picture in the Midwest. Silver and full of smells and smiles, and all the waitresses hospitable and motherly. Skin milky and pure.

"Everything okay?"

"Yes."

"Everything still okay?"

"Yep."

I was asked by so many that I forgot who my waitress was. I felt love all over and suddenly realized that love is everywhere—not just in one person, place, or thing. I wanted to stay. I watched a cook scrape burnt bacon bits from the stove. Maybe I'd take his job.

Fueled by coffee, I hopped back into the Chevy and sped through southern Illinois, down through the rolling plains of Missouri straight into Kansas—the blandest, damnedest stretch of land that offered no pleasing distraction from my inescapable thoughts. Regret, guilt, and indecision continued to plague my conscience, and my mother played the emotional keys and heartstrings. Even in Kansas I could still turn around.

But it wouldn't happen.

I was so close I could taste it.

I was licking the granite, dragging my tongue along the turnpike, an American Autobahn, cars whipping past at ninety, tearing across the tarmac as if trailed by tornadoes. And the big rigs blared just as fast, reminding me of the trucking days; the inherent loneliness in states like these. Softly bouncing in my seat, watching little cars zip around and wondering about the people inside—where they were going, where they lived, what they were like. Wishing I could go with them, especially towards the end when the glamour wore off and the states became boringly united—all too similar—connected by gravely veins and a corporate cranium.

By and by, I found myself seeking character in people rather than places, for people comprise the places and speak for the land. I thought of Kansas City and what life might have been like had I stopped to live there. It was a sad afterthought with all the horizontal humdrum howling ahead.

I raced to keep the sun in sight, and when it dropped I began to nod off, well past my limits and knowing full well what they were. I stopped for gas in Salina and booked a room for the night—a full moon night where a slight chill nipped the air and carried cigarette smoke as fast as I blew. I drank my two-pack and ironed my most professional attire, as I still planned on interviewing come hell or high water. Surely there was no water to be found between here and Colorado; therefore I prepared for hell.

—

I FINALLY heard from Bill.

In the morning. A simple email that read:

JUST GIVE ME A CALL WHEN YOU GET INTO TOWN.

I slammed a bowl of granola and was back on the road, buttoned up and buckled in for the final stretch. The closer I got to the state line the better I felt about the whole trip, and thus is something to be learned about movement: the more we continue, the stronger we become.

Clouds filled the sky and I skimmed under slashing rain until I reached the edge of Kansas, stopping at a convenience store and running into a wall of humans inside. Tall, thick humans with cowboy hats and leather boots, towering above as if carved from mountains and set free into the world. I looked around for their overgrown, mythical horses.

After soaking in the sun with my black coffee I was back at it again, emerging from the dust of western Kansas, gulps away from rocky redemption. The Camaro roared forward, floored pedal and churning metal, burning, with me behind the wheel yearning, following the landscape as it led west.

West! West to zest!

Tumbleweeds drifted past, snagged into brush, and I wanted to collect one and buckle it next to me just so I wouldn't arrive alone.

A little further and there it was:

WELCOME TO COLORFUL COLORADO

White paint against a wooden sign, leaving much to the imagination color-wise. But I knew there would be color, just as I found neighboring New Mexico enchanting. With hours left to Zephyr, I stopped for a final fuel-up. And as I stood at the pump, I admired my gleaming vessel, amazed at its reliability—a trooper thankful of his tank.

Back into the driver's seat, a turn of the key and . . .
silence.

Again and again to no avail, she would not start.
Wouldn't even crank.
So there we sat, tired trooper and tank, and not a mountain in sight.

12

STUCK IN THE GRASSLANDS, little Limon, cigarette hanging, leaning against the ol' Camaro which was bubbling at the brim and I felt for the poor heap. The attendant, a squirrelly teen who helped push the car to a safe place, told me of a local mechanic I could drive to, if only she would start.

I waited.

Wandered the store for awhile looking for a pretty girl I saw during my trucking days. It was in a place just like this, and suddenly I felt a heavy sadness, as I was certain I wouldn't see her again.

I started remembering all the women of the road. The waitresses and cashiers and even the border patrol girl in Laredo—the Latina with faraway eyes which made me want to quit the damn job and take her up in my arms.

"Are you alone in the cab?" she asked.

I wished I didn't have to say yes. Wished I could've undone her tied up hair and uniform. Laredo girl, I called her. Ah she was a woman! And I drove away that day and God knows where she is now. Sitting in a living room, perhaps tending to children, or off at school studying, dating, living—certainly not in Limon.

Does she dream of me? Does she imagine climbing into the cab that day?

Or was she simply in a somber mood?

How often does another reciprocate our yearning?

If only we didn't walk around with these masks, maybe we'd be bold enough to find out.

—

EVENTUALLY THE BUBBLING settled and the Camaro sprang to life. I shot down the meager main street and found the garage. No coincidence it was next to a truck stop.

The mechanics lumbered forward, bushwhacked as the brush, and swiftly went to work—even the shop owner pitching in his time. Meanwhile I walked across the street to the truck stop in search of my damsel, or a damsel. The sun was warm and wind cold, and as it blasted my face I could nearly smell the pines from the canyons it came. There was no damsel to be found but plenty more grease to load up on, and I sat in the convenience store eating, looking around at the truckers and seeing myself in them. They watched TV with glazed eyes, sometimes noticing when I passed by, flinching a greeting—raised eyebrow or slight opening in their mouths. But no. They were only licking dry lips. Truck stops gave me the same I-need-a-shower-feeling as the retirement home my grandfather stayed at.

—

"ALMOST READY, BUD," said the larger of the two mechanics. "Whereabouts you from?"

"Mary—Cal—Pennsylvania."

"'Swhere I'm from!"

"Yeah? How do you like it out here?"

"It's okay. Freezing winters, blazing hot summers."

I glanced around, suddenly in awe at the flatness of the land.

A completed coloring book page.

Striking blue sky striped with clouds, as if it had all been conceptualized by the genius of a careless child. I did not desire to live there, but these men, like the others, were carved from its surface—even the one from Pennsylvania. It's as though we all find our way home eventually.

—

I PAID MY BILL and said goodbye and was westward bound again, full tank and hours left to Denver. I looked forward to seeing its skyline, but more importantly kept my eyes peeled for the Rockies. This wasn't a trip to Denver; it was a trip to the mountains.

Mountains!

Now the excitement returned, replacing fear, leaving nothing but smiles and tousled hair. Everything gleaming. Cars washed, trees trimmed, not a stone out of place. The moment was a gift and the further I drove the more it unwrapped. Shiny, sprawling, colorful Colorado and its colorful sunlight raining down—a baptism if I ever felt one. The Abyss was behind and all the signs read WELCOME TO DENVER, and for those few hours I was freer than ever.

There they stood in the distance. 13,000-foot peaks demanding I live up to their height.

I felt strong. I could do anything.

Past the Denver skyline, barely taking notice of its splendor, the mountains couldn't come soon enough. I was a child running into his mother's arms—running and running—no matter how far away she was I could not stop running. That is, until I saw a Walmart.

Then I stopped.

Not for everyday low prices, but to prolong entering Zephyr. Abruptly afraid. Worried that it might not meet my expectations, that I may regret the whole drive, and what about Sage? Francine? Cobbler? Oh God. Did I make a mistake by coming? I hadn't even entered the damn town yet and these were my thoughts.

No!
Unchain me!

I got back in the Camaro and booked it up the canyon. Shadows clipped at my heels and with each curve and switchback I lost them. Sloping sections of highway pulled me downward, sucking me in, a warm vortex. The road seemed to curve forever, and I delightfully tackled the twists and turns like a Christmas Matchbox car. Other vehicles sputtered up the canyon with me. Kayaks and backpacks strapped to trunks and trailers, RVs crawling along, pulling off to the side for sports cars with tops down and topless female bicyclists reading maps and oh God! This is it!

My ears popped at eight thousand feet and I saw a stone sign engraved with ZEPHYR HEIGHTS. Spread before me lie a valley, a picturesque postcard of a town nestled within the rocky embrace. Pointy peaks rising to the sky—past the sky! Peaks piled on top of peaks, snow-capped despite impending summer, defying both gravity and season. I descended into town, crossing the low bridge over Lake Zephyr, easing up on the throttle so as not to disturb Pleasantville. Quaint shops and cozy cafes, cute people and their cute dogs. A western cardboard cutout town with the renowned Watson Hotel perched above as elegant overseer of its empire.

I stopped at the edge of it all, pulling into a parking lot next to a river lined with cabins and benches. But I chose to sit on the rocks, meditating on the journey, catching my breath on the high clean air.

I craved a beverage.

Nearby was one of the aforementioned cafes. I strolled over, greeted by a graying lady with a youthful face who smiled at me like an expectant oracle. "Nice young man," she said, upon handing back my license, followed by a beer, locally brewed and sweating in my palm.

I slumped into a surprisingly comfortable wooden chair, sipped my bliss and tripped off the scenery. I knew immediately that this was meant to be, all regret disintegrated. The only regret was that I spent weeks worrying about whether it would be worth it. Lost time. And yet it would happen again and again in coming weeks.

—

WEEKS? Hours.

I was still without a job and roof, calling Bill to no avail, leaving voicemails in the cold evening. I dug a phone number from my pocket—a guy named Vick who I connected with over the internet just before my trip. Vick sought a third roommate for his house and, upon calling him, invited me over straightaway. I got there just before dark, passing a herd of wild elk on the way.

The house was nice, but the room small and smelly. I didn't mind except for the high price of it. Vick and I sat in his living room chatting without drink, mouth dry from all the dry talk, and as the sky disappeared so did his face—an eerie shadow man of forty with the voice of a teen. He told me all about Zephyr, how he'd come from bustling Fresno, and still it was too big a town for him. The fact that he failed to turn on any lights began to creep me out and so I got up to leave not knowing where I'd sleep.

Vick outlined a couple of places on a map and suggested camping, to which I responded I had no tent.

"Don't need a tent!" he laughed. "Just a blanket. Stare at the stars. But you're a city boy, I can tell."

—

BETWEEN ALL THE DRIVING and talking I was beat and willing to crash anywhere. Still, I sought rejuvenation in the form of a warm bed, driving up and down the main street scanning for vacancy signs.

Memorial Day weekend at ten p.m.—I was pressing my luck.

Red buzzing laughter, yellow love beaming inside cabins, white moon illuminating black hope.

I took chance on a low budget hotel, greeted by two heavenly Nepalese faces—exotic women that further mystified Zephyr, piquing my interest among other things. No rooms were available, but they allowed me to bum around the lobby for awhile.

I sank into plush couches and nearly fell asleep when their angelic voices called out, letting me know of an opening. I snatched the keys and dragged myself upstairs into the room—weary and wrought, horny as hell.

—

COME MORNING, I stood in a long line waiting for waffles. They smelled good and everyone was fighting over the waffle maker.

I felt eyes upon me.

It seemed people were looking at me as if I was a martian who had just fallen through the ceiling. If I were a martian, the waffle line wouldn't be a bad landing spot, but I wondered why all the stares. I considered that it was only a reflection. For anytime we're placed in new and unfamiliar circumstances, we too appear new and unfamiliar, wide-eyed, glowing.

It was a scorching day and, itching to explore Zephyr, I roared into town amazed by the distant high snow. The Watson Hotel immediately caught my attention. It was part of what drew me to Zephyr—famous for its hauntings and having inspired artists who've stayed there. I nearly accepted invitation to a writers' retreat at the hotel months earlier but didn't have the cash.

Somehow I had manifested this.

And it was a glorious place, gleaming with elegance and dense with energy—a sense that there were twice as many occupants at any given time. The windows milked with unnatural light that showed up in photos as a faint, fuzzy presence. Top floors were closed off to the public and I was dying to see what abyss hung above. Thinking it could be an interesting place to work, I went to the front desk and applied for a job.

—

SOON HUNGER SET IN and I hit downtown for food and further exploration. Mostly I was looking for a place to stay since I could no longer afford hotels, or rather felt that I shouldn't, having already spent a sizable portion of my "Bank of Dad" loan. I ambled from one end of Main Street to another, imbibing the ambivalence of its small town charm: Nepalese restaurant, bookshop, back alley boutiques, a music store (aptly named The Rolling Stone), and little plazas with bridges to cross.

I felt like I'd break the town if I didn't watch my step.

Old movie theater, old saloon, old mountains.

Neon t-shirts, knick-knacks, candies, backpacks.

What fresh heaven is this?

Then I walked down an alleyway and saw a slightly darker side of Zephyr, lined with dumpsters and chattering bums. It was there that I came upon an international hostel. An adobe-style building with bright blue shutters, two travelers sat on the upstairs balcony playing guitar. Immediately my gut told me that this was the place for me.

I walked up the crying steps into the building.

"Hello?"

No one in sight. Cramped kitchen.

I entered the living room and found one Theodora Schneider hiding in the shadows. Seemed the inhabitants of Zephyr preferred their shade and she was no exception.

"Come in," said Theodora. "Welcome."

I couldn't discern her features, only noticing large, round-rimmed glasses, round face, and straight smirk. The walls were painted with dark colors like a circus on a sad day; plants perched on windowsills next to bookshelves, pin-pricked maps, abstract artwork, and an ancient loom. Corridors were lined with small bedrooms that harbored sweaty stenches and climbing gear.

Theodora gave me a tour of each room, ultimately showing me a private space that suited my taste, although I was still hesitant.

"So do you think you want to stay here?" she asked. "Thirty bucks."

My gut screamed YESS!!!!!!

"Y—yeah," I whimpered, and went downstairs for my stuff.

I nearly bolted.

I thought creepy thoughts.

She was going to cut off my dick in the night and sell it on Black Market eBay. It wasn't even a real hostel, I thought. A human meat factory, Soylent Green for the mountain mouths. I muted the maniacal thoughts and went back to pay for the night, dropping my bag onto the hardwood floor, next to the bed and broken blinds and sad lamp.

I walked out onto the balcony and found another hosteller, offering some relief to my paranoia. He was skinny and meek, from Tennessee, sunk into a couch and lightly strumming chords on a cheap guitar. He told me that he and his brother were bicycling from Denver up through the Rockies and back down again.

We spoke of life and travel; everything we loved about the great American West. And now as I eased into the waters of the hostel I desired more people, more noise, more character! The fear of jumping in faded and I was ready for the full experience. It seemed that everything was fearful until you *began*, and then you realized there was no such thing as fear in the first place; only cruel jokes of the imagination.

—

THE SUN SET and the Tennessean went to bed, having to wake up at five o'clock the next day. I ventured across the street into a bar for a cold beer and warm body, finding one of the two. I gulped it down and walked around and stopped in front of a framed collage of barflies of the past. Smiling mustached faces with mullets and redness and arms around shoulders. I wanted to dive into the collage and jump from moment to moment, grabbing each face by the collar and asking whether or not they were truly happy. I wanted to track them down in this exact moment, find out where they lived and how they lived, whether they remember the smiles and what they were smiling for.

Nah. Just walked away.

I zigzagged across a parking lot and found another bar, coincidentally named the Tahiti Bar, billed as an 'island in the sky'. I had another beer and joined the jokers and smokers outside where live music played. The guitarist was black—the first black man I'd seen in Zephyr—and it felt strange to be struck by the sight of him. He sang cover songs, "Hotel California", and I thought about the balmy distant state and desert between us.

An older woman joined at my table, grooving to the music—long brunette hair that shot straight down from her scalp reminding me of a flower child that decided never to grow up. She told me she'd come from Michigan fifteen years ago and found home. She smiled the smile from the pictures. The smile I fell asleep with.

—

CROWS CAWING. A dream maybe.

Hours later the windows burned with daylight and I knew I had slept in far too long. I crept out of bed, cracking bones and toes, and heard the clinking of silverware outside my door. I peeked out to see a man hunched over the kitchen table, straggly hair stemming from a bald spot. Mad musician composing a crunchy bowl of cereal. He breathed a hello as I hurried past to the bathroom, wanting to know nothing and everything about him.

Today was the day that I would formulate a plan of how I'd sustain summer in Zephyr.

Job, place. Place, job.
Whichever came first.

It was a sweltering day. I squinted my way to the Camaro and drove straight to the ranch to track down Colorado Bill. Stepping over mounds of horse shit, I made my way into the office where a couple of blonde cowgirls greeted me like costumed waitresses of Illinois. They radioed Bill and I waited for the moment I had waited for; traversed half the country for.

In walked a lanky man with cowboy hat and Florida tan. He took off his sunglasses and shook my hand, immediately showing me around as if I already had the job. . .

"Here's the microwave if you decide to bring your lunch, and the monitors and equipment," etc.

I was ecstatic. I had the job without even interviewing!

Then Bill had some bad news. He told me that because I arrived late I wouldn't be able to work full time—he already hired replacements. I'd also have to wait another week to find out the exact amount of work he could offer, if any at all.

What a tease.

Bill sputtered off on his ATV and I left deflated.

I drove downtown again, scattering seeds of hope across real estate offices and businesses. There were plenty of jobs to apply for, but very little in the way of housing.

Everyone came to Zephyr in the summer.

Decked in adventure gear, ready for the world. And the world was directly in front of them. A town where everybody knew everybody save for the tourists. I had no place among either group; a drifter floating alongside old creatures of the west—flowing white beards like mighty gods turned mortal and poor. Vacant and vibrant all at once. And the women! A hardy stock of women with short haircuts who walked with intent—arms swinging at their sides, makeup-less and bra-less. Women are men and men are women. RVs and hippies and rusty campers with dog snouts sticking out. The population swelled from seven to fifty thousand.

I wandered among them all, seeking home, looking for locals and tapping into the town's truth. What I eventually found was that I gravitated toward places that appealed to me, and in entering those places found like-minded people who understood me. This is how I met Joolz, a barista at Friendly Coffee—two parts punk, a third hipster, and one hundred percent Colorado.

"Live here or just passin' through?" she asked (as they all did).

"A little of both. Staying at the hostel."

"Why'd you come to Zephyr?"

"Mountains." (as we all said)

"Freewheelin', huh? Got a job?"

"Looking for one. You guys hiring?"

"Not right now," she said, glancing back at the crowded kitchen. "Should try Circus Cafe, though. Pretty rad place. Talk to Rocco. He's a fellow writer, you'd get along."

Rocco.

I scribbled the name and made note to visit the following day.

It was getting late by now, and as I left the cafe I saw the most peculiar thing: Across the street, an elk waiting at a crosswalk. The stoplight changed color, cars halted, and the majestic creature trotted across. He made it with time to spare and continued upward toward a shopping center.

—

THEODORA AGREED to let me stay a few more nights at the hostel so long as I helped with chores. And when I returned that night, I opened the front door to a staggering sight—an Asian beauty, tall and slender with silky black hair, making soup at the stove. Aromas that transformed the musty building into a sacred temple.

"Soup?" she asked, handing me a cup.

"S-s-s-sure."

We sat down together and traded synopsized life stories. Xiu had just graduated from school in Minnesota and was on her way back to California to see family, stopping in Zephyr for a hiking adventure. I was lost in a trance, somewhere in the Wild East surrounded by cherry blossoms and orchids.

I fell asleep soon after, hoping to continue my fantasy or at least my vision of the summer.

Mountains.

But nothing came.

Only blackness and more crows and daylight washing over the white-walled room.

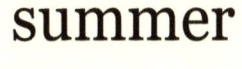

summer

13

IT HAD BEEN A WEEK living at the hostel and I was still unemployed and homeless. It was Maryland all over again, except now I had these damn peaks to live up to. I no longer circled around an empty house, but found myself on the balcony of the hostel each morning, following the ridge of the nearest mountain with my eyes. Or the Mexican shop owner who would park his bright orange Mustang in the alleyway and check a dumpster lock before bellowing off. Or the lovely ladies who walked past in their summer skirts and shorts. And the stars weren't stickers, but still I stared. Each one a tick on the clock. Are there as many stars as there are ticks?

I tried my damndest to stay in Zephyr.

Shadowface Vick's room was still available, but he was charging more than I could afford and besides my gut was telling me no. Trusting my gut became daily practice, sometimes a very confusing one. Logically the decisions never made sense and I was left in a pit of self-loathing.

Why wouldn't you take the room? It's a place to stay. You're an idiot!

I sought other options, at one point connecting with a guy named Evan—a lanky, gaunt-faced kid who drifted around in a haze. He was in his sophomore year at college, desiring a summer in the mountains before he had to settle down at his new job. It sounded ridiculously fatalistic and I was disturbed that anyone his age should feel such pressure.

Evan found a place to live atop a wood shop. A cramped little room with just enough space for bunk bed and dresser. He offered me one of the bunks and drawers for a few hundred bucks.

Inhabited by exchange students, the entire building smelled of Nepalese food. One couple peeked out to say hello, barely opening the door, embarrassed by the upkeep of their cell. I thought of my grandfather and sympathized. They were the kindest people I'd ever met and living in a windowless closet. The kitchen was bare and black; showers moldy. I couldn't believe the owner rented every room. I wanted nothing to do with the place, but kept Evan hanging just so I had the option.

—

ON THE SAME DAY I met Evan, I walked across the street to Circus Cafe to find Rocco, but alas he wasn't there. Instead, a middle-aged woman with a short bob, bopping around to her own beat—a Jimmy Buffet concert in her head. She reminded me of a coastal girl, but I later heard that she was from the mountains and it baffled me. What puzzled me more is that I never saw her again afterwards, as though she disappeared into the beach of her brain.

"You can leave a message for Sam, the owner," she said.

Sam.

I thought of a big burly man who carved and constructed the cafe—a building that rose higher than the others in town, peaking into a triangular roof that pointed to the heavens. I left my contact info and wondered about Rocco and the writers' group and what it would be like to work there.

With nothing to lose, I continued driving around town knocking on doors, stopping by a motel called The Nifty Nickel, as someone told me they rented rooms on a monthly basis. Upon entering, an oddball eyeballed me from behind the desk, snickering like a porn director. I asked if any rooms were available to which he replied they were all occupied by Russian girls. Young Russian girls.

It was hot again.

I sat down in the Camaro and let the heat consume me. I rolled up all the windows and held my breath for a long time, waiting until the very last second to kick open the door. It was like jumping into a pool.

I closed the door and prepared for another round when my phone rang. It was Howard, manager at The Watson Hotel, who requested a job interview with me the next day.

Yes! Potential!

Things were looking up and I hurried back to the hostel to prepare, bumping into Theodora.

"Theodora! I might have a job. Mind if I stay at the hostel a couple more nights?"

"That's fine," she said, "but I need your help."

"Sure. Whatever."

"I need you to clean the bathrooms."

My mind wandered down the hallway. The mess.

"Alright, deal."

And with that, she shoved a mop and bucket into my hand.

I slipped on gloves, goggles, and a dust mask, and appeared ready for the apocalypse. On my hands and knees, scrubbing months of grime from porcelain. Scrubbing entire countries from tubs and commodes. The irony. All these years wanting to travel the world and now hovering above it; worshiping it on my dirty jean knees, an entire planet succumbing to the power of my sponge. I sweat profusely—hours and hours— and at one point Theodora brought burgers and asked me to stop and have lunch with her.

My appetite was non-existent but I obliged and sat down, joined by her college-aged son—a recent dropout fixated on his inventions. Theodora spoke of life as a textile conservator and how she was still working in the far reaches of Nebraska as an anthropologist. Her life was amazing. She'd been a nomad up until the age of twenty-eight when, during a kayaking adventure, had become capsized and nearly drowned, reshaping her plans for a more purposeful existence. She was in her fifties now and her son was but twenty, drifting through life as we all were. I knew his type. He was seeking a calling—the lost generation of the twenty-first century—fed up with the lost American dream. There was something purer to fight for, something screaming from the depths, and for whatever reason it was no longer easy to ignore.

—

WHEN IT CAME TIME for my Watson interview, I dug clothes from my bag and ironed them best I could. I walked the long steps toward the hotel and entered, meeting Howard in the acclaimed dining room. Tables crafted of aluminum and wood. Glass bottles glowing behind the bar.

Howard was a model for hospitality.

Young, brawn, buzz cut, blazer and black tie. Despite his youth, his eyes were already disappearing into his face, and I thought about Evan and Theodora's son, and all the young people I kept meeting who seemed to be fighting for their eyes. Howard immediately took to me and my knowledge of horror films, and wanted me as part of the team—to be a guide for Watson Ghost Tours. We spoke details over sparkling water and, finally, just as I went to shake his hand, he stopped me.

"There's one last condition you'll need to meet," he said. "You've gotta shave your beard. Hopefully that's not a deal breaker."

I'd had my beard for seven years. It was an uncomfortable thought.

"Not at all," I replied.

The interview ended there. We were to meet the following week for orientation. I proceeded downstairs to greet the rest of the team and they all welcomed me as if acting in a commercial for the place—"Hiiiiiiii!!"

An older lady with purple hair approached. They called her Midnight Maggie.

"You have such good energy," she said, placing a hand on my shoulder. "I hope you'll *join us*."

I looked around for the ghost of Jim Jones.

"Do you live in Zephyr?" she asked.

"I'm staying with my aunt," I lied.

She closed her eyes. "Your aunt. Does she have a little white dog?"

Despite my lie, my aunt did have a little white dog.

"Yes."

"I can see it wagging its little tail. You should invite her to our ghost story night."

"My aunt or the dog?"

—

MY SEARCH for home continued.

I hung out with Evan a few more times, eventually going on my first hike. Evan was a bewildering kid. Every tidbit story he told was Hallmark material—full of sap and cheer and a smattering of sadness. It was as though he'd just burst from a bubble, pure as packaged soap. Be that as it may, Evan had loads of physical stamina. He was an experienced hiker as well as a bicyclist, mountain climber, and something else requiring energy. I was huffing after our first mile and quickly realized how out of shape I'd become. My street shoes didn't help, ineffective at gripping loose gravel.

The valley was spotted with shadows that kissed the sharp evergreens while inky crows flapped past. We continued on through aspen trees, spaced apart like white bamboo sticks (nature's toothpicks), and then climbed upwards where we bumped into a fellow hiker—a lost soul who reminded me of Ronald from Moonshine. A hat covered most of his gray hair except in the back where it sprouted out the sides. He was staying at the YMCA and told us about all the lives he'd lived, from Alaska to Australia.

Evan skipped alongside while I meandered behind, suspicious of the man's nervous ticks. The difference in our trust levels was apparent.

Was there a correlation?

Do we transform into vigilant prudes with age?

I wasn't much older than Evan, but there I was encased in a hard shell, painting the hiker as some backwoods serial killer; just like Theodora, the black market butcher. It's ridiculous. Evan just burst from a bubble and there I was inside of mine.

Soon I said my goodbyes, finally telling Evan that I wouldn't be rooming with him and that was that. Life would whisk him off to thousands of new experiences, as it would me.

—

BACK AT THE HOSTEL, I convinced Theodora to let me stay another week under the condition of continued chores.

"Come with me to the basement," she said.

Upon entering, I ran into a wall of boxes. They were stacked everywhere. Boxes on shelves. In closets. Boxes inside of boxes.

"And they all need moved somewhere else."

It was essentially a storage area that she wanted converted to a functional living space. Her son showed up with a friend and I was happy to see that I had a small army, however it was still quite challenging. Theodora stood by as we heaved the boxes into each other's arms, all of which had to be brought to her attention—"Yes, that can go in the truck for disposal" and "No, that needs to stay and go in the attic" and "I don't know what I want to do with that one."

I was cleansing her life of clutter and couldn't believe the amount uncovered.

"I'm *not* a hoarder!" she proclaimed.

She bought burgers and we laughed about it.

—

THE FOLLOWING DAY I stopped by the DMV to trade in my temporary Pennsylvania tags for Colorado plates. I held one of the plates to my nose and sniffed it as I would the binding of a new book.

It was the smell of potential.

One day it would reek of mud, rusting in a junkyard buried under mounds of scrap metal. I smelled the bumper of the Camaro, then the plates. Maybe they were both smells of potential. Did the car not provide me opportunity just as well?

I looked over and a family of four were sitting in a van staring at me.

Slightly embarrassed, I sat back down inside the car.

Something didn't feel right.

My nose was filled with the aroma of potential and outside the windshield was a landscape worthy of a hundred postcards. But in my mind, I saw the black backs of my eyelids. And then I realized that my eyes were actually closed.

Where were the mountains of my Maryland couch?

I thought maybe I had been searching in the wrong place. Maybe there was more to the mountains than the mountains. Maybe I'd placed too much emphasis on those poor peaks.

Where were my people?

—

FEELING AS THOUGH I wouldn't find camaraderie at The Watson, I dropped by Circus Cafe again to speak with Sam.

Again, he was nowhere to be found.

Instead there stood a barista behind the bar, motionless as a statue. A man in his early thirties with dark, intense features. Hair like a surfer. Spirit like a monk.

"You Rocco by chance?" I asked.

"Yeah, what's up?"

"Joolz at Friendly Coffee referred me, said you might be hiring."

"Couldn't say for sure. You'd have to talk to Sam, the owner."

Sam, Sam, where was Sam?!

Rocco didn't budge. His aura was of another era. It was as though he stepped out from a painting, flummoxed by the particulars of reality.

I waited for Sam, shuffling around the store.

Half of the establishment was a gift shop, and most of the merchandise was imported from Paris or Italy—boutique greeting cards, journals, paints and canvases. A playground for artists upstairs, complete with extra seating and tall windows. Board games for boredom. Turntables for turned tables. Books scattered like intellectual fairy dust.

Upon returning downstairs I bumped into a petite lady with silver hair perfectly trimmed to her round head.

Rocco nodded, "That's Sam."

—

SAM INVITED ME into her office, which was just as cozy as the rest of the place, and soon began an impromptu interview that I was half prepared for; handing her a wrinkled resume with a wink.

"Ever been a barista before?" she asked.

I shook my head.

"Any experience in food service?"

Shook my head.

She dropped the subject and settled for small talk.

A recent divorcee, Sam was rebuilding: Attending college in her fifties, changing careers, lifestyles, thoughts, and hairstyles. She was a changing woman and understood change and knew why I was in the mountains.

"I like you," she said. "I like your energy and think you're a good fit for the job. Interested?"

Once again I was struck with indecision, having just accepted the offer at The Watson.

Which was better?

I thought of Francine and Sage, and Pennsylvania and Colorado, and all of my other choices. I loved the options and wanted more, more, more! So I left Sam hanging and went back to the hostel to sit and ruminate.

I sat and sat.

And before long, I realized that by not taking action, I had chosen the option of sitting.

—

THEN I MET HANK. Hank got me moving.

A man of epic proportions, he thundered out from his hostel room and greeted me with a Santa Claus smile—rosy cheeks, minus big white beard. He told me that he was from Albuquerque, spending a week in Zephyr while waiting for his teenage daughters to finish summer camp nearby. We moved our conversation to the local bar, which was empty save for the bartender, famous black musician, and girl doing tricks with a hula-hoop.

A big kid, Hank out-joked me and was always first to laugh. It was delightful to discover such enthusiasm in a man who worked at a corporate accounting firm; a man opting for hostels and bottles. I told him about my dilemma—wondering whether or not to stay in Zephyr or continue on to California.

"Couldn't imagine spending a summer in this tiny town," Hank chuckled, looking around.

Maybe he's right, I thought.

But days later Theodora would tell me that a summer in Zephyr could be *life-changing*.

—

AT DAWN Hank and I packed our daypacks with snacks and essentials and off we went on a hike that lasted approximately ten miles.

I wasn't prepared for any of it.

I had a bag full of Slim Jims, raggedy shell toes, and no hat. Hank was nice enough to lend me the latter, including a pair of sturdy boots. I slipped and scraped my way up the trails, shrugging it off as a walk in the park. We passed by burnt crisps of trees from recent brush fires and ducked under rock formations resembling faces, ultimately winding up at a lake for lunch.

Hank had even brought an extra sandwich along.

He was clearly a responsible parent and for the moment I considered him my Colorado father. I wondered if he thought of me as his Colorado son. Sometimes we talked and sometimes we just sat. Our time together was therapeutic; hiking itself was meditation. I focused on the land in front of me—the contours, patterns. There were no petty worries about life. Only immediate action.

—

IN THE COMING DAYS Hank and I continued our hiking excursions, exploring the wonders of the windblown land.

Quartz Lake, Black Lake, Spruce Lake.

The hikes were yet another version of sitting in parking lots, hiding under covers, and wandering supermarkets—a way to distract myself from the questions. I knew this. I knew this like I knew it when I drank. But I'd much rather this. This was physical; this felt good.

Ah but I yearned for a drink!

Yearned for drama, yearned for stormy nights!

Why? Why couldn't a good hike suffice?

Why must we fight?

14

I WAS ABOUT TO LOSE my Colorado Dad as he had his Albuquerque family to return to. Like everyone else, he would go back to his life and leave me to wander. This is all before I learned to accept my drifting and found solitude to be some kind of curse. It was as though God was playing tricks—introducing me to great people only to yank them away at the pinnacle of our bonding.

I even took to calling Sage a couple of times and the conversations went something like this:

"Why are you calling me?"

"I miss you, I want to talk."

"I don't see the point."

"I thought maybe you could come to Colorado."

"Why would I want to do that?"

"Because I miss you."

"Then why'd you leave?"

I had no answer. I left because I had to.

We do what we have to do. Sage couldn't understand because she wasn't me. I couldn't understand her because I was me.

—

AND SO I BUMMED around the hostel a while longer, helping Theodora with various projects. I cleared out her entire basement by the end of my stay. Sometimes I dug up old photos of her younger days—sitting in boats and on beaches, sun-baked, toes dug into the sand like living fossils. She was a beautiful spirit and we swam together for the time being. She saw me down in the doldrums and told me things like "This is your *twenties*, you're supposed to be having fun!"

One day Theodora handed me a dry cleaning bag and I unzipped it to find a white vintage blazer inside, worn by a professor apparently. She said that I could have it so long as I wear it to The Oscars upon nomination for my first hit film.

I kept finding little jewels in her boxes.

Picture books drawn by her son with western themes. Oregon Trail. Lewis and Clarke. I meditated on the drawings, every little scrape of crayon. The history of America and a single human being. Still I grew bored and thought that I should move on. Despite Zephyr being my dream town weeks earlier, I hesitated to settle. None of the options seemed good enough. I kept thinking about palm trees and paradise somewhere else. Always somewhere else. Really it was my hesitation that I grew bored with.

—

I PISSED AWAY DAYS in parking lots—usually McDonald's where I could get a meal for a buck or two, then hit the library to replenish brain cells lost from chemical food. I went to McDonald's not for the food but the people. Because the restaurant's design is so consistent, I found the differences in people more obvious.

Sometimes I went early in the morning to catch sight of the old folks clustered together, talking about the good old days, reading job listings and joking about coming out of retirement to wash dishes. Their laughs were slow and they savored wisecracks for minutes. "Time goes fast," they'd say.

The words stamped the surface of my brain.

"Time goes fast."

One morning a group of elderly women were huddled around an iPad, which I thought was quite progressive. I waited until one of them looked up and saw me, and I stared into her eyes and tried to see her decades younger. I wondered if she saw me decades older. Or maybe we saw each other the same age momentarily.

Sometimes I sat outside for fresh air and watched the homeless people beg at the entrance. There was a tattooed lady with a shopping cart and poor dog tied to it. A human being like everyone else, yet invisible to the world. Cowboys in chaps offered her a bag of food. They made small talk. Afterwards, a long-haired man approached. They compared tattoos by lifting up shirts—"Whoaaaa! Check out this one!" He ran a homeless shelter in Denver and tried to recruit her.

She declined. "I like Zephyr Heights."

—

MY RUN-INS with the homeless didn't end there. When I returned to the hostel, Theodora told me that a mother and daughter would be joining me in my room. She said that they had nowhere else to stay and couldn't refuse despite her reservations. I thought nothing of it and met the woman upon waking the next day. She was a tan-skinned, stout lady from Brooklyn. She looked like Brooklyn and talked like Brooklyn. Her father was dying of cancer and she was about to go back to Brooklyn to be with him.

"Got a toothbrush?" she asked.

I handed her my spare.

"Paste?"

Yep.

"Comb?"

Nope.

"Well how do y'comb your hair?"

She was needy and I tried my best to provide companionship and good conversation. A peculiar woman. I watched her grab a glass from the kitchen cupboard, fill it with water, take a swig, and put it back, lipstick stained and unwashed.

"So where you headed?"

"Somewhere," I told her, as I told everyone.

She laughed.

"You a believer? Believer of The Bible?"

"In my own way."

"Let's pray right now."

She gripped my hand and it was then that I realized the power of faith for the homeless. Everything holy, everywhere church.

Later, her teenage daughter entered our room.

Dark skin just like her mom and the same stuffy voice that made her sound like she had a cold. Wet hair, tattoos, attractive in a way. The next morning I heard her and her boyfriend having sex in the shower.

—

WITH NONE OF my options looking pretty enough, I planned to leave town.

Wednesday.

Yes, I would leave on a Wednesday.

And on Tuesday night I had wicked nightmares of giant bulls chasing me through a field. I was running and running until I grew a pair of giant balls that dragged the ground and halted me to a stop. I turned and faced the bulls and, likewise, they stopped.

I stood defiant. They bowed. I woke up.

I looked at myself in the mirror and knew that it was Zephyr or bust. There would be no more sitting on the balcony with beers and loitering in parking lots.

I grabbed my electric trimmer and proceeded to shave years off my face, clumps of hair falling into the drain. And then came the blade. Cold steel against steaming pores, breathing deeply while trying to remember that I was a human being and it was just hair.

Upon finishing, I saw a stranger in the mirror. I looked both younger and older. The skin of my chin and cheeks was bare and smooth, but my discolored teeth had become more obvious. Black coffee and stouts, I thought.

My eyes reminded me of my father and uncle, and for the first time I saw a physical resemblance to them. It startled me and I gently reminded myself that I was not them. I loved them but did not want to be them, and suddenly I wanted my beard back as an extra layer of self. No turning back. I had shaved for The Watson and promptly set off to accept the job.

—

I WAS SWEATING in the HR office of the hotel.

Paperwork. Sign here.

Date of birth. Start date.

Taxes and timesheets.

Howard walked in with one of the corporate heads, an older guy in a three-piece suit. They greeted me with hearty handshakes.

"See?" said Howard, "Clean shaven now!"

"Seems like a bright young man," said the head. "Happy to have you on the team!"

My gut danced like the devil.

And yet I signed everywhere and smiled everywhere, and the secretary in particular smiled back at me—a blushing Puerto Rican girl with cheerful eyes and long dark hair. I wanted to take her away and leave the rest. Her name was Valerie and we had coffee together afterwards. I told her that I didn't really want the job and was thinking of leaving Zephyr. She smirked as though nothing mattered in life. Her English bounced from syllable to syllable like a ping-pong ball. I loved every mistake.

"Just think about it," she said. "No pressure or anything."

We agreed to meet the next day for a spontaneous trip somewhere.

—

IN THE MORNING I was officially homeless.

Theodora ran out of rooms and could no longer let me stay at the hostel for free. I could have paid, but was subconsciously pushing myself to make decisions by creating dire circumstances.

Before leaving the hostel, I had a big oatmeal breakfast and stuck a pin into one of the maps on the wall. There were hundreds of pins from travelers all over the world, each one marking their hometown. I found myself lost when I thought about the concept of home and didn't know where to put the pin, so I grabbed a handful and started sticking them everywhere. Places I'd lived or wanted to live, or just places I wanted people to notice which had no pins at all. Then I drew my own island in the middle of the Pacific and named it CHEVROLET, CAMARO.

Pin.

—

WITH A FEW HOURS to spare before my date with Valerie, I decided to drop by Circus Cafe just for kicks. Maybe to say goodbye to people I would never come to know.

This time, yet another guy stood behind the bar.

Slightly older than Rocco with a pair of keen eyes— kinetic laser beam eyes that shot right through me. His hair was neatly combed to the side and he leaned across the counter with a smirk that made me think of Lorenzo, my favorite bartender.

"I like your eyeglasses," he said.

"Thanks."

"I'm Ezra. You applied to work here, right?"

"Sure did."

"Gonna take the job?"

"Don't know yet. Might be leaving town."

"That's a shame. Heard you're a writer. We're all writers here, you know."

Behind Ezra stood a barista youngest of all. Curly hair that sprouted like a Chia Pet. You could barely hear him when he spoke; he seemed locked in a perpetual state of bashfulness. He nodded a greeting and went back to work.

I started to really dig the atmosphere and was once again thrown off my axis.

What a place!

Unlike the hotel, there was no sweating here. Only butterflies.

—

I LEFT THE CAFE with a smile. Somehow I knew that everything would be okay.

I picked up Valerie for our trip to Lamont, the closest town to Zephyr of a much smaller population. It was a mere twenty-minute drive but felt like forever because we had nothing to talk about. I barely knew the girl and was barreling down the canyon with her. Her hair blew all over the car and my invisible hand reached out and felt it. She looked free as the wind.

In Lamont we walked around, admiring the small town glory. It was as though all the misfits moved there and kicked in doors, claiming spaces like the original pioneers. A fairytale land similar to Zephyr with pinball arcades and breweries, cafes that closed at three p.m., and in-home art galleries advertised from front porches by French expatriates. *Bonjour!* And then back up the canyon—Valerie handing me pieces of baked seaweed or something. It was clean food and a clean day and I craved dirty wine.

My wishes were granted later that evening when I met one of Valerie's friends, Jackie, who worked in a winery—an older lady who looked Native American—tan and tattooed. I imagined her on the back of a motorcycle, engulfed in the flowing white beard of a mangy man, racing through Arizona in the middle of the night. We drank in the winery and by the time Jackie clocked out, I was comfortably buzzed.

Too drunk to drive, Jackie drove Valerie and I back to her apartment. I was grateful, given I had nowhere to stay. We continued our partying there with goodies laid out on cardboard-boxes-turned-tables, watching classic westerns, reveling in all the jagged cinema when suddenly the room flashed with light as if someone were taking pictures outside.

Jackie opened the front door.
"Oh my God, guys, come look at this!!"

Lightning.

Thunderless lightning contained within a single cloud centered in the sky, everything calm around it. We sat and watched.

—

MY CAR BECAME HOME.

I popped the trunk each morning and pulled out clothes, empty water bottles, bags of trash. I showered in the laundromat for five bucks. Six including towel and bar of soap. The sweet old ladies who worked there welcomed me each day with a smile warm as the summer and allowed me to vent all my frustrations to them.

"This is one of those times I'm glad I'm not young" they told me, laughing and reassuring that everything would work out as they knew from experience. One afternoon I bumped into Sam at the laundromat and she asked whether I'd made my decision about the job. I wanted to say yes but found myself paralyzed yet again.

"Unfortunately, I still don't have a place to live," I told her.

"I know a person who has a condo for rent," she said.
"Yeah?"
"You know Lonnie, who manages the record store?"
"Heard of him."
"We're good friends," she said. "I'll talk to him and get back to you."
She winked and walked off.
Shit. If she found a place for me I'd have no more excuses to give myself.

Being indecisive sucked, but it was easier than taking action. Action required commitment and trust. But at the time, I felt like everything I did was wrong and didn't want to screw up any further. The next decision *had to be right*, and with that self-imposed pressure came the fear of stepping in *any* direction.

—

MOUNTAIN NIGHTS were cold, but I continued to sleep in my car, covering up with a blanket that Jackie gave me. I was told there was a five hundred dollar fine for camping in parking lots, so I ducked down as far as I could and covered my body in black.

No matter how tired I was, it took me forever to doze and sometimes I'd pop a couple of sleeping pills. They bought me a few hours before waking up again, cold and cramped. There was no straight logic as to why I chose homelessness over the hostel. I was pushing myself into something. Or away from something. All I knew was that this was an unsustainable way to live and something had to happen soon.

—

COUPLE NIGHTS LATER, I met with Valerie and we walked around town holding hands—flirting in and out of shops—her speaking Spanish and teaching me phrases, rounding out my rough pronunciations. Likewise, I helped with her English.

She told me about the beaches of Puerto Rico and showed me pictures of sandy shores and cities skirting along their edges. I wanted to be there. We sat together on a park bench and listened to a musician cover John Denver songs. He sounded like John Denver, looked like John Denver, and I could've sworn it was John Denver—the ghost of John Denver who fell from his ghost plane and splashed onto the ground with his ghost guitar.

Disappointingly, his name was Ted. Cowboy Ted.

It started to rain and Ted played on while Valerie and I sat with arms around each other. The sun poked through the clouds and encouraged Ted's enthusiasm.

"It's just rain, friends! Let's sing it away! C'mon clap with me, I think God is listening. There's the sun, see!"

—

AFTER DINNER we sat in the Camaro, in a deserted parking lot. We sat for a long time and created a silent rhythm, waiting for the proper beat to kiss at. Eventually my lips found hers and we fondled for a few minutes. Hours maybe.

She was a good kisser. It felt like every cell in my body had crammed into my face to join the party.

"What do you have?" she asked.

I didn't know what she meant but liked the way she said it, just like Laredo girl at the border patrol.

"What do you have?"

We kissed some more and I bottled the feeling of love. Love, lips, and her whole likeness—the entire night right into the bottle. It seemed that I collected feelings and options the same.

—

AT THIS POINT it was clear to the managers at The Watson that I wasn't taking the job, and just to make things clearer I went to visit Howard and told him myself.

"So you shaved the beard for nothing?" he asked.

"I had to know it wasn't the reason."

"Okay, fine. *Good luck.*"

Eventually, Valerie came to tell me that we couldn't be together if I had taken the job due to company policy and I thought it was amazing—the decisions we do or don't make in life and their consequent effects. Truly our lives are defined by our opportunities, and at the end of the day if you love life you can't go wrong. Every day is going to be incredible because you're alive.

Live, dammit!

There are no rules, as Ronald from Moonshine would say! There's only insecurity and bullshit, and love and courage.

Love is courage.

—

I RETURNED to Circus Cafe, this time with Valerie, and Sam quickly approached with open arms.

She noticed Valerie and gave me a nudge.

"You work fast," she whispered. "Come, walk with me!"

"Where?"

"To see a friend."

Valerie waited while Sam dragged me across the street to the record store to see the manager, Lonnie. There he stood, smirking from behind the counter—a thirtysomething with small eyes and cheeks like a chipmunk. He wore loose fitting clothing and sandals and flopped around when he walked, speaking in a slow drawl and saying things like "Yeaaaaahhhhhhh" and "Riiiiggghhhhhtttt?"

The embodiment of Zephyr slow life.

"So you're looking for a placcceeeeeee?" he asked.

"Yeahhhhh."

It was infectious.

"I've got a one bedroom condo we can share if you're interested. Four hundred a month. Come by and check it out tonight."

He seemed cool and so did Sam, and there was something about all the good vibes that calmed my spirit. Again, this was it and I just *knew*.

And everyone will give you their own advice based on their own strange lives. Hank would tell me to get the hell out of Zephyr, Theodora would tell me to stay forever, and Valerie would just shrug and twinkle.

—

WITH THE PIECES falling into place, knowing that I would take the job at Circus, I went back to Friendly Coffee and thanked Joolz for the job referral weeks earlier.

Sure enough, Rocco was there meandering about.

"Hey man, find a job yet?" he asked.

"Might be working with you at Circus."

"Serious?"

"Yeah. Have to see about a place to live first."

"Cool, man. Do you have time to chat right now?" he asked.

"Of course."

We sat among a crowd of milky Midwesterners—young people mostly—along with those who ventured up from Boulder for higher elevation and adventure.

Swallowed by couches, Rocco and I bonded on the subject of literature.

"I'm reading a book on Toltec Wisdom," he said, "Ever heard of it?"

"Nope. Ever heard of Watts?"

"Yep. Read the Beats?"

"Mhmm."

We were long lost brothers.

"Where you from?" I asked.

"Jersey. The good part."

His jokes were cut thick and served deadpan so that I could never tell funny from facetious. We spoke with enthusiasm and set the cafe on fire, and a group of college students emerged from it, ready to absorb our ideas with anime eyes. They were all freshmen on a Christian retreat of some kind and riddled with anxiety about their futures like Evan.

"What are your ambitions?" we asked them.

They hadn't the slightest idea.

"This and that, you know . . . like that. And maybe that."

What I mean is that they spoke about the things they thought they ought to be doing rather than things they wanted to do. Granted this is natural for young people, I saw the same waffling patterns in older folks.

"Forget what you've been told, do what you feel!" is what we said. More courage, more enthusiasm, more passion! Those are the types who will lead the future!

—

SOON I LEFT to meet Valerie, as she was to accompany me to Lonnie's to check out his bachelor pad. When we arrived, he opened the door and we entered a colorful apartment with stacks of records and a turntable. Outside, a small balcony with barbecue grill and thick pines in the backyard.

I was sold. It took me thirty minutes to move in.

We lit cigarettes and watched the sunset.

15

"WHAT DO YOU HAVE?"

Valerie kept asking me while we made out.

I didn't know how to answer or where any of it was going, but enjoyed being around her because she loved so passionately and was a genuinely positive person.

We went everywhere together. Valerie even tagged along to the grocery store when I went shopping for the first time, helping me pick out the "healthy foods."

"How about this? Healthy?" I asked.

"No," she smiled.

"And this?"

"No."

Everything was no bueno.

Then we stumbled upon the sausage and she hovered over it like a pot of gold.

"No," I said. With a smile.

In one of the aisles we bumped into Howard from Watson. He saw us together, feigned a greeting and continued on. Valerie turned red.

"What's the matter?"

"Nothing."

Then I stopped hearing from her.

I sent text messages only to receive single-word responses. It was peculiar and I backed off, jumping into my new job.

—

THE FIRST DAY at the cafe, I worked with Ollie, the sixteen-year-old barista prodigy who poured lattes with leaf designs and served them with a smirk. His curly hair was extra bushy and he was dressed in earthy colors that made me think of a hobbit. Far too pensive for his age, he shrugged all the time as if nothing mattered—first listening to everything—"Mhm" and "Uh-huh"—and then tossing a crumb into the conversation.

As the day went on, a familiar voice returned . . .

Why would you work here? Nine bucks an hour? It's for high schoolers, see? Get a real job.

These thoughts multiplied with the menial tasks Sam assigned to me on the first few days: take out trash, wipe down tables, refill napkins, gaze upon African goddess.

Huh?

Cozyed in a corner, flipping through a safari picture book was a sight that made my jaw drop and roll across the carpet.
"My father is from Kenya, so I love looking at these photos," she said. "Would love to go someday."
"I'll take you right now."
Except I didn't say that. I said "cool" and prayed that she lived in Zephyr. She did. I memorized her face—the caramel complexion that reminded me of Sage and short frizzy hair that bopped when she talked. Dimples and dark eyes and demonic smile. Yet there wasn't an evil bone in her body. Her name was Neema and she was a hostess at a popular lodge in town.

—

NEEMA TIMED her visits so that we could have mini dates when my shift was over. I'd run upstairs to the seating area and meet her in the corner by the big window where we could people-watch and talk philosophy—just as I had done with Rocco and the midwestern kids.
Despite my lusting, Neema had a Great Wall erected around her, and every time I tried to get close she would build another layer. Again she reminded me of Sage, and I

thought maybe there was something wrong with me that caused this melding of mortar.

One night I went to visit Neema at the lodge and walked into the tavern where she was assisting the bartender. A band was playing and I felt good, ordering strong local brews—beers with names like G'Knight. Next to me sat a lady named Wanda, fiftysomething, sad eyes, who rambled about her three divorces and how Zephyr had been her home for a decade. We talked a good deal about the word home and what it meant to each of us. She told me that Zephyr was meant to be home for me—"The mountains want you here. We want you here."

I thought of Midnight Maggie.

We were getting drunk and the Abyss was nigh. I could feel myself wanting to escape the world, and so I grabbed Wendy's hand and hit the dance floor. I thought about the wise women in McDonald's and looked into Wanda's eyes because I knew there was no difference between any of us. The entire planet just one big ball of flesh.

Neema glared from behind the bar. I'd temporarily forgotten about her—my African goddess. Wanda caught me glancing and said "She's a great woman, that one." And I knew it was true and only wished I could get over that great tough wall. Neema was undoubtedly a tough chick—an athletic chick. I imagined her spiking volleyballs into oblivion.

Spiritual, physical, beautiful.

Maybe she was out of my league.

As with Valerie, these were younger women and innocent at that. I was the man in black with crumpled cans in my hand.

—

I CONTINUED WORKING at the cafe with Rocco, Ezra, Ollie, and sweet Sam, the owner who wasn't always sweet especially during chaotic days when customers flowed through the door like the town river.

She took to calling us children—

"Children, you're forgetting to wipe down the bathroom."

"Children, you're not keeping track of milk stock."

"Children, we need to start making backup pots of coffee."

It was the one rule I remembered and made so many backup pots that Ezra nicknamed me Backup Pot Bach, after the musician.

We all had nicknames.

Rocco was Chai Wallah, Ollie was Olivier (French pronunciation), and Ezra became Maestro, as he led the circus as store manager.

Ezra was an enigma.

A family man with recent newborn, he remained a mystery despite his fatherly facade. It's as though he'd already endured five lives and was now beginning a sixth. He hinted at stories of living in Russia and France and his nomadic past. Long hair recently cut, just before the arrival of his "tiny human." Everything was a mystery with him, and that's how he seemed to like it.

—

I SLOWLY GOT the hang of the espresso machinery.

For the first couple of weeks I felt like a child again, not knowing a thing about anything—having to be shown how to steam milk, grind beans, press buttons, ring up customers, and where's the key to the bathroom? What's the combination for the dumpster lock? I wanted to get everything perfect right away. I hated this period of infancy and watched all the lovely women line up at the register, ordering specialized drinks that I knew nothing about:

"Lemme get a triple shot latte, soy milk, no foam, with two pumps sugar-free vanilla. And a little bit of honey. And not too hot."

Luckily Rocco was there to help during times of such crisis.

He'd look at me—"I got it."

Or Ollie, who would smirk and shrug and do it himself.

Or Ezra, who had the drink ready before the customer finished ordering.

Sam played the teacher role, dragging me over to the machine and quizzing me the entire time—

"Now what's the next step? How hot should that milk be? Test it with this thermometer. 160. Good. What's next?"

I went home exhausted each night, smelling like espresso beans, hands cracked and split and darkened at the rough patches. Boutique blisters. I dreamt of screeching, screaming-banshee steam wands and overflowing pitchers of burnt milk, and customer's eyes burning holes into my back and Sam burning holes into my face as she watched and evaluated.

Ah! I remembered having similar nightmares when I started my trucking adventure—backing the trailer off a cliff or forgetting to engage the brakes so that the truck rolled forward while I slept in the cab. I'd wake up and throw open the curtains only to glance around at the black parking lot, heart beating like bongos.

—

I STILL HADN'T found my groove in Zephyr and was sliding back into the Abyss, thinking of Valerie and Neema disappearing, my money disappearing, and my family calling for me to come back home.

And screwing up the drinks and feeling stupid for not remembering the right combination of syrups, milks, ratios and subsequent slang—cortados, macchiatos, flat whites, and the Starbucks terms that didn't even belong.

Somehow I forgot all the great things that had happened: finding a job and housing simultaneously, meeting Rocco, making new friends.

And mountains!

What about the mountains? How could I forget?

Where was the person who sat on the couch in Maryland, giddy and grinning? I knew where he was. He was in the future thinking of another mountain.

—

I SOUGHT the experience that I dreamt.

I was there and now I needed to *be there*. Hikes and bikes and committing myself—committing myself—to the land and people. And eventually I learned that damn espresso machine. And the more I learned the more I became comfortable; the more I breathed. And when I allowed myself to breathe, everything changed. The dream became a dream. Possibilities opened like a revolving door with endless entrances. People approached who reflected my enthusiasm—artists and travelers and eclectics.

The more of myself I gave, the more that flowed into me, as though I had broken down the dam and opened channels of energy, accumulating into waters where everyone could bathe in my spirit and I didn't give a damn because there was no dam.

Why not.

Why build your Great Walls?

I whipped up drinks faster and faster and grooved to the tunes. People from all over the world walked into the cafe.

People!

People with their foreign faces and flashy handbags, digging for dimes and snacking on pastries. None of our baked goods were labeled, so I had to run the gamut each time . . .

"What's that?" they'd ask.

"Pumpkin bread."

"And that one?"

"Poppy seed."

"And that?"

"Oatmeal cake, gingerbread, quiche, cherry pie . . ."

We did this all the time, even when lines were backed out the door (just one of the quirks of Circus Cafe). Like Sasquatch, our three-foot figurine that stood atop the display case, donning a messenger bag and thick-framed glasses. Hipster Sasquatch we called him—keeper of the bathroom key, looped around his wrist on a chain. Everyone loved Sasquatch and all the regulars knew where to go when they needed the key.

Newcomers had to figure it out.

Sometimes we were so busy that we could only glance over our shoulders and yell "Sasquatch!" to a desperate, dancing customer.

"Sasquatch?" they shrugged.

"Big foot! Yeti!"

—

Late in June, Valerie called. It was her birthday.

She wanted to meet for dinner at an upscale restaurant near the town lake. I was eager to see her after her mysterious disappearance.

I waited, lying on a bench anchored so close to the lake's edge that water rolled beneath me. The evenings were still chilly and I bundled up in my sweater, watching birds swoop down in search of suppers, then back up again towards the sky, which drew my eyes to the peaks. I could have seen them just as easily by looking down into the mirror of still water.

When Valerie arrived, we kissed and entered the empty restaurant, which was near closing time. Valerie knew one of the servers, who hooked us up with a seat despite glaring busboys and waitresses. We drank wine and sat awkwardly until the wine drank us, and then we began talking about the awkwardness.

"There's something I have to tell you," she said.

No way she's pregnant.

"Go for it."

"Remember the day in the grocery store when we saw Howard?"

"Yeah?"

"Well the next day he called me into his office and told me that I shouldn't be seeing you; that you're no good for me and that he doesn't want to see us together ever again."

"Howard told you that?"

"Yes. And he said that he could make things very difficult for you in this town, and could run you out if he wanted to."

"You've got to be shitting me. Is he your boss or father?"

"I know. It's not right. But I need this job. So we have to be careful."

"He's pissed that I didn't take the job and now we're together," I said.

She looked down at the ground, red-faced from the wine and truth.

I was furious.

—

WHEN I ARRIVED back at the condo, I noticed the balcony doors were open. I heard voices and saw two specks of orange floating in the darkness. Curious, I walked outside to find Lonnie and his friend, Paulette. She too appeared to be a goddess of some sort and I wondered how I kept meeting such epic women. Her hair was curly like the other goddesses, nose pierced, native, looking misplaced, like she dropped from the sky into the parking lot of a thrift shop. I dug her style and her swaying movements and the way she smoked her cigarette—as if it were her last.

"Yeahhhh." Lonnie went on about something, possibly introducing me to Paulette, but I wasn't in the mood for the exchange of life stories, not even synopses. I was just happy to be surrounded by stars.

Paulette worked at a glassware shop and suggested I stop by sometime for further talks. I promised her and excused myself to bed.

—

I KEPT MEETING interesting people at the cafe. It seemed that the whole world came to visit for a hot cup of java. One day an old Persian man caught me staring off into space and snapped his fingers in my face.

"Petit mals," he said.

"What?"

"Petit mals they're called, what you just experienced. When you were staring at the wall."

"I was just zoning out."

"Yeah, but that's a seizure. Some are very tiny like that."

"I get them all the time."

—

THEN THERE WAS Ed.

Ed was tall and slender and always wore a ball cap. He was the owner of a local hiking shop that sold adventure gear and enjoyed getting the scoop from young folks about new styles. He would sometimes venture into other subjects, and on The Fourth of July when fireworks were exploding over rooftops, Ed and I similarly lit the dark corners of life. We spoke of physics and the economy and the way people choose to live their lives.

And enthusiasm! We spoke of enthusiasm.

And when I was enthusiastic, so was Ed, and I could see in his tired eyes that he still had it and was pissed that he ever lost it. "As you get older," he said, "it's like your brain has wormholes. It's harder to take risks or deal with change. I'm getting older each day and wondering what to do with my life in this old age."

Walking down the sidewalk, I thought about life and the time-goes-fast theory of my McDonald's mentors. Neema strolled past with a friend of hers and waved a greeting. Our eyes met and I thought of Africa, the place I traveled to the day I met her.

She kept walking and so did I, stopping at a crosswalk to wait for the blaring traffic to halt. The lights turned and I started across the street when—

VRRRRROOOOOOOOOOOOSSSHHHH

A car zoomed past three feet in front of me.

A car that I did not see because a large truck blocked my view of the lane.

Death drove it, I thought.

16

I AWOKE ONE MORNING in the condo and walked outside with my black coffee and bowl of cereal, only to look over at our neighbor's deck and notice an old woman slumped lifeless in her chair. She looked uncomfortable—neck bent sideways and mouth drooped downward, quiet as a shrub. I imagined hearing the shocking news later. I wished for it to give me perspective on life; some major push or transformation.

Look at her wrinkles, I thought.
Look at her hair.
Look at that body which has been through so much.
She stirred.
I finished my cereal.

—

I HADN'T SEEN Valerie in a while and was starting to miss her. Neema was coming around again but remained distant, batting eyelashes on occasion. And on the night I planned to visit the glass shop to see Paulette, she came to see me, along with a friend who was much shorter but just as beautiful. A woman of Spanish descent with long, shiny black hair and eyes that seemed to contain galaxies, outlined by dark makeup and aura. Everything about her was dark except for her clothing which was overly colorful—old purple Chucks and a rainbow of shades leading up to ruby red lipstick, and then darkness above that. But it was a warm darkness and I thought of Sage.

"Meet my best friend, Helena," said Paulette. "She works at the glass shop with me."

Uh-oh.

They both twinkled, shifting in fabulously flirtatious ways. I whipped up their drinks—two soy lattes—and off they went upstairs to sit. Meanwhile I began closing the shop, wiping counters and forehead in the steamy kitchen, eventually making my way upstairs where the divas remained.

"Closing in ten minutes, just to let you girls know."

"Okay, thanks!"

I started downstairs and stopped myself. What was I doing? Two gorgeous women and I'm ushering them out like stray cats?

Back upstairs I went.

"By the way, if you two aren't busy tonight, would you like to join me at The Fox & Hound for drinks?"

They looked at each other.

"Sure!"

So I finished mopping and met them in the parking lot where we caravanned to Fox & Hound—the best bar in town where you could order a delicious meal and beer for twenty bucks. We sat in the lodge-like atmosphere of wood and mounted elk heads—the wonder-women at one end of the table and me at the other like a job interview. The best damn job interview ever.

They asked me questions—fiery questions. Questions that I loved to answer like "What do you think of modern society?" Questions that put me in the boxing ring with others, but not them. These women were like-minded and open-minded and had minds of their own, wowing me throughout the evening.

They sipped and stirred drinks: Helena a gin and tonic and Paulette a water with lime (I thought of Ronald). Paulette controlled her thoughts, straining them into clean, neutral sentences; whereas Helena poured them out as they were—controlled but brutally honest. She was a woman of conviction. Atheist, vegan, anti-consumerist, politically independent, generally independent. I imagined her living in a commune. She talked about communes and Jim Morrison and books, books, books. Both loved books, but Helena lived in them.

We were feeling good by midnight and Paulette wanted a cigarette, so we all went outside for a smoke. At some point I felt drunk and started speaking to them as I spoke to Sage—wild dreams—testing the two for ultimate truth. Testing them like Francine tested me with her love. Testing them like Dad tested me before handing me a check. Testing like teachers test children, wives test husbands, and nations test citizens.

Alas, the test only revealed that we were all tired.

—

SOMEHOW I had manifested all this. It was turning into the summer of my dreams, the original vision from the Maryland couch. Despite the fact, boredom set in and I was already thinking of the next place.

Already!

I knew that I had to go somewhere to cure this itch.

Anywhere.

I'd wanted to visit Boulder for a long time, having heard of the wild children of the west who went to live there, and the movements that happened in the sixties and seventies. And so one sunny Sunday I hopped in the ol' Camaro and twisted down the canyon straight into the innards of Colorado, its bohemian bowels.

Now I was alone again in a strange land, looking for something to wow me and twist my logic into pretzels. Sadly, I only found shopping centers and famous Pearl Street lined with glass-front buildings. Handbags swung from elbows and the occasional street performer with guitar and harmonica.

I closed my eyes and listened to the performers and imagined what old Boulder must have been like. I knew I'd find pieces of it if I looked closely enough, so I hit the cafes and crevices. I walked through neighborhoods, alleyways, bookshops and back rooms. I looked under carpets and between car bumpers.

Eventually I came upon The Orange Moose, a cafe full of energy and scarf-wearing intellectuals, shifting eyes around the room then back to their screens. It was a great place and soon the lights dimmed and audio equipment was brought in by a guy who carried himself like an original Boulder beatnik. And I could tell that he was by his age and attitude. Although white, the man looked like an eastern Buddhist master with a goatee and long hair, graying fashionably.

Guys like this were role models for me.

Diehards. Craftsmen of their existence.

Just like the bikers that I witnessed while trucking through the neverlands of Nevada, watching them ride straight into nowhere. They thundered along like the voice of this man. While he was setting up, I went outside for a cigarette and loitered with the hipsters and street rats who lounged on the concrete. One of them was a black kid who blasted old school hip-hop through a boombox. He was creating psychedelic art with highlighters. I sat down to watch.

"Where you from?" he asked, pointing a felt tip at me.

"Lots of places. Zephyr at the moment. Yourself?"

"Originally? LA."

His hand was moving in circles along with his eyes.

"What are you doing here in Boulder?" I asked.

"Came to make art. Came for the spirit."

"Did you find it?"

"Found drugs, man. That was the problem for a long time. Been here awhile. I'm forty-five."

"What!?"

"Don't look it, do I? 'Cause I keep moving. But you see these bitches walkin' 'round? Fine as hell, but they won't ever pay attention to me. My dad? Won't pay attention to me. He's got money but I won't see any of it. It's our generation, man. We're left in the cold with these tired visions of America. Yo, can I get a cigarette?"

I handed one over.

"What do you think drives the world nowadays?"

"Power," he said, lighting up.

"What's behind power? What do you think people are really searching for?"

That's when I lost him. He rambled on about women and trying to get laid and other guys trying to get laid.

Maybe he lost *me*.

Maybe there was meaning to be found in his mania.

Maybe I was overcomplicating the whole thing. There was nothing more than the old primitive act.

When he finished ripping across the canvas, he turned and showed it to me—a dizzying array of squiggles and swirls. I shook his hand and went back inside Orange Moose just in time to catch a poetry reading in session. The place was packed now, and I pushed my way through the bulging crowd to catch glimpse of the spirits on stage, pouring their hearts out, each with unique styles and rhythms.

I must come back, I thought.

I must bring the mountains.

—

THE ENERGY of the reading infected me and I took the virus back up the canyon to infect everyone else. Rocco ran a writers' group at Circus, but it had been weeks since he'd held a meeting. I convinced him to start it up again, and on the first night it was slow-going with only myself, Rocco, and Ollie present.

We gathered upstairs with the house lights off and old lamps on, getting very little writing done. Instead the event turned into group therapy session, mulling over relationships and life. But it seemed okay, as we were purging the bullshit, and bullshit had no place in our minds.

We bitched about everything—life and sometimes death. Ollie looked particularly interested in what we had to say. Most of the time he sat quietly, twiddling thumbs, occasionally lifting his head to smile or frown. When we spoke of life, we spoke of all we loved about it. And when we spoke of death, it's usually because we started talking about something we hated about life, which ultimately brought us to death.

Our venting led us to believe that a silent fear of death was driving the world, and that all of our problems, big and small, were caused by the knowledge that one day everything would end. We're obsessed with our ages and faces and beauty and whether or not our lives hold any meaning—running in circles, trying to create tornados of truth.

Afraid to live, afraid to die.
Afraid of it all and not knowing what to do.

—

ONE NIGHT we were joined by Cassie, an Ohio beauty of Olympic proportions with short hair and taut muscles. We were all revved up from fresh wine and spoiled talk, and when bitching only served to suffocate us in the big hot room, we proposed a spontaneous trip to the Grand Canyon to watch the sunrise. Cassie had never been.

"Why not?" I said, "These are the moments we have to take advantage of! We're all on the same page here. This may never happen again."

"What's holding us back?" asked Rocco.

"Well, for one, I have to work tomorrow," said Cassie.

"Me too," I said.

We shifted uncomfortably.

"It's certainly a risk," chimed Roc. "But what are we risking by not going?"

Still, we worried what others would think. Whether we'd lose our jobs; the fact that we didn't have our clothes packed, or our toothbrushes, or phone chargers.

Suddenly we all had to go home to sleep.

—

THE NEXT DAY I opened the shop to hoards of humans. Hollow eyes hungering for a cup of caffeine. It was a group of painters, and as with most artists they could not begin without their coffee. I was bitter from having not followed through with our plan the night before, shuffling around the bar, mind in Arizona.

Ezra popped in to fix himself a latte and helped thin out the crowd. I told him about our idea—how we almost ditched town.

"Nice! Why didn't you go?"

"Who would've opened the shop?"

"Someone."

—

TIME PASSED and I kept meeting women at the cafe. Women from all over, and they were all supreme—spawning from some Venus vortex.

One day I glanced across the bar to see a long-haired Latina sitting nearby, picking at her sandwich. She looked up at me with big eyes.

"Where you from?" I asked.

"Guess."

"Don't know. Spain?"

"Nooooo."

"Mexico?"

"Nooooo."

"South America?"

"Yes. That is the continent. And country?"

"Brazil?"

"Nooooo."

This went on for a while until I was crouched next to her scanning a tiny map, eventually landing my finger on Columbia, the correct answer. We spoke of travel and coffee and Columbian cafes until Sam walked in and glared from across the room. We exchanged numbers and that was that. She was marvelous and skipped around the cafe as though she owned it. Sam hated her.

Women, women, women.

Can't forget Carrie, the voluptuous security guard who always fixed her hair beneath her cap. Again I thought of Laredo girl. She was always smiling and blushing, blurring the lines between friendship. And I blurred right back as I did with all the women, only because they were all wonderful and I wanted them all. It's as though life were one big tease, leaving me to teeter on the edges of my own tightrope.

Eventually I honed in on the one I adored most—the one with the glassy, galaxy eyes—Helena. We ended up going on a slew of dates; most of them ending up back at my apartment where we sat on the carpet and played Lonnie's records in the dark. We lounged and listened to Pink Floyd and drank cheap wine, and Helena seemed completely at home, as if nothing could make her happier.

She took off her shoes and I noticed that she had mismatched socks. She smirked and shrugged when I pointed them out and, again, everything was right in her world. We quickly polished off the wine and I began digging through the cupboards for a second bottle.

I felt Helena's eyes on me everywhere I went.

I'd leave and return to the room only to see her smiling as before. I wondered if there was a black hole in those galaxy eyes. For some reason I wanted to go to the Abyss with her. Maybe to rescue her. Maybe for company. I sensed that she too was there, behind the smile, behind the color and cuteness.

17

HELENA AND I SAT OPPOSITE at The Fox & Hound one night, eating our vegan dishes piled high with green beans and avocado, nuts, seeds, sauces. I ordered an organic beer, thinking I might taste the mountains in it.

Helena leaned in, "Now there's something I must ask of you, and I hope you don't mind."

She had the most delicate way of handling things.

"When we're in public," she continued, "I would appreciate that we remain unaffectionate for various reasons. Small town, you know?"

"Sure. No problem."

"Great."

Her smile spanned the room and snapped back to a grin.

We ate the wholesome food and it was delicious, and then we drank and talked. Helena spoke of the mountains as her promised land. She'd come from San Diego and never felt more at home, and I thought it was fascinating that a coastal girl could pinch herself between landlocked peaks and valleys. Again, the soul transcended all physical and historical boundaries.

Helena had the soul of a mountain girl, possibly, or a German girl from the Black Forest. Perhaps Tabitha the Manhattan psychic could better explain all this. Helena probably didn't want to hear it.

She lived for the moment and spoke of death as her next-door neighbor—

"I look forward to death. I think it will be a peaceful thing."

"You don't fear it at all?"

"No."

"So why all the concerns about food and health?"

"Because I don't want to be sick. I fear pain, not death."

"So you're a hypochondriac who doesn't fear death?"

"Uh-huh."

She didn't flinch.

Then Paulette walked into the restaurant and she blushed.

"It's Paulette, isn't it?"

"Yep."

Paulette walked over to greet us, and we pretended as though we were merely having a friendly candlelight dinner.

"This is the only problem with living in a small town," Helena told me as we dodged out the door afterwards.

—

WE STOPPED FOR MORE alcohol on the way back to my place, just before settling down on the couch to watch a movie, sipping wine and doing the old cuddle game. Helena looked stunning. Her shiny black hair enveloped me. Her skin was warm and soft.

The longer we embraced, the further the couch seemed to suck us in.

I sank like a dummy.

Further, further. We fell through the couch, through the floor, and dropped at least a mile or two below soil and sediment until all went black and my brain buzzed with silence. I turned to Helena and we began making out and, just as I expected, she was a woman of passion. We became one. I lost all sense of where my body ended her hers began—love, love, love. All I could think about was love and how I loved this moment and loved her.

Society banged on my eardrum—*You cannot possibly love this woman! You just met her!*—and I defied the voices through continued loving.

Movement!

We were strolling the shoreline at the beach of the Abyss, where we could not see anything but felt the wet sand beneath our toes and heard the crashing of waves in the distance, foaming in our direction.

Soon we left the couch and entered my bedroom, and as I began undressing and exploring her body, she stopped me.

"We can't," she whispered. "Paulette is my friend. She really likes you."

"Okay, but I'm not with Paulette. I'm with you."

"I can't, I'm sorry. This has happened before."

I laid there for awhile staring at the ceiling, then got dressed, guzzled a glass of water and drove her home.

—

O HELENA! A cavalcade of colors trotting through my life. Talk to me about death in the dark; tell me that you're not afraid. I'm here to listen and look into your two beautiful eyes and watch them flutter like an old film projected onto my heart. I'll kiss you without kissing you until you're ready to kiss back.

This relationship continued for weeks—a push-pull paradigm in which we weren't allowed to show public affection; everything contained within apartments and car interiors.

"You're going to leave like all the rest who pass through Zephyr," she said.

"Won't you give it a chance?" I asked.

"Why?"

"Love is a beautiful risk."

And she closed her mouth and the smile was still there.

—

ROCCO AND I began working together more often.

We shot the shit during shifts and afterwards went to the pub for kicks. Drinking and smoking on the outside patio, our minds ran amok and we talked about the world and its madness, and all the mad people in it. I knew we'd have to get out of Zephyr together. I sensed a quiet desperation in him, a yearning for the moon.

He spoke of his travels to India, living in an ashram—attempts at an ascetic existence. He was slightly misplaced in America. Something leeched onto him overseas and he now dabbled in the portal between eastern and western cultures. An immense talent welled behind his eyes, but he seemed stuck in many ways. A blocked brain. He was a few years older than me and I could tell that he was being choked by pressure, constrained to the box of *shoulds*. Forcing his way through unhealthy relationships because he *should* be in one. Fretting about work because he *should* have a better job and *should* be making more money. He took long drags and blew all the shoulds into the atmosphere and looked at me as though I should have an answer for him.

All I had were ears.

—

ONE EVENING we hopped inside the ol' Camaro and went for a delicious drive into Boulder with Helena. Our plan was to read poetry at The Orange Moose; Rocco an epic piece about India and me a quick something-or-other I scribbled. We barreled down the canyon. Rocco rehearsed in the back seat while Helena smiled at me from behind her galaxy. Magic electric guitars emanated from the speakers, hissing and crackling with our voices. Somewhere along the way I pulled over to remove the glass tops so we could feel the evening air and look up at the sky.

The night was alive and we drove ourselves mad, straight into Boulder, finding the perfect parking spot outside the Moose. The enigmatic emcee with ponytail and goatee was still setting up when we arrived, so we left to grab a quick cocktail.

Or two.

Or more than a few.

And soon we were outside a pub instigating our own poetry session, forgetting about the one we came for. We were raising hell in the heavens of Boulder, and when the ice began to melt in our glasses, we remembered the reading and hurried back—drunk—pushing each other into poles and laughing because it was all fun and games and no one got hurt.

We shoved through crowds in the cafe, ordered more booze and sat with the hipsters, listening to the emcee pour himself silly with verse. We were hopped-up on liquor and adrenaline and ready to tear down the walls.

"Okay, good souls," said the emcee, "This is the end. Thanks for coming out."

He began packing up. I ran over.

"Hey man, we'd like to read if you can hold on wrapping."

"Sorry," he shrugged, "just yelled last call five minutes ago."

"We've got some really good stuff. Can't you work with us?"

"Next week."

I sat down, disappointed.

"There will be other times," said Helena. "Besides, we had a great night at the pub. Can't forget that."

"I need to practice my inflection anyway," Rocco said.

Fuck that. I was pissed.

Halfway through the year and all I wanted to do was make shit happen. Any missed opportunity was a blow to the gut. Helena continued to smile. I wanted to kiss it right off her face.

—

WE PACKED OURSELVES back into the car, northbound for our beloved mountain town and stopped to fuel-up at a gas station. I leaned against the cold Camaro and closed my eyes, meditating on the moment.

....Om

I left my body propped like an action figure and floated above it, seeing myself alongside the gleaming red beast, and the red faces of my friends within its unwashed windows. I zoomed out and saw the stars in the sky and the silhouetted mountains in the distance. Even further and there was the big blue earth ball spinning through the universe, the sleepy sun, and quiet moon, and galaxies beyond. And then I saw everything rolled up into one and was suddenly grateful to be part of it.

I got back in the car and smiled at Helena because I finally saw the galaxy that she was reflecting. And then we continued on, climbing the canyon, screaming Johnny Cash songs into the atmosphere.

I hear the train a-comin'
It's rolling 'round the bend
And I ain't seen the sunshine since I don't know when!

HOOOONNNNKKKKK HOONNNNNNNKKKKK

Laughter and smoke all the way up to eight thousand feet where the air became chilly and reminded me of Father Time and the fleeting summer season. It reminded me of the Abyss, nipping through the air, nipping at my heels—the darkest winter of my life perforating my Colorado dream.

—

THE WRITERS' GROUP was still going strong and Rocco and I showed up every Wednesday to light the literary candle. Sometimes it was just us, sometimes Helena showed, and sometimes young Ollie came with his young friends—wide-eyed—notebooks in hand as if they were arriving for their first day of school. We told them to burn the notebooks and set their brains on fire.

Some nights we fell back into bitchfests, especially when the downers showed. Like George, a man in his mid-forties with Uncle Wallace eyes. Rocco introduced George as the talented writer who had completed five novels and once retreated to the backcountry of Idaho to write for a year. I was impressed and nodded in respect. He hardly said a word, hunched in his chair, gazing at the table. The room seemed to shrink.

We all spoke about the creative spirit and great artistic journey. I was beaming, Rocco was deadpan, and George was dead.

"It goes away!!" he shouted, slamming both fists on the table.

"What goes away, George?" I asked.

"The gusto, the *motivation*!"

He opened the door to his life and told us about divorces and women, and wanting a woman to love but not being able to find one at his age. He spoke of money and how he needed money and how only rich guys his age got the women. Then he talked about money some more, and then his age, and eventually ended on a poignant note about money.

I was sick of hearing him and wanted to pound my fists on the table, but instead stood up.

"Okay, George, I'm your puppet. I'm the younger you. Tell me what to do."

He laughed and looked away.

There were no answers. There is no standard formula or guidebook for life and he knew this. There is only following your gut and pouring wine into it. Which we continued to do until about two—a bittersweet end which left me slamming fists against the inside of my skull.

—

THE SUMMER FLEW right along and soon it was August. My mother was calling again, inquiring about my plans—"You can always come home." And I thought of the blueberry cobbler decomposing in a landfill. Cobbler and Colorado, and Mom sitting in Pennsylvania on a balmy summer day, where leaves rustle against her porch and rabbits run around, and all is right except for the three empty chairs at her kitchen table.

I just wish we all lived closer, came her voice.

My gut swirled with guilt.

I told her to come visit, come see the mountains, come drink a beer.

Bring Kelsey, bring Art, bring cobbler!

—

DAYS, DAYS, DAYS. Nights, nights, nights.

Chilly, hoodie-wearing nights when August felt like November and the elk bugled from beyond thick black sticks. Nights that ran crisp, when I stared up at the fading bubblegum skies of Zephyr and wondered about the entire world and what was happening that very second.

Nights when Helena and I would sit together and talk until one night we made our way back into my bedroom, undressing and me guessing whether she was just teasing again—

"What are we doing?"

"I don't know. What shall we do?" she said, unsmiling.

—

DESPITE BEAUTIFUL HELENA, I was still restless and speeding around the dry snow globe of Zephyr. Wondering if I'd ever get out, straining my neck to see beyond the peaks. There was no cure for this. Only movement. And sometimes I moved too fast.

One evening I left the cafe and sped home, six-pack in my lap, ready to drink and forget that I was human when I saw red and blue lights in the rearview mirror. I pulled over and cut the engine. An officer approached—older, balding, bearing the face of a man who wants to retire but can't bring himself to hand in the badge.

"Know why I pulled you over?"

I pushed the six-pack off my lap.

"Speeding?"

"Mm-hm. License, registration, proof of insurance."

I handed everything over. He paused and furrowed his gray brows.

"California license, Maryland insurance, Colorado plates . . ."

"I'm a bit of a traveler, officer."

He shrugged. "Beautiful vehicle you've got."

"She's for sale," I blurted, not knowing why.

"More than I can afford probably."

"Thirty-five."

"Thirty-five thousand? Can't swing that."

"Hundred."

He was shocked that I was selling for so little and convinced me to raise my price considering the Camaro was a rarity.

"Sorry I gotta do this to you," he said, ripping a ticket.

I drove home and cracked open a beer, surprisingly calm about the whole thing. I thought about the old cop and old Zephyr and how everything was beginning to feel old. Seemed Boulder would not stave my hunger. I needed a new place. Somewhere different than all the other places I'd been. Somewhere they spoke a language that I did not, where people walked with a bounce that I did not have, and water flowed with a viscosity of purpose.

I devised a plan right there to sell the Camaro and use the money for an overseas adventure. The finger of my brain landed on Paris. No particular reason. It sounded good. Felt good. I decided not to tell anyone; instead posting ads online and going about my business as usual. And of course, as soon as I made this decision sentimentalism reared its head.

Aww, the mountains. Aww, the cafe. Aww, the elk.

How could I leave such a magical place?

I set the price of the car unreasonably high, effectively sabotaging myself. When little interest was shown, I knew why. I knew what I was doing. I was hiding. Afraid of myself and the uncertainty of a foreign land. What awaited me there? Who would I become if I went? What if I changed for the worse? What if I changed for the better?

18

ADULTS ARE AWKWARD.

Little children encased in growing, fleshy vehicles, constantly changing and evolving. Shedding skin cells, shedding hair, shedding weight and gaining weight, shedding money and maintaining money, relationships, love, houses, new carpets and silverware.

We grow things. Plants and babies.

We kill things. Bugs and boredom.

We kill thoughts that enter our heads. We choose what to embrace and what to disgrace. It's a roaring rollercoaster. And because of that we want to scream.

We want out!

Children inside fleshy trains on the steely tracks of life.

I felt deeply for adults, having been one for quite some time myself. I stared at them, usually their eyes, and saw truth. The rest is dressing. Layers upon layers of clothing, even if we were to stand naked apart. Everything's in the eyes, I knew.

—

IN THE COMING WEEKS I continued working at the cafe, seeing Helena occasionally. One night we met for drinks and I got to telling her about my Paris plans, and she got the gist that I was leaving town soon as the Camaro was sold.

Telling her this was like spraying her with a fire extinguisher. Any flames left between us were smothered like those mashed potatoes I used to eat at Margaret's Truck Stop Diner. Now I watched the batting eyelashes from afar, a telescopic view of the galaxy. God oh God, what was I doing? Pushing away—always pushing towards something else. The grass never greener, yet I had to see for myself.

I WAS SICK from all the thinking, so I took a day off and went for a hike with Lonnie. The mountains were misty and we made our way up the trails with backpacks and bottles of water, granola bars, and stories. We traversed the land and stopped for pictures, and I noticed Lonnie's socks were colorful like Helena's but did not dwell on the minor mystery. Sweeping views swept us away and we kept climbing to higher sweeping views—sleeping views. Views to set up tents and snooze to.

We spoke of life near swamps between swigs of water.

"So do you think Ezra will ever get married?" asked Lonnie.

I thought about my barista friend and how I knew so little about him.

"Don't know."

Lonnie had just divorced his wife and was now with another woman that he was set to marry in a few months. There was a lot of marriage talk that day and I thought about Francine and tried not to feel remorse. No, I couldn't. I was certain of my choice—had to be.

We finally reached the end of our hike at Quartz Lake and sat down to watch its peaceful waters, eating sandwiches. I meditated on the stillness of the water and wondered how it could be so calm and people so crazy. At one point Lonnie climbed high into the mountains and I got lost looking for him, alone with nature. I sat on a rock and felt the mosquitoes landing on my skin and the wind blowing the hairs of my skin, and the sun fighting its way through the clouds to reach my skin. And I had no clue where Lonnie was, but I had a clue of where I was.

I was on Rock, Planet Earth.

And it felt good to sit there and do nothing with my mosquito companions. I wanted to marry one of them and fly into the atmosphere with my buzzing beauty and watch the ground below—all the green rolling beneath us knowing we would die in a matter of days—weeks maybe—but not caring because life was so short that worrying itself was a waste of time. And rather than wasting it, looking into her mosquito eyes and buzzing above the moss, having mosquito sex, and in the morning we would make mosquito meals of sweet honey and tree sap and live happily ever after.

Eventually found Lonnie.

We were headed back down the trail when I felt my knee give way under loose gravel—a sharp, shooting pain. I began to hobble and Lonnie suggested finding a cozy rock to sit on and rest. Sure enough we found our cozy rock, and I clutched and nursed my injury while Lonnie smoked cigars.

—

ONE NIPPY NIGHT I was sitting around feeling glum when Valerie called and invited me to a shindig across town. Still aching, I hobbled to my car and raced over, and then hobbled through a door where I met her standing straight as an arrow, smiling her smile; the smile that a thousand other smiles would bow to.

The apartment belonged to a guy named Andy—a fifty-year-old with the attitude of a young surfer. He looked like a surfer, spoke like a surfer, and seemed to surf through life. I watched his feet surf across the carpet as he walked. He drank oceans of wine, flirting with Valerie's friend, Jackie.

Seemed we were all on the same boat together.

It wasn't long before we joined them for drinks. Andy pulled cold cervezas from the fridge and said things like, "Mannnnn, you gotta try this bro! With lime. Yeah man, with *lime*!!" And I stuffed the slimy limes into the cold cans and gulped everything into my body. And meanwhile Valerie taught me Spanish, laughing at my mispronunciations, only to correct and kiss me.

I thought everything was hilarious. Andy pulled out a bottle of wine big as the room and heaved it onto the counter.

"Ten bucks, bro! Can you believe it?! The only rule is that if I open 'er we gotta finish 'er."

I hesitated when he told me the price, well knowing it would taste like acid rain, but we went ahead and popped the cork with a POP and the tide came crashing in.

I drank big glasses, stumbling and spilling, splotching Andy's floor and then asking for more. At one point he told us a story about wrestling a bear in his college days—"Yeah man, I had the sucker down on the ground"—and I saw a little boy inside of his adult face and it freaked me out, causing me to leave the room and watch TV. But Andy followed and told me he wanted to see the Camaro; so we went outside and sat down in the tired beast, and I revved the engine a few times and, again, sensed the small child in him.

I felt bad.

I could see pain in his face, as though he was being forced from his skin. And time plagues us all it seems—ticking leeches licking pieces from our better genius. Stifled by the second hand, by our own hand, by the same brain we're trying to maintain; reminding ourselves of our own mortality instead of seizing its remainder.

Back inside the apartment we continued watching the fabulous glowing TV until Andy muted it and turned on '90s rap and began passing around a bottle of rum. We all took shots, and Valerie passed her shots onto me, and before I knew it I was dancing and rapping alongside Andy and we were both the same age.

—

AT THE CRACK OF DAWN, shreds of daylight squeezed through cracks in the blinds and I cracked the window for a gasp of fresh air, grasping for a glass of water, aghast at the mountain sunrise. The TV hummed in the background. Must've been on all night.

I was still drunk, zombie-eyed, watching religious programming where a priest in oversized glasses spouted sermons in front of a tired choir. They all looked tired. They all looked like children. I wanted to pinch their cheeks and send them off to play with a colorful ball.

—

SOON VALERIE walked downstairs and I went to make coffee. We sobered up and talked, and as with Helena, I told her about my Paris plans. But unlike Helena she was accepting and supportive, even suggesting I meet up with friends of hers who lived there. We kissed and I promised to see her again before I left town.

She went off to a funeral with a big smile on her face to celebrate the life of an unknown woman, and I stood there amazed by her soul, astonished at the differences between the souls of everyone I met.

—

DAYS, DAYS, DAYS.

Night, nights, nights.

It just keeps going, I thought.

On this particular day, I walked into the cafe groggy due to a nasty nightmare where I visited the Abyss—a place that truly existed! Filled with floating balls of lightning, mannequins, plastic babies. The day was foggy and wet, and when I walked in Ezra was juggling pitchers and mugs, and customers stood with their arms crossed—a line forming from one end of the shop to another. I rushed to his aid and grabbed a gallon of chai only to drop it and watch it splatter across the floor.

"Aaaghhh!"

Now the floor was sticky—SQUISH, SQUISH—and meanwhile the line kept growing.

"Where's Rocco? Isn't he supposed to be working, too?" I asked.

"Roc had a mental breakdown during a phone call with Nicole. Went to go have a talk with her. Just walked off."

He snickered out of stress.

Rocco and his girlfriend, Nicole, had a volatile relationship. We always joked that one day Roc would leave to break up with her for good, only to return hand-in-hand: "Guys, we're getting married!"

But that's how it was with them.

So there we were, left to manage a crowd of caffeine-deprived monsters. Tourist monsters from across the globe. Damp dollar bills and slippery coins, and me tripping all over the place with my brain at the Abyss and not thinking clearly about anything. I spilled coffee beans and dropped plates, burnt sandwiches and skin, and couldn't keep myself from cursing.

The bad energy was contagious.

We thought it must have been leftover from Rocco, and soon Ezra was making the same mistakes—forgetting to charge customers as they walked out.

I shattered a cup.

"Take a break, man," Ezra told me.

"I'm good."

"Go take a break before you break something else."

—

LATER THAT NIGHT Rocco returned and all was well again in our tiny kingdom. I found out that he and Nicole were taking time apart, and meanwhile I could sense that he was at the Abyss and looking for temporary escape.

Lo and behold Helena stopped by the cafe and now we were together again—the terrible trio—and our sights were fixed on The Fox & Hound.

We trotted into our favorite locale and bought glasses of ethanol enthusiasm while a bluegrass band strummed and strung their hearts to our feet. And we picked up the hearts and danced with them and danced with each other, and before long I was drunk out of my mind, screaming at the fiddler, passing beers to Rocco, twirling Helena, watching her smile twist through the air.

Everything was beautiful and I couldn't stop stomping.

Roc had to drag me out of the place, plop me by the bonfire and pop a cigarette in my mouth. The entire night burned like the logs, and the last thing I remember was staring at the wavy faces on the other side. All of us burning with the fire, melting in the most romantic way possible.

—

THEODORA.

Where was Theodora during all of this?

Cleaning her basement? Digging up some magnificent fragment of fabric? She was my mother for a few weeks and now where? The interconnectedness was mind-boggling. People come and go, hopping around like fireflies, glowing in and out of our lives.

—

THE TOWN SHRUNK just as everything shrinks.

Tired old Main Street.

I kept wanting to get out and go somewhere else. Boulder—always back to Boulder—each time hoping that it would be better. Hoping old dead poets would emerge from its alleys and carry us across the moonlit streets onto Cloud Nine. Helena sitting with legs crossed, book cracked in her lap, smile cracked with her laugh, and Roc next to her staring off into the distance.

All we wanted to do was float.

And so late one August night, we made our final excursion into Boulder with no fixed plans except to enjoy the journey. We sought out bars on the quiet streets and unfortunately everything was closed; lights turning off as we walked past windows, our faces darkening with them. But we skipped along and took refuge in a cafe that did not serve alcohol; rather, strong matte and vegan entrées. It was a warm sanctuary, and all the servers were dirty blonds with freckles and slim bodies, and they smiled like Helena. We munched and told stories and jokes, and at one point Rocco pointed out that we hadn't had one sip of booze.

We left the cafe to stand by the Camaro under the pale moon and Roc found a spot on the grass to lie down. I leaned against the car with Helena at my side, lightly rubbing her back, trying to start a fire with little friction.

"What a breathtaking night," said Helena.

"Completely sober—how 'bout that?" I mused. "Why do we feel the need to drink anyway? What are we escaping?"

Roc sat up to join the discussion.

"Well. It's as though we have voids, right? Each day we wake up with holes that need filled, and we're looking to fill them with love by the end. And if we don't receive love, we find other things to fill them with. Booze, drugs, shopping, ice cream."

I thought about my voids and whether or not I was trying to fill them through travel. I thought about Helena next to me and how I started something beautiful with her only to run away again. Did I have to take these journeys alone? What was I seeking that I couldn't find with her?

19

MY COLLEGE ROOMMATE was an interesting guy.

Dale was balding but grew a mullet for the hell of it, had never drank 'til he turned twenty-one (at which point he became a full-fledged alcoholic), and one chilly night on a walk back from the liquor store, he told me something that stuck with me for the rest of my life:

"I wouldn't care if I died right now. I've done everything I wanted to do."

As with Helena, he said it with such conviction that it shook my core.

"You're kidding. There's nothing else you want from life?"

"Nope."

I thought of Dale's drinking and wondered if it was the last box to be checked on his bucket list. I wondered if each of us had different bucket lists of varying lengths. I wondered what the hell a bucket list was even good for.

"You could die today and be okay?"

"Yep."

And with that we went upstairs for a night of boozing. But I could never look at him the same again. It stuck with me.

—

SO THERE I WAS, still in Zephyr, my dream of the spring falling with the leaves. I couldn't stop looking at the stars and asking the sky questions, which is exactly what I did one night on the deck while huddled over hot coals with a cold stout.

"If I am to leave town and take this journey to Europe, give me a sign—a shooting star."

It was a clear enough night and I knew that I'd see one if there was to be one. Within seconds, there it was, blazing a trail through the atmosphere.

I wanted to dismiss it as mere coincidence:

There are tons of shooting stars.

The sky is too clear.

I got lucky.

—

I KEPT POSTING advertisements online, attempting to sell the Camaro, pushing for Paris despite my fears of leaving Zephyr and losing everything I held dear. There were very few bites at my price but many offers to trade vehicles: diesel trucks, motorcycles, ATVs, and in one case a boat.

"Not unless I can sail it across the Atlantic," I replied.

One day I met with a Mexican guy, Victor, who was interested in the old heap and I made sure to shine her up beforehand. Victor was doing the whole mid-life crisis thing and wanted a Camaro like he had in high school. One test drive and he was drooling over the dashboard. He told me that he was going to gather up the money and meet with me the following week to finalize the purchase . . .

I left excited. My dreams were just around the corner. Everything was about to change.

Then came the rain.
Ridiculous rain. Rain for days.

Rocco and I joked that Zephyr had become Portland, and beyond Portland—that it was monsoon season. And the cafe was packed all the time because people were tired and wet, looking for caffeine to dry their soggy souls.

One afternoon I met an interesting girl amid the mist, Tammy, twenty-six, donning adventure gear and short brown hair. She was looking to buy a new journal and showed me her old one—full of quotes and photos from recent travels. There were pictures of burning red sunsets from foreign lands, and her beautiful body leaning out of tents in the wilderness. I couldn't look at the images any longer without falling in love.

I went upstairs to meet her at the end of my shift and we listened to the rain and spoke about life, and she told me about her upcoming trip to New Zealand. Maybe Helena was right, I thought. Everyone who passed through Zephyr was on their way somewhere else. I asked Tammy if she wanted to go out for dinner and she agreed.

By now it was really pouring. We huddled together beneath an umbrella and ran across the street to the closest burger joint. Like Helena, Tammy was vegan, and I joined her in having a veggie burger while we continued talking about travel. I couldn't believe how similar our paths were, and in a strange sense felt that I had finally met a woman who was exactly like me—so much so that it freaked me out and I took extra gulps of beer.

"I'm sleeping in the camper of my truck," she said. "Been in Wyoming the past two months."

"Wow, you're just *out there* aren't you?"

"I'm *out there!*"

"And your family?"

"Well they support me, but you know . . ."

"You're the black sheep."

Tammy drank beers with me, sparkling from two feet away, and I pictured us sharing a night together inside her camper beneath the clouds, wet and naked and cold. Curled up for warmth and loving each other until the end of time, which would surely be when she departed for Oceania.

She promised to visit me at the cafe the next day and promptly set off to her campsite somewhere in the Monsoon Mountains.

—

EVERYONE OKAY OUT THERE?

Ezra's text messages seemed a joke until photos came pouring in and I saw the flooded alleyways spilling onto Main Street. Dirty, murky waters sopping up the city. When I heard that our cafe had been sandbagged shut, I crawled out of bed and went to see the damage with my own eyes.

By the time I reached downtown, Main St. had truly become a river and people were standing around, watching their lives flow past. Everything gray and cloudy. Even the mountains hid behind the ominous fluff. The cute little town I had come to know was cleansed of its energy. Somber faces, slumped shoulders. I couldn't even reach the cafe, as I would have to forge the road, which by now had risen quite a bit.

"Worst I've seen since '76," an old timer told me.

A woman with hair curlers cried into her hands.

Everyone stood separated, as though they had to fight this battle alone. And then came the tourists that stuck around to witness the devastation as an attraction—cameras flashing and suppressed smiles. Oh drama, don't we just soak it up?

Needless to say I was dour for a few hours, humbled by the flushing destruction of my promised land. I began looking for Roc and Ezra and Helena, but the cell phone towers were down. No one knew where anybody was. We were wandering in the dark, beaming love from behind raincoats.

Finally, I bumped into Lonnie.

"Heyyyy mannn, doesn't this suuuccckkkk?"

"To put it lightly, yes. Wondering if we can escape to Boulder."

"Cannnn't go to Boulder, mannnn. Roads are closed."

"What?"

"Yeah dude, couple miles of road washed away. Won't be fixed for months."

Now I was really panicking. Not only was I mentally stuck, but physically.

"Well how are they going to get food into town?" I asked.

"There's talk of helicopters dropping bags."

"What?"

"Or bringing goods in from the back range by truck."

"Dammit."

So I blared around town in the Camaro, grabbing milk and bread and all the other things people do in these situations. Whiskey.

I went home to drink and wondered about the cafe, as I still hadn't heard any news from Ezra, Rocco, or Sam. Then I remembered Victor and the Camaro. I was supposed to meet him to finalize the deal. But the rain continued to pour.

—

A KNOCK AT THE DOOR.

I opened it and Rocco stood before me, hyper and disheveled.

"You hear about 53 and 19!?"

"Closed off."

"Yeah, and so is Route 8. What are you drinking? Have smokes? Can I come in?"

He paced back and forth, fussing with his hair, sitting and standing. Standing and sitting. I couldn't keep track of him.

"I've been real prolific over the past few days," he said. "Writing. You been writing? Write anything new?"

"Written a little," I said, handing him a highball. "You seem anxious. What's up?"

"Thinking of gettin' out of town. What are your plans?"

"Really? Where to?"

"My mother is headed back to Jersey for the winter; needs someone to drive her to the airport. Gonna take the back roads before they get shut down."

"And where are you going after that?" I asked.

"Don't know. What are your plans?"

"Probably stick around. Help out."

"You think I should stay, too? Feel like shit for leaving."

"Do what you gotta do, man. But if you're leaving, we should hit Fox & Hound one last time."

And so we headed off to our favorite pub, splashing our way down the streets, not knowing where Helena was but finding solace in our flowing friends, Jack and Jameson.

"Who would've thought that a mountain could become an island?" I quipped.

We laughed and tried to ignore the fact that our summer had been washed away.

We spoke of money, for I was almost out of money and using credit everywhere.

"I think I'm maxed out on this one, but we shall see!"

The bartender overheard:

"Uhh, I can't accept that. Our systems are corrupted as it is."

"Uggh."

Rocco threw down his card to cover the cost.

"Hey, did Jesus have a credit score?" I asked.

"Probably not," said Rocco.

"Yet he's followed as a leader by billions. A sandal-wearing, penniless bum."

We were delirious, laughing at everything and trying to remain strong. After a good hug, Rocco departed to Jersey and wherever else the land would take him. I kept picturing India because whenever I looked at him I saw India—the highlight of his high life.

—

EVENTUALLY THE RAIN subsided and there was lots of cleanup to be done. I went to visit the cafe and bumped into Ezra and Sam along the way, sloshing down the sidewalk, carrying coffee pots with forced smiles. We hugged and I rushed back to the shop to help make drinks for the locals.

The cafe was dry as a bone and we were open. Not for business, but to serve drinks to construction workers and such. I promptly started a new pot, looking outside the windows at all the slop. Mounds of mud and muck. CAT trucks piling it all up. Beep, beep, beep all afternoon. Ezra and Sam returned and we all sat around trying our best to keep spirits high with salsa music and slices of tea bread.

Soon Neema showed. My African queen of the mountains, still a mystery. She was saddened and wanted to show her support, and eventually, sauntering around sipping tea, she grabbed a twelve-string from the wall and started to play. She and Sam both played, bellowing gospels and uplifting tunes until I stumbled over and requested Johnny Cash.

Neema was shooting daggers from her eyes. I caught them before they hit me. They were daggers of love. Look at the darkness in her eyes, I thought. Look at the eyelashes. Look at the curly hair and dimples. Gonna go jump off a bridge now.

—

ONE NIGHT EZRA held a party at his house to stimulate our smiles and senses, which included alcohol aplenty—whiskies that Ezra tended to stomach without qualm. I on the other hand saw a bottle of gin and filled a glass half full, adding a splash of something just for color. I sat and listened to Ezra, Sam, and beautiful Helena. They all talked about the state of the town while Ezra's chubby baby was passed around like a slow game of hot potato. Then Neema showed. And then I was swirling into my drink, hearing words spaced apart, trying to tie them together in my head. At one point I heard Sam tell me, "You should probably look for another job."

Next thing I knew, I was sitting in the back of a Volvo. Neema and Helena were in the front seat slapping me awake, asking about my address and whether or not I had the keys to my apartment.

"Of course I have my keys.... uh... I don't have my keys."

"Okay," Helena decided, "That's an issue."

"Hey girls, girls, girls . . . What is happiness to you?"

It's a question I'd ask anyone, drunk or not.

"I think it's a state of mind," Helena said, turning to Neema. "What do you think it is?"

"I think it's a choice."

The car went silent. Then, laughter.

"Take me to Frank's Diner!" I yelled.

"Where's Frank's Diner?"

"I don't know."

—

ZEPHYR REMAINED QUIET. There was no work. I was done at the magical cafe. My fantasy obliterated into fragments. Where was the Zephyr of the couch of Maryland? Where was the Sage of the mountains? Where was the love that I sought?

Fuck it. I was focused on Paris.

Alas, nobody wanted the Camaro and I kept driving her through the mountains and laughing at the world because I felt alone in the soggy land.

Occasionally I volunteered around town, arriving at houses to drain water through hoses. Poor basements and faces. One lady lived on a hill and I couldn't imagine her house being flooded as it was so high up, but running water from the slope had seeped through to the floor. I helped her pull carpet and by the end we pulled every piece, tossing scraps into wheelbarrows; borrowing tools from neighbors—everyone pitching in just as you'd expect from a small town.

—

I SOON HEARD from Victor. He called to tell me that he was no longer interested in the Camaro. His business was sinking due to the flood and he couldn't afford to splurge on a high school fantasy. Subsequently, I told Lonnie that I could no longer afford to stay at the apartment and, without knowing where I'd go, gave myself no less than a week to figure it out. I started putting feelers out to friends, asking if anyone would let me crash on their couch until the car sold.

It had to sell. It was my only way out.

After awhile, Ezra's girlfriend, Danielle, introduced me to friends that she worked with at a local high school. They were creating an event to raise money for relief efforts—a mud volleyball tournament. My job was to design a logo for the event, which they would use for websites and t-shirts. I was told there would be no pay, but they offered to give me free lodging at one of the fancy cabins in town. Words like jacuzzi and fireplace had me hooked. I promptly set off to work on the logo, finishing in a couple of days. Everyone loved it. Despite receiving zilch for the job, it was a confidence boost that kept my head above water.

—

ON THE NIGHT that I took advantage of my free cabin, I invited Helena over to enjoy it with me. The place was enormous. I imagined a dozen people partying at the long dining room table, reveling under the high ceilings and toasting by the fire. I imagined Helena and I leaving them to their own vices, running off like homebody vagabonds into our distant fantasy bedroom-land.

Helena certainly showed, but sadly it was not what I pictured. We sat on the couch and talked about this and that, and ultimately she told me she had to wake up early and that was that. She left and I had the cavern all to myself.

It was a sad place without Helena and I couldn't stand it, so I went outside to the jacuzzi, removed all of my clothes, and drowned my body in heat. The air was crisp, and when it met my warm skin I thought about the merging of summer and winter and wondered what would fall between.

Then I sank like a

stone

autumn

20

I LEFT LONNIE A SIX-PACK and pack of cigarettes, and off I went with the ol' Camaro crammed to the roof. It was a somber day and everything was gray—the energy still depleted from town. I had no clue where I'd go or what I'd do and scolded myself for being back at square one.

Why can't you just settle down and be normal?

I didn't want to leave Zephyr.

It was happening all over again. Mom and cobbler. Francine and Kiwi. Sage and her face.

I hummed around the city and wasted time.

I thought about life and its big cycle spinning me like laundry, wishing it would cleanse me of all my dirt. Sometimes I found myself at church, or wandering outside the church, marveling at the marble Mother Mary. I was looking for answers over and over, but mostly I was looking for a place to sleep.

—

ONE AFTERNOON I received a call from Danielle. She told me about available housing at the high school she worked at, Rocky Start Preparatory. It was a progressive school established for troubled teens seeking alternative environments. I thought it might benefit from a name change.

The bunkhouse was usually reserved for visiting professors, but Danielle hooked me up for free so long as I helped sell t-shirts at the volleyball event. I was booked ten days.

—

IT WAS EARLY OCTOBER and there was already a light coating of snow on the campus when I arrived. A few kids were hanging out in the commons area, shouting at me— "Sweet car, man!" And me shouting back, "IT'S FOR SALE!"

I dragged my luggage up a set of stone steps into the bunkhouse, which was completely empty. The room was dark and dusty, and when I turned on the lights it reminded me of the hostel, and all the places I'd ever stayed which had bunk beds and linens, and community this-and-thats. I sat on a hard mattress and rubbed my itchy eyes, distraught with thoughts of what I'd do next.

In that moment I was hungry and seeking food, so I hit the cafeteria at twilight and found a room full of energetic youths bouncing around to pop music, scooping food onto trays from the long buffet. I was uncomfortable and out of place. The kids kept asking "*Who* are you?" and "*Why* are you here?" And I could only shrug and say, "I'm a friend of Danielle," hoping she would show because she was the only one who could give me any credibility in the place.

I found a table and sat down with my greasy pizza— observing everything with wide eyes. Deep down, I reveled in the new experience.

"BACKUP POT BACH!!" I heard from across the room.

I looked up and saw Ezra strutting towards me, Danielle close behind.

"Welcome to the Abyss!" he said, sitting down with his plate.

"What?"

"I said welcome to Rocky Start! Isn't this place great?"

"Oh . . . yeah."

"Government funds the whole thing, built the campus in the '90s. Great community. Everyone bonds."

It was true. The students shared an obvious connection.

"So, have you heard from Roc?" he asked.

"I have not."

"Think he and Nicole finally took off for the chapel?"

"Who knows."

164

"What are your plans for after the volleyball tournament?"

There was the old question. I had no answers.

A group of students came to gather around us. Black-haired teenage girl holding Ezra's baby.

"Who are you?" she asked me.

"He's a new professor here," said Ezra. "Teaches physics."

I blushed, giving away his joke.

"Whateverrrrr!" she said, punching him in the arm.

Ezra excused himself and got up to tend to his little guy, bombarded by more students who cooed and tagged along. He looked genuinely happy among them. It's as though I were watching a stranger, allowing myself to forget all his stories of lost love in faraway lands.

Ezra had shed several skins already. He once told me about waking up one morning in his early thirties and putting on a suit and tie for the last time—the six-figure desk job he relinquished in lieu of a life true to himself. His boldness anchored me, kept me going. It was my big epiphany, right there in that cafeteria, that we all serve as anchors for one another—the bolder the action, the bolder the influence. And possibly the boldest action possible is unconditional love: for others and yourself. Do what's best for you and others will learn that it's okay to do what's best for them.

—

FOR THE REMAINDER of the week I met remarkable students. They all wanted to know who I was and why I was at the school. I told them variations of the same story, but the main theme was that I was leaving on a plane to Paris or not leaving at all.

One warm afternoon, I was invited to sit with the students outside. I squeezed into the picnic table, feeling faces all over mine, and when I looked up it seemed that I was the center of their curiosity and I suddenly felt much older. I began asking what they wanted from life and who they wanted to be, and little by little they left the table until only one student remained. A shaggy-haired boy with spotted acne, Dimitri.

Dimitri loved comedy and spoke of comedy as his superpower—the thing that brought joy to himself and others around him.

"I don't feel like I'm good enough, though," he told me. "Some people don't like my style."

"There will always be people who don't like your style," I said. "The world is a pool of personality. Do you like peas?"

"What?"

"Do you like to eat peas?"

"They're okay."

"I hate peas. What does a pea think of itself?"

"It's a pea. It doesn't think anything."

"Exactly."

"So I should be like a pea?"

"Be a pea."

We clicked on our favorite comedians and artists, and after awhile a freckled soul named Mackenzie joined. Her red hair was curly and tied up; a sturdy woman with ice cube eyes and fiery smile. I figured she was one of the assistant teachers and it turned out to be true. She vibed with us for the next half hour and I thought I might see her again because she was a traveling spirit, and we all seemed to find each other along the grand journey.

—

I WENT BACK to the bunkhouse to sit and read under its tall sunny windows, and before long there was a knock at the door. I turned around and sure enough it was Mackenzie—

"Hey! Sorry to bother. Just wanted to know if you'd like to join me at Earth Cafe. There's live music tonight."

My first thought was 'no' as it had been most of my life, but I quickly remembered my new philosophy of movement and decided to go.

We hopped into her truck, which had a camper on the back, and I thought of Tammy, the traveling beauty I met on the night before the flood. I hoped that she was okay and didn't get washed away; but if she did, I was certain that she rowed her way out and was halfway to New Zealand by now. I was saddened by the thought that we would never see each other again; that I would never know if anything could have become of us. We swam together for a blink. We shared the lifetime of a gnat. And now with Mackenzie, I knew that I was about to enter another world simply by being with another unknown person.

We parked outside Earth Cafe—the place I arrived at on my magical first day in Zephyr. The once clear pond was now brown from the flooding, and the trail that surrounded it had washed way like the tourists.

Mackenzie and I sat outside sipping coffees, enjoying the foliage, agreeing that it was nothing like that of our native east coast. She was from Manhattan and we spoke for a long time about the coast, and family, and beauty, and why we chose to leave the beauty, and the beauty we'd found since leaving.

She was a sports-addict: hiker, climber, bicyclist, swimmer, and now there she was in front of me painting pictures of Utah canyons from memory. As with Ezra, I was inspired by all that she had seen and done, and even more so when she mentioned that she was only twenty-four.

"Do you sell any of these paintings?"

"No. It's just for fun."

"You should."

"They're really not that great."

I was taken aback because they were some of the most marvelous watercolors I'd ever seen. I thought of my discussion with Dimitri.

She put her brush down and clapped her hands together. "Wanna take a trip somewhere cool?"

"What's cool?"

"I know a place."

WE SET OFF in her truck again, roaring past tumbleweeds, trailing our tumultuous thoughts, staying just far enough ahead to laugh. Mackenzie pulled out a plastic bag and turned to me—"Pot cookie?" Without thinking, I grabbed one and stuffed it in my mouth. We both did.

Our destination was Mackenzie's recommendation—an overlook at the top of town where there was an abandoned cabin that burned down eighty years ago. Somehow the frame remained standing, rendering a perfect haven for those with a hankering for pot cookies.

We walked up the easy trail and I could already tell that Mackenzie was a well-experienced hiker. It seemed like she wasn't even breathing, just gliding across the dirt. I looked up and saw that it was a clear night, and I was ready for a clear brain, and Mackenzie and I joked around in the old dilapidated house and found a stone ledge to sit on; watching the twinkling lights below. It was as though the curtains had just opened for the most silent show of the year.

Suddenly my skin tingled on the rock that I gripped, and the rock felt like *felt*—some mossy fabric—and from that point on I had entered the Abyss, or the ultimate escape from the Abyss (as you wish).

Mackenzie and I continued to snuggle under the sky and at one point I joked myself right into a kiss with her and couldn't remember who she was or why I was there but desired every bit of it. Everything had compacted into this one moment.

We began slow dancing in the center of the crusted structure. I opened my eyes several times to see Mackenzie and *only Mackenzie*. Total black around us. It very well could have been the Abyss, which prompted me to contemplate light and dark, and whether *Abyss* was just a gloomy term for an infinite unknown that was equally enchanting and scary.

Then the strangest thing happened.

Mackenzie began to morph.

I mean her face began to morph and transform into all the women of my life. It was like one of those dolls whose head spins around within their bonnet. One minute I was making out with Francine, and the next Sage, and then gorgeous Helena! And then a European-looking femme that prompted me to ask Mackenzie, "What's your heritage?"

"Ohhhhhh let's see. Russian and . . ."

Before she continued, I saw an old Russian lady.

". . . Irish . . ."

Then she was Irish!

Then I was dancing with all of Europe at once, maybe even the world. Mackenzie was a single woman of the universe and that's exactly how I saw her.

We ceased our dancing and sat stoned in the unwalled house. I began to worry about what I would do next with my life, for what could top a tango with the world?

"I feel so lost right now," I admitted.

"You just need to see it, be it, feel it," she said.

"What do you mean?"

"See it. Be it. Feel it."

The wind picked up.

Her words hit me like bricks. For a long time I sat still while the wind blasted my face. It just kept blowing, as though it would never stop.

Mackenzie massaged my hand and it disappeared.

—

I STUCK AROUND Rocky Start, waiting, wondering where Rocco was. Wondering where the world was and what I was waiting for. The mud volleyball tournament turned out to be a success. I stood behind a table selling shirts, occasionally peering out at the playing field, watching teams splatter themselves while smacking the wet ball across the net.

I was happy to see everyone so happy, and happier to see the t-shirts selling—stacks of money handed over, numbers tallying on calculators. It was a cold day and everyone was half naked and shivering, covered in earth, posing for cameras and clamoring over final scores.

At one point I saw a man I thought I recognized wandering about—long hair and jacket—staring blankly like Van Gogh with a canvas. It wasn't until he approached my table that I realized it was good ol' Rocco, back from wherever.

"Roc, Roc, buddy ol' Roc!"

He looked shell-shocked.

"Where you been?" I asked.

"Denver with Nicole," he said, brushing a stray hair aside.

"It's damn good to have you back. You're back, right?"

"I'm back," he affirmed.

"How are things with Nicole?"

"They're okay. Hey, I heard you might be looking for a place to stay. My condo's available if you need a bed."

"Yeah, that'd be great. When can I move in?"

"Whenever."

He was tired and needed to rest, and I had to continue volunteering but told him to meet me at the after party.

I kept selling shirts—two thousand dollars worth—and by the end I had a fist full of bills to hand over to Danielle who smiled ear to ear. Everyone was freezing by five o' clock and we looked to The Fox & Hound, our promised land where whiskey awaited for the warming of bones.

It was an impressive night.

And what I mean by impressive is that I was back to guzzling liquor as though the sky were crumbling. No explanation. Maybe I knew that my Colorado days were over. Maybe I knew Helena and I were over. Maybe I missed Sage. Maybe I had a bird named Kiwi on the top of my head, and maybe I knew that one day it would all end.

Rocco eventually showed.

I ran my credit card to the limit, purchasing drinks for everyone, at one point turning to a couple of older folks—

"Who wants to come with me to the Grand Canyon tonight!?!"

They just stared.

But I asked with such immediacy that I could see them considering. If even. For a second.

21

"YOU HAVE A PROBLEM."

O Helena and her beautiful face.

I wanted to take her with me in the Camaro, light the tank on fire and blast into the desert, rocketing and camping wherever it stopped, stripping off clothes in subdued sunlight.

"A problem?"

"A drinking problem. I saw you at Fox & Hound last night."

"And?"

"You have a problem. I'm only telling you because I care."

I never thought I had a problem until now when Helena stared into my eyes and, with her contagious conviction, unleashed her advice. She was distant. A Great Wall. Over and over—"You have a problem" and "When are you leaving?"

"How 'bout a kiss?" I asked.

"Thaaaaatttt's not going to happen."

"Just one kiss."

She smiled and walked away.

What a beautiful girl, what a beautiful world! What a beautiful tragedy to be in such close reach yet so far removed. When all you want is to give your love away and the mighty flow meets its drain.

—

I HAD A PROBLEM, and I drove over to Rocco's and we drank it away. Roc's condo was great. Tall ceilings, long kitchen, fireplace. Enough space for the clearing of minds, and a short little driveway where we stood outside and smoked, clogging our brains with ideas before going back inside. The house was meticulously maintained by his mother, traces of her throughout. I thought of my mom when I saw the knick knacks and love—the whole place filled with love which hung on hooks, mantles, shelves, and smells! Soaps, creams, cupboards, seeds. The cutest damn condo to rest my ugly head.

Despite all the warmth on the walls, nights were cold and I shivered my way through the house. Dark and lonely nights when Roc ran away with Nicole and I sat at my laptop alone, fiddling my thumbs, thinking of the fiddlers and drums from our summer.

Could have been anywhere.

It was no longer about places, warm or cold. Dirty or clean.

I kept running into walls.

—

It was nearly November and I began losing hope for selling the Camaro, as the weather was fast-turning and it became unlikely that anyone would want to buy a rear wheel drive sports car in the mountains.

One night I opened the garage door to see the ground dusted with snow.

"Noooo!"

I spelled PARIS in the driveway with my toe, then proceeded inside to sit at the computer, redoubling my attempts to market the Camaro.

Days later, my efforts were honored, as I awoke to an email from a guy named Shep who was interested. Shep was from Wyoming and wanted to drive down to Colorado to buy the car, but not before haggling me through text messages, lowering the price to unreasonable offers. Ultimately I hooked him on a convincing note about the Camaro's "classic coolness." We found an agreeable price and scheduled a time to meet the following week.

I was reeling, already pulling cardboard boxes from the car and cleaning it up. The boxes went into the garage where I taped them shut, ready to ship my life back across country.

Preparing the car was a battle in itself. I'd fix one thing only to have something else break.

Change battery, radio fuse blows

Fix radio, coolant fan stops working

Fix fan, lose cell phone inside bumper

Recover phone, hood latch sticks shut

Pry open hood, chip paint on bumper

I made a terrible commotion, neighbors walking outside to see what the clamor was about and me trying my best to keep a friendly smile for the sake of Roc's reputation.

—

WHILE WAITING to meet with Shep, I began making my rounds in town, saying goodbyes. I met Valerie at The Fox & Hound one night and we sat by the fireplace and drank beers, and I felt that she had changed quite a bit since the beginning of summer. Physically she looked the same, but now radiated a confidence that seemed to transform her features. It's almost as though I were meeting an entirely different person. Her English improved; my Spanish worsened.

We hung out for awhile before heading back to her new apartment where, after a quick tour, made our way into her bedroom. It was a good night. I helped her make pancakes in the morning, but it was a quiet breakfast, as we both knew our time had come to an end. I drove off, smoking a warm cigarette, ingesting every piece of the town into memory.

—

HALLOWEEN NIGHT, the wind whipped through town and people crawled out of their cabins to celebrate. Zephyr came alive for the first time in weeks: children dressed in character with their bags of candy, aromas of cocoa and smoke.

Roc and I were at the Abyss—walking around, pockets bulged with whiskey shooters. There was a lot of energy and we were glad to be around it. Roc was full of enthusiasm, dancing to music from speakers perched atop a fire truck, spinning and dripping spiked coffee everywhere. Party lights flashed across his face and I saw the portrait of a madman. A man who had removed his mask and revealed the costume of himself.

Then I thought madman was too extreme a word. He's just a guy with a lot of enthusiasm. Why couldn't it be that simple?

Anyway, we found ourselves back at The Fox & Hound—there I was again! And there were all the people asking, "Why are you still here?" But I kept Paris in my pocket until I had money in my pocket because I still couldn't believe it was happening.

Paulette was sitting at the bar—Helena's best friend who lured me in with her own brand of smile. Our friendship had been quiet up to this point, but the tension of tiny magnets existed between us, causing just enough connection for conversation. Her hair was extra curly and she was dressed like a piece of sushi or something that made me laugh. We made small talk and I promised to see her before I left town.

—

IT WAS A FROSTY blue morning when I drove to the car wash for a last minute detailing of the Camaro. So cold, in fact, that water froze onto the car as I hosed it down. I was supposed to meet Shep in Fort Collins by noon and, rushed for time, didn't clean it as thoroughly as I wanted. But she looked good. I forgot how well she cleaned up.

And so there I went, tearing down the canyon one last time with Rocco trailing behind (he was to drive me back after the whole ordeal). It was a melancholic journey. I felt like I was breaking up with a faithful friend, and I spoke to her as I had earlier in the year, rubbing the dash and reassuring that Shep would take proper care. Still, I felt a large resistance against selling the car, and the closer we got to the city the more uncertain I became. By now I recognized this feeling as fear and tried to ignore it by enjoying the warming morning—

The foliage! Look at the foliage!

Light streaked trees with birds fluttering from branch to branch. Everything seemed to reassure me with unspeakable grandeur. Still I felt resistance. Just like seeing the shooting star and brushing it off as coincidence. We're constantly being reassured and feeling unsure.

With only five miles left, I was craving one last blast of the throttle. A final moment with my metallic comrade. I found my chance at a stoplight: straight road ahead and farmland on all sides. On green I buried the pedal. The exhaust moaned at the world and the ol' Camaro sprinted forward, and suddenly courage was coursing through my veins just as when alcohol coursed through them. I gripped the wheel and waited for the tires to lift off the ground—the feeling of weightlessness. And when I looked down at the speedometer I saw that I was rapidly climbing, but the gauge needle was broken and bounced between 90 and 120 so that I couldn't tell how fast I was going.

Go, Camaro, gooooooo!

There was nothing but road and land and a small cluster of traffic vibrating in my rearview mirror. I felt powerful; alone with everything I could ever want. I waited and waited for the car to lift, but alas she did not. I let off the gas, let her drift, while I bottled the adrenaline—the courageous feeling that anything is possible—brought to me by the very car that made Zephyr possible. By the love of my uncle who donated the car and father who helped repair it.

Now I was cruising along slowly and steadily, allowing Rocco to catch up. I crested a hill and saw a police car casually pulling out from a side street. Whew, I thought, and sighed relief, as there was no way he could have nabbed me from a mile beyond a hill.

He switched lanes and got behind me.

"Hm?"

Lights and sirens.

Here we go again. I pulled over as traffic caught up and howled past.

NOT SMART, MAN! texted Roc.

The cop approached—a frail, older gentleman who twitched every other sentence.

"Know why I pulled you over?"

"I'm not sure, officer."

"You were clocked by air patrol for speeding."

I imagined a bird's eye view of the Camaro as a red blur; fighter jet chasing it down, gunning at the back tires while I stirred dust in my wake. That's how I planned to tell the story later, at least.

"How fast was I going?"

"Seventy-seven in a fifty-five."

I'd add to my story that I outran the radar. Was clearly going faster than that.

"License and registration."

I handed over my paperwork and waited for his puzzled expression.

"I'm a bit of a traveler, officer."

"Obviously. What do you do?"

"I'm a writer."

"And where do you live?"

"Zephyr Heights."

"Not much work for a writer in Zephyr, is there?" the cop laughed.

I shrugged, thinking of the magical summer. He ripped a ticket for three hundred bucks and let it fall into my lap. I pulled away slowly, trying not to beat myself up, but the voices in my head tore me to shreds.

Idiot! Rocco is right, why would you do that? You were only five minutes away. Now you're going to be late. You might not even sell the car anymore. You suck. You don't deserve to sell the car. You don't deserve to go to Paris.

I la-la-la'ed these voices away, but they were relentless. I grew tired and let them play on my conscience for a short while until they became tired and silenced. Then I gently reminded myself, "I am human, I am not perfect, I make mistakes. Everything is okay."

And suddenly I felt good. I was ready to sell the car.

—

ROCCO AND I pulled into the Walmart parking lot where I met with Shep and his brawny wife. A wholesome couple with whole-grain faces—colored like the golden fields from which they came. Shep approached with a firm handshake and went to work inspecting the Camaro. He was meticulous, combing the car front to back. Crawling under it, pulling off the glass tops, sniffing around like a bloodhound.

"Shep knows vehicles," said his wife. "Was a used car salesman for seventeen years. If there's a problem, he'll find it."

Shep started up the car. It reminded me of the day she was unveiled in the Pennsylvania shed, hearing her for the first time.

"Burn any oil?" asked Shep's wife.

"Not that I know of."

"Maybe jus' a little?"

"Not that I know of."

"How old are the tires?"

"Still have some tread."

"Look bald."

She walked over to the bumper and began pointing at the paint, and then patting the seats, frowning at dust, sniffing around like Shep. I backed off, tempering with clenched teeth, giving them space. It dawned on me that Shep hadn't said a single word and I wondered what he thought of the car. Rocco stood off to the side, entertained.

Then came the negotiating, full on from Shep and his wife. They fussed about petty problems and eventually threw me a lowball offer, which I threw away, meeting them at four-thousand dollars—"Take it or leave it."

Shep walked over to the car and sat down inside like a hopeful child.

"It's a 25-year-old car," I said. "She has her problems, but you can't deny the beauty."

"He looks good in it," nudged Rocco.

The wife looked at Shep. "Your car. Think it's worth it?"

Shep nodded, his wife nodded, I nodded. Everyone was nodding and then a wad of money was pulled out. And with each hundred dollar bill placed in my hand, I saw pieces of my dream coming true: one thousand miles in a plane, one week in a hostel, one month's worth of metro rides. At the end I thanked them and told them my plans—the big adventure they helped actualize. I wanted a group hug but settled for handshakes.

"Be very, *very* careful in Europe," urged Shep's wife, holding onto my hand.

Normally these would be words of advice, but when she said it there was something of fear in her eyes, as though she was trying to transfer it onto me. The lady finally let go and I went over to kiss the ol' Camaro goodbye.

I got inside Roc's car and, looking back, saw Shep drive away in a separate direction. Now I had four grand in my pocket and an empty keychain. No house key, no car keys. I was feeling deflated but happy to have it over with.

"What invisible key is attached to this poor ring?" I said.

"Maybe it's the one inside you," replied Roc.

——

THE FOLLOWING DAY I borrowed Roc's bicycle and rode into town. It was windy and I pushed against gusts that seemed to defy everything I pedaled for. I went to the bank and pulled out the thick wad of bills—its cashy scents swirling upward, teasing me one last time before it all turned to digits. Then I went over to Circus Cafe, sat down and booked the flight to Paris. It was done. I gave Sam one last hug and left the shop, trying to shake her sad eyes from memory. I couldn't. They followed me, jumped into my pocket, and now I had two slimy, sad eyes to carry around. How would I go to Paris with these?

While waiting at a crosswalk I felt a presence—footsteps? Something that beckoned me to turn around. And wouldn't you know it was gorgeous Helena, colorful as ever.

"Is this your new ride?" she asked, motioning at the bike.

"Momentarily."

"So you sold your car. What are you going to do now?"

"I'm going to Paris."

She puckered her lips and nodded, and I couldn't bear to look at her eyes. One pair was enough to carry.

"When are you leaving?" she asked.

"Few days."

"Cool. Are you *excited*?"

"Sure am."

She looked tired of me. The whole town, tired of me.

"Well, see you later maybe," she said.

Then off she went in a separate direction.

A disappearing rainbow.

22

"Moving?"

"Kind of."

"Won't you miss the beautiful mountains?"

"Yes . . . yes I will."

"Well, you can always come back."

By God it was happening again. The postal clerk took the taped-up boxes and I slid my credit card to pay for their eastward shipment. Rocco stood by like an angel—the angel I didn't have in the City of Angels and it was nice to have someone to walk away with.

Now I was left with only the clothes on my back and backpack, which carried more clothes, and laptop for my lap, to keep my brain sane when thoughts spilled through my fingertips. Roc and I bummed around together, bumming smokes off one another, and eventually he had to leave to see Nicole. I knew this meant goodbye as I was flying out the next day. We tried not to make a big fuss about it.

Back at his house we took shots of whiskey, toasting to nothing and everything, and then he left.

I started pouring another one for myself when he burst through the door.

"CHRIST, MAN! You have to come outside!"

I slipped on my shoes and slid through the garage into the driveway where a herd of elk roamed freely, grazing a mere ten feet in front of us. There must have been fifty of them, spaced across the street and spread into a nearby field. Trotting peacefully, glancing up every now and then to acknowledge us with chomping jaws. Dark marble eyes, thick muscles and fur, everything flexing within their steps. And the alpha male with antlers shaped to sharp points, looking after his brown women.

"They've come to say goodbye," Roc nudged.

"Maybe."

We couldn't help but stand in silence. I thought I was dreaming. It was an elkpocaplypse. Even when I went back inside, I saw elk outside the blinds—all around—peering in like furry, four-legged zombies.

—

LATER THAT AFTERNOON, with Roc gone and Helena gone and the elk gone, I was bored and walked to the liquor store where bottles glistened on shelves, competing for my sobriety. I wasn't sure why I was there aside from being bored, and when I thought about it I wasn't really bored. I just missed everyone and didn't know why I kept leaving everyone, suddenly afraid that I would be alone for the rest of my short life. I saw my body shriveled inside a casket, clenching thorns while people bent over to marvel at the mystery of life.

I'm going to Paris, I thought. My dream is coming true! Why the misery?

Then I realized I hadn't told my family about my trip. Shit. I didn't want to tell them. I felt guilty for taking the money and spending it on myself. All this debt and I'm going to Paris. Why should I get to go to Paris?

Selfish! Always thinking of yourself!

Despite *knowing* this trip was right for me—that I needed, wanted, and deserved it, I couldn't shake the voices. I was experiencing the same should-syndrome that Roc had. I *should* be in an office somewhere with a good job and nice salary, and I *should* have a family, and babies, and benefits, and so forth.

Selfish!

I knew I had to go to Paris, but did not want to tell my family because I did not want to hear this. And whether or not they voiced any opinion or said anything at all, I always felt this self-imposed guilt. Where it came from I did not know.

O guilt! It's one of the torturous three along with jealousy and regret. They're the worst, and they're all linked like a chain of bombs. They kill us not physically, rather, spiritually. Weapons of soulful dissolution. The brewing maggot-basket of waste. And tonight I would take the waste and suck it down my throat in an attempt to digest it as happiness.

So there I sat in the dark condo with my pint of cheap whiskey, wondering why I felt this way—why I couldn't seem to tell anyone about something I was so enthusiastic about. And suddenly it dawned on me that my becoming happy around people who weren't happy made me unhappy, and that maybe the reason we're all unhappy is because everyone's afraid to become happy.

The more I drank, the more it made sense.

God how the glasses glinted! One after another, I knew I would kill the pint or myself. Empty stomach, empty brain, empty conscience, can't complain!

I made up songs, man!

I was singin', man!

I was dancin' with myself, man!

All was right in my world.

This is about the time that everything went black and the gates of the Abyss opened up. I walked straight through them and there was nothing. Only more blackness. I was suddenly naked and felt scaly hands on my skin reaching to pull me in, but I dodged them and kept walking. I proceeded toward a swirling center that was so dark that it made everything else brighter and the demons came into sight. I approached them, and similar to the bulls and creatures from my nightmares, as soon as I stopped running, they stopped.

Fear only works when you run from it.

The scaly faces receded into the darkness, and then I stood there motionless, and it was just me.

—

I AWOKE at eight in the morning drooling on the floor of the living room, then stumbled upstairs to find a bed. When I went to lie down, I felt a gurgling in the pit of my stomach and dashed to the bathroom. Sure enough, all hell broke loose and I spent the next six hours hugging the toilet and sleeping on linoleum.

I couldn't keep anything down, not even water. Sometimes I missed the toilet and dove head first into the trashcan. I looked at myself in the mirror and hardly recognized the gaunt cheekbones and sunken eyes. It stung when I swallowed. My joints throbbed like xylophone keys, and when I moved about I heard bells ringing in my skull. My eyelids ached. At the end of my spouting bout, I held a plastic bag saturated with stale yellow fear. I hoped I had purged it all.

—

I SAT ON THE COUCH, sipping water, trying to comprehend how any of this happened. The recurring question was "Why?" Clearly I drank for a reason—surely not for the taste. Not this time.

To *feel* something—that's why I drank! The feeling in the bottle! The stormy night at Salamander, the texture of Sage's hand, kissing Valerie in parking lots and outrunning jets in the Camaro. The feeling of being *alive*. I didn't have energy to dig much further than that. It was the most convenient excuse.

I took the rest of the day to recover and by night I was back on my feet, stuffing my backpack with clothes and preparing to leave. It was then that I decided to call my family and tell them about my plans.

184

I was met with some resistance—"Why would you want to travel this time of the year?", etc—but it wasn't nearly as painful as I thought. More uncomfortable than anything. It was similar to selling the Camaro, moving to Colorado, leaving Francine. The fear of doing these things was infinitely worse than actually doing them.

Then it struck me: I was working against myself. My own worst enemy. Was the Abyss a self-made hell? The distortion of a void warmer than expected?

—

IT WAS LATE by the time I finished packing, and I called Paulette because I wanted to see a pretty face before I left. Not only that, Paulette was a wholesome girl from Kansas— a devout Christian—and I needed to be around someone who exuded poise before taking to the skies.

I walked the dark neighborhood streets looking for the lone lamp we were to meet under. As it turned out, there was more than one lamp and I wandered for quite some time until Paulette waved a flashlight at me in the distance. I hugged her when we met and felt at home in her arms.

"So I hear you're leaving," she said.

"I am."

We started walking and Paulette pulled a case of clove cigarettes from her pocket, handing me one.

"Your send-off gift."

I lit hers and mine, and then we continued on through the chilly air. Not a single car drove past as we walked along the main highway. The sky was clear and the moon illuminated the clouds, rendering them transparent around the edges. In the clearings, the entire universe revealed itself to us.

I enjoyed the taste of the cigarette, and upon taking drags could hear the faint crackling of tobacco. Between the taste and smells and sounds and Paulette's presence, I began to feel much better. Somehow I had gone from hell to heaven in a matter of hours, and I had to chuckle because I couldn't believe how stretchable life was.

"You still haven't told me where you're going."

"Paris."

"Paris, Texas?"

"Paris, France!"

She snickered at her little joke, then nodded approvingly—"That's amazing. But won't you miss our lovely mountains?"

I glanced around at the black earth rising up and down and thought about how much I hated the question about missing things because eventually I missed everything.

"Of course. But I'll return."

"Will you?"

"I will."

We floated back to her apartment, which, to my surprise, was a mere ten-minute walk from Rocco's. I couldn't believe I had been this close to her the entire time—sitting in our empty kitchens, eating dinners, watching movies, living beat by beat. Wishing for love, failing to look in our own backyard.

So there we were sitting in Paulette's living room, happy to be out of the cold. Snuggling on her couch, holding hands, trying to make up for lost time within final minutes.

A fluffy white ball jumped onto our laps—her puppy—which peered through curls of shaggy hair, face disappearing into its own wilderness.

After entertaining the sweet bichon, Paulette and I went outside for another smoke, looking up at the stars—looking for a shooting star—a sign that everything would be okay now and forever.

"We should lie down on the ground!" Paulette exclaimed.

And so we did, continuing to look.

"You know the trick to spotting one?" she asked.

"No."

"Don't look in one area. Scan the entire sky."

By now the clouds had completely dissolved and there was nothing but a glittering canvas to observe. I remembered lying in my childhood bedroom earlier in the year, looking up at the star stickers. Bonfires with Sage. And the time I sat on the furry stone ledge with Mackenzie, or looked through the roof of the Camaro while Helena's hair blew across the heavens. Hiding under sunny blankets with Francine. And now I looked over at Paulette. Every moment swirling together in the sweet soup of life; no single flavor overpowering.

"Think you'll see stars like this in Paris?"

"Not like this."

"Oh. . . just saw one!"

"Where?"

"It's gone."

I was looking at her. Sometimes we miss one beautiful thing in place of another.

23

THE CLOUDS BURNED while I peered out the small window, waiting for the moment of weightlessness. And soon the bouncing airplane pierced the skies, and there were my eyes—wide open—watching the red clouds and big orange ball behind them. A bald sun, glowing like the tips of the cloves I shared with Paulette the night before. I watched the land disappear. My beloved mountains in the distance rising like America's piecrust.

Up up up we went, and I looked around the stuffy aircraft, knowing we would soon be crossing over the ocean in my airship of the Atlantic. The passengers were falling asleep as though a poisonous gas circulated throughout the cabin. I squirmed around for an hour, eventually dozing for ten minutes.

—

THERE WAS A SHORT layover in Reykjavik, Iceland, and when I stepped outside the plane, icy air penetrated my clogged nostrils. Each breath was like a sip of cola. The cheapest soda I'd ever drunk.

Two in the morning, wandering the terminal with all the weary-faced travelers, I had already begun to sense that I was far from home. And what I mean by home is anything familiar.

"Two donuts and an OJ please."

My Iceland cashier gods spouted off a figure in the hundreds. Strange currencies and currents, icy six-foot princesses in boots up to their kneecaps, click-clacking across the glass island of lost souls. Souls between mainlands. I didn't know who was who. Who was European, who was

American, who was human, and who was alien. Tired eyes at two o'clock, everyone looks like an alien.

Back on the plane I tried sleeping again, but alas it was not meant to be.

I thought about the vast waters beneath us and began to imagine scenarios of crashing into it. Would I be able to float my way to Paris? Maybe on a piece of wreckage, arriving as the burnt, soaked soldier from America, and people would speak of me in history books one hundred years from now. That, or we'd simply hit the water and die on impact. Better not to think such things, I thought.

Outside my window I noticed the sky beginning to lighten into a violet hue, and suddenly I pictured Paris with purple skies and got excited about all the strange experiences I was about to have.

No rest for the adrenalized. Soon I saw shapes forming beneath of us, growing with our descent. I knew that it was the foreign land of France, and as we neared I watched the plane paint light onto patches of farmland—no different than the outskirts of any other town. Yet I knew it was to be very different than anything I'd seen before.

—

LUCKILY MY LUGGAGE came tumbling down first. I heaved the backpack onto my spine and began walking away when I noticed a painful burning sensation on the back of my ankle. I sat down and removed my shoe to find a patch of raw skin—a blister from the new sneakers I hadn't quite worn-in. I promptly changed into another pair, but it was too late. The blister was there to stay and my shoe would chafe its way into my conscience with every step over the next few weeks.

I stopped by a store and tried speaking French to the clerk, suddenly aware of how little I knew. All I wanted was a pack of bandages, and I mimed and "oui'ed" my way to their location, "merci'ing" my way out. But not before bumping into a locked door that was not an exit.

I left the airport only to realize I had the slightest clue of where I was going, so I went back inside and searched for my friend's address—a Frenchman I met online prior to my flight. His name was Virgile and he was an artist apparently—an animator. He agreed to let me crash on his couch for a few days until I got my feet wet in the city. And quite literally I was about to get everything wet, as the day was pouring down.

On the bus I sat next to a window so that I could see all the stops as they came. Directly in front of me sat a couple with their cute toddler daughter. The little girl spoke slowly, usually in single-word responses, and I began learning more from her than I had all the guidebooks in previous months. The bus started moving and we hit the highway. Steely industry, flat-faced buildings. Everything was worth seeing. We dipped down into the urban outskirts of Paris—low-income neighborhoods where we stopped frequently and picked up more passengers.

Now the bus was filling with energy. Faces.

Too many faces that I wanted to breathe in all at once. Some were looking at me and I wondered if they could sense my American-ness. I kept quiet so as not to give it away. I wanted to blend. I wanted to disappear into the soil and become as ingrained as possible. With the faces came the language, and clothing styles, new sounds and smells, and I regulated my glancing back and forth between the scenery inside and outside of the bus. Graffiti-sprayed walls, street signs with unique symbols, and oh God it's still raining.

Nothing looked like the Paris I imagined—not yet.

But as we continued to move I began to see the cityscape change. Buildings became refined and corner cafes sprouted like daffodils; the whole garden of Paris blooming before my sleepless eyes. With all the stimulation I nearly missed my stop, snapped from my trance by the driver who reminded—"*Monsieur! Nationale!*"

—

I WAS BACK ON FOOT, wandering the city, distracted and forgetting that I had any destination. Forgetting that I was alive or that we die, or that anything mattered at all. My brain was a vacuum. Everything went straight through my eyes into memory. Soon my left lobes kicked in and told me I needed to get out of the rain and find Virgile's place, as I was still lost to the specifics of his address.

So I boarded a metro train, threw down my wet backpack, and listened to the tracks thumping along as we moved through the tube. I began to feel how tired I was and hoped Virgile was a drinker (I craved a beer). We popped out from the tunnel onto the above ground tracks where I caught further glimpse of the city—Place d'Italie and culture that bewildered me because I was seeing Chinese restaurants in the Italian section of Paris.

At my stop in Chevaleret I walked down three flights of stairs, aching along, a wet rat from the States. There was a pharmacy nearby and I knew that they would have a phone I could use, or an ounce of compassion. Pharmacy workers deal with sad, sick people all day, right?

I walked inside and fluorescent light kicked me in the jaw. Once my eyes adjusted, I saw people in lab coats and gravitated towards them like a jellyfish in a white ocean. One out of three spoke English and I was in luck—he was a man of compassion, handing me the store phone. I dialed Virgile.

"Hello?"

"Bonjour, Virgile! It's Johan!"

" . . . "

"From the CouchSurfing website?"

" . . . "

"American guy?"

"Ah yes! Johan! Where are you?"

"I'm at a pharmacy around the corner, but I can't find your apartment."

"Wait right there."

And so I did.

I waited outside in the rain, staring at all the street people, not knowing what Virgile looked like. An old woman approached from nowhere and asked for the time; except she asked in French and I shrugged. Then she pointed at her wrist. Then I told her the time. Then I was bored. Rain splattered on my shoulder and made little piddle sounds, and the train roared past with its stale green windows. Then a young guy approached. He was the shorter French version of me. It was Virgile.

Virgile walked me through the rain and we spoke very little until we reached his building. His place was interesting. We rode a tiny elevator up to the room, creaked through the door, and before me lie a small studio flat with kitchen and hole-in-the-wall bathroom. I was happy just to be dry. My backpack hit the wooden floor with a thud and I hit the bathroom. My bowels were confused—the ten a.m. shit at seven p.m.

For the next couple of hours, Virgile and I hung out in the apartment making small talk. He had drawings and concepts pinned to the wall—animation projects—including a few posters of Los Angeles.

"I love LA," he said. "Was there last year."

There was a Hendrix poster.

"Funny," I chuckled. "People in America have Eiffel Towers tacked to the wall. You have Hollywood and Hendrix."

"We always want what we don't have," Virgile reflected.

I nodded, looking across his balcony at the lighted windows of the next building, wondering who was behind them and what they were dreaming of.

"Hey man," said Virgile, "my friends are having a party tonight if you want to join."

———

AH, NOW WE'RE TALKING! We sat on the train together, me with a six-pack and Virgile with a bottle of wine. Where would the night take us? My French friend. I wanted to put him in a headlock because he was so cool. I wanted to put planet earth in a headlock and give it a noogie.

When we arrived at the party, it was likewise a teeny little flat with few rooms, but far more packed with people, and we unloaded our bottles on kitchen counters like bags of treasure.

People greeted me from all over.

Women approaching with their fabulous greetings—a kiss on each cheek—*Saluuuut!* I didn't know what I was doing, but enjoyed being kissed by so many exotic beauties at once. I wondered if there was a lip-to-lip version of the greeting.

So there we sat drinking, and I kept quiet as I had on the bus—watching the faces, listening to sounds. They all spoke French, but not all were French. There was a short Aussie guy, Brazilian chick with dark skin, Scandinavians. Most knew English and we made small talk. It seemed they all wanted to practice their English by talking to me, but all I wanted to do was learn French.

The Brazilian stood up unexpectedly and shouted, "I'M GOING TO BAKE A CAKE!" She was drunk and we were hungry—no one complained. We stood around like wolves, drooling on her shoulder while she whipped various ingredients together into some kind of foam. An hour later, she pulled a pan of fluffy chocolate from the oven and cut it into squares. They were delicious.

"How do you say delicious?"

"*Délicieux!*" the room rumbled back.

193

By now I had been awake nearly twenty-four hours and anything that entered my digestive system was sure to put me in a coma, so I went to sit down with my sugary sedative. This is when I suddenly became aware of my ankle again and pulled up my pant leg to notice skin swelling over the side of my shoe. I panicked, and soon the entire party hovered around me, making jokes . . .

"They may have to cut. What's it called when you cut?"

"Amputate," I said.

Finally the Brazilian rushed to my side. Apparently she was also a medical student and quite possibly Wonder Woman. After careful examination, she determined that I was not going to die and brought me an ice pack and another piece of cake.

—

I awoke around two p.m. the next day.

Virgile was still asleep and the sun was already low in the sky. I looked down at my ankle: still swollen. Regardless, I wanted to explore the city and tried to ignore the pain, slipping on my shoes and jacket that now smelled like a wet dog. Inches outside the door and I realized it wasn't going to work. The rubber of my shoe prodded my fat ankle like a farmer with cranky cattle.

I wanted to explore, dammit! I was going out that door somehow.

I took off my shoes and put on a pair of ugly sandals. Beach sandals with thongs. And I kept my socks on, to boot. Virgile laughed and said that my feet would freeze after awhile, but I shrugged and left, limping down the street, savoring the disappearing sights.

It was a gritty section of town in the southeast corner of Paris, and I enjoyed all the grime, as it was raw and unexpected. At one point I heard children's voices and stopped to listen. A playground nearby, guarded by a tall

wall as though it were a castle. I imagined stubby little kings
and queens skipping around hand-in-hand—tiny people with
serious agendas. Conquering sandboxes.

I kept walking. Hobbling.

Dragging the bum ankle like a bum, and accepted it as a
sort of disguise. I entered Chinatown, and all sorts of
shadowy figures walked past in the trash-strewn streets. To
my left, naked, headless chickens spun on rotisseries behind
squeaky clean glass, and a stout woman stood hypnotized in
front of it.

I soon caught sight of a pharmacy and walked inside
looking for something to resolve my swelling. I couldn't read
any of the packaging. Not wanting to walk out with a tube of
toothpaste, I flagged down the cashiers and found the one
out of three who spoke English—a man in his early thirties
with stubbly beard. He was kind and handed me ointment
and bandages.

"Beer is a good painkiller, too," he snickered.

"Yes, I've used it many times."

"Where are you from?"

"America."

"Do you like to party?"

He tore off a piece of receipt paper and wrote down the
addresses of hip clubs and hot spots. I folded it up and
walked away in my ripped socks and flip flops.

I would not party that night,

But I did continue to wander.

I loved to wander.

Even as I limped, I loved it.

I think I loved it more.

—

PARIS WAS A DARK PLACE, or at least for the night it was. I
walked alone feeling invisible, face enshrouded in my hood—
a nobody in the eyes of everyone near.

No phone, no pool, no pets.

No map, no language, no nothin'.

I looked up and Paulette was right: no stars.

What I did have was a bag of sliced raisin bread and banana. I ate the banana in one bite and picked at the bread for the next few blocks. A homeless woman reached out with a wrinkled hand and, as I had on Sunset Boulevard, I reached back with food. She was genuinely hungry—"Merci beaucoup!"

Good Lord. What's a woman her age doing with ass on cold pavement? What unforgivable act has she committed?

I saw homeless people everywhere, lost in the ambience of mopeds and sirens and throbbing church bells. Swallowed in the shadows of a babushka. I wondered whether I'd be able to go on at that age, in those conditions. Something had to be behind those eyes keeping that woman alive.

—

I SPENT A COUPLE MORE days at Virgile's place but didn't do much. He worked from home and I tried to keep my distance so as not to distract him. Sometimes I peered over his shoulder and saw the cartoon characters he was developing for some kind of story-based video game. It looked interesting and he was excited about it. He sat straight and determined. All the craziness that plagued other artists had found its way out through his scalp, blossoming into a jumble of hair.

One night after another day of wandering, I returned to Virgile's place to find a pretty girl sitting on his couch, cup of tea in her hand. Her name was Mya and she had a porcelain face. I thought it might shatter if she spoke. As with other women, I felt daggers shooting from her eyes—beautiful daggers. And the fact that she knew very little English made it worse because all I could do was communicate by glancing into her eyes and falling into them, as though I were bungee jumping from heaven into the ocean.

Three days into my trip and I knew nothing had changed. I still had the longing, I was still infected.

"Sorry we were speaking mostly French," Virgile told me after she left.

"All good. You dating her by any chance?"

"No, no! Just friends."

"Is she dating anyone?"

"Ah. Your first French crush!" he laughed. "Yes, unfortunately for you she just began a relationship two weeks ago."

"Only two weeks? So I have a chance."

—

THE NEXT DAY I decided to get lost for a second time. It was evening. My swollen ankle had improved; I was now able to wear shoes and felt civilized again. The only problem was, after dragging my leg for miles and miles, I agitated my knee which made it difficult to climb up and down stairs. This was an issue since the main mode of transportation in Paris was the metro, in which you must sometimes descend two or three flights to reach the train.

Stairs everywhere and stares everywhere as I hobbled around like an old geezer.

The metro stations were a world of their own. Hallways of characters. Colorful people with nowhere to go, artists with nowhere to perform. Scraggly gray man singing to jazz emanating from an old boombox. African playing xylophone.

And then there were the ones who jumped aboard trains and shoved accordions in my face as we barreled through the blackness. Accordions on one train, saxophonists on another, pouring themselves silly. They were good and shaking coin cups.

—

I DID NOT DESIRE to do anything touristy. I just wanted a cafe or beautiful relationship; to meet beautiful souls and swim with them for a bit. Because of that, I didn't really care where I was. I found the Eiffel Tower without looking for it. Just saw it glowing above the treetops and meandered over. It was impressive. Like a candle lighting the way for some invisible beast stomping across Europe. Then I followed the Seine until I drew closer and closer to it, passing men who sold miniature versions of the monument—"Two Euro, Two Euro!"—noticing how my neck bent upwards the closer I neared.

Suddenly I stood directly beneath it, gazing at the web of steel beams and cables rising through the center like bones and veins supporting the heart of the city. Without warning, the entire structure sparkled from top to bottom.

These must be the stars of Paris, I thought.

—

I WALKED A LOT that night. I think I walked half the city. The walks were meditative, and usually I thought of people from my life. Being so far away made me picture them more clearly, like figments of a vivid dream. I thought about trucking and my other adventures. Sometimes a thought would pop into my head that seemed to come from nowhere, for no reason, like the jukebox at my grandparents' house. Francine's hair clip. Sage's boots. And then I was thinking about the gold leaves on the trees outside Circus Cafe.

I wondered if one day I would recall the things I was experiencing right now. Sometimes I stopped and tried to freeze time by soaking in everything wholly and completely.

Châtelet, Châtelet! Look at you shine!!

I took my tongue and stretched it across the entire street, licking it up and down. Licking the light that splashed its surface as though it were painted by some gargantuan hand above. Lapping up the light posts and flower pots hanging from shops, and statues centered carefully in front of columns. I chewed through the rock and stone and kept eating the city because I wanted to taste its fibers. I wanted to carve through brick and mortar and bleed crimson across the land. I wanted people to know that I had been there; that I had existed in such beauty. That I *existed!*

Alas, I licked my lips and looked for a drink.

Paris at night does not feel like night. It feels like day with the lights turned off. The energy of day remains, and although the sun may be hidden, every bulb in the city continues to burn as its own electric, neon galaxy. Diners seem unapproachable, gleaming like chrome portals. Even the birds continue to chirp. 2am, 3am, 4am.

In some areas I was completely alone, walking past stained churches that shot to the sky—looking up, looking down. You use your neck a lot in this town. I stumbled upon a side street that was alive with energy. It appeared so abruptly that I thought it might be a mirage—an oasis of sensational cafes with immortals seated at terrace tables. I wondered if I returned the next night, whether they would still be there in the same positions, drinking the same drinks. One man peered over his glasses at me. He looked like Hemingway with his white beard and hair.

I continued walking and turned at the next block. It was dead.

Now it was really late and nearly every shop had closed. Even the metro was closed. A few young people stumbled out from a bar, wearing scarves and smoking cigarettes as though they had just been invented. Taxis zoomed past left and right; but I was looking for a bus, aware of high prices. The problem is that I didn't know anything about the bus system.

Why wouldn't you take a map? Idiot!

I hopped aboard the first bus that came my way, asking the driver which bus I needed to be on, but he knew very little English and only pointed ahead, speaking in French. I watched his finger flap around like a dog watching a treat in its owner's hand.

"Where?" I asked.

He flapped some more. "Straight, straight."

Didn't know where the hell I was.

I dragged my ankle around another corner and there were five more stations with nobody around. How was there nobody around?

Suddenly an angel surfaced on an elevator. A young woman who worked for the Metro.

I ran over to her.

"*Excusez-moi...* uh... uh... *Parlez-vous anglais?*"

"A little bit."

"Can you tell me which bus to Chevaleret, *s'il vous plaît?*"

She pointed. "Straight."

"Which one?" I said, looking at the five stations ahead.

"Come with me," she said, grabbing my hand.

Her skin was soft and I didn't want to let her go until I knew everything about her. We stopped and she pointed— "Straight." Then she smiled and pranced away. When the bus finally arrived I asked the driver whether or not he was going to Chevaleret, but no. He was not.

Idiot!

I kicked cans around, wishing one was cold and closed and full of beer. Then a guy approached—a black Frenchman who spoke decent English. He directed me towards an information booth where I picked up a map and asked the attendants for help. Eventually I found my bus and was thankful for my two angels of the night.

—

I NEARLY FELL ASLEEP on that bus when the driver yelled, "Chevaleret!"

In my daze, I thought of the Camaro.

I stepped down into the street and realized I still didn't know where to go. I had the address but forgot the layout of Virgile's neighborhood. It was now three a.m. and I was meandering in the seedy areas where birds did not chirp.

I took gambles on streets, squinting at dark signs, listening to my gut. It only grumbled. I was grumpy. Even the mannequins looked well fed. My frustrated whispers echoed off walls. How could this be Paris?

Then I heard a crunching noise from behind and whipped around.

A taxi cab slowly approaching.

I motioned for the driver to stop, and a middle aged man with glasses rolled down the window.

"Where do you need to go?" he asked.

I showed him the address.

"That's only a five minute walk," he said. "You just have to go——"

"I know," I interrupted. "Straight."

24

IN THE MORNING I said goodbye to Virgile and was back on the streets, trying to maintain my posture while the backpack bounced on my shoulders. My next temporary home would be a hostel, and I was headed straight for it.

By now I had learned the metro system fairly well and enjoyed riding the trains. There was always someone to see that I'd never seen before. On this particular day, I watched an ancient-faced Native American-looking Frenchman that blew my mind. His cell phone disappeared into humungous hands.

Across from me sat a woman in a black dress, legs crossed and book in her lap. Watching her was a landmark itself. The morning light and her rising breasts bathing in the warmth. I had the urge to smell her. I was sure she smelled good.

When I stepped off the train I immediately looked for the hostel, not wanting to get lost again. I stopped a man pushing a stroller and tried to appear friendly while asking directions. He pointed me down an alleyway.

I was in the trendy neighborhood of Montmartre, but it felt very touristy near the famous Sacré Cœur church which is where my hostel was located. There were shops everywhere, selling everything to anyone. Souvenirs and clothing. Racks of post cards and baskets of fabric overflowing onto piss-stained sidewalks. Scarves. Everyone wearing a scarf, fashionable and fashion-conscious. Boots and scarves, hats and bags—all of Paris one big circular catwalk. And the magnificent church perched above like a shrine to street swag.

Inside the hostel, I waited in line with a crowd of tired travelers doing the traveler-hunch with their bulging packs. The place was colorful with maps and flags, and it reminded me of Theodora's little hostel back in Zephyr. There was a kitchen with microwave and hot plate, communal area with wooden tables and chairs, and lockboxes for storing valuables. Bass thumped throughout the room—techno that made me smile because it sounded distinctly European.

I checked in, stowed my laptop, and ascended the creaky wooden stairwell with my creaky knees, into a room on the first floor. It was small with two sets of bunk beds and a silver chair plopped in the center of the room, which looked like a porn prop. Black Market eBay, I thought. They're gonna force me to do a porn flick and sell it without giving me any of the residuals.

Techno continued to thump and vibrate the floorboards while I put my stuff down and sat in the dark. Outside, sirens and mopeds. Foreign voices. Just like truck stops. The unknown is cleansing; a shower for the soul.

Then I heard a loud click and the door pushed open.

In walked two Asians—a girl and guy, both about twenty. They shook my hand and introduced themselves as Joanna and Lee. They were full of energy, moving like bees, buzzing around the room, making their beds, bobbing their heads, flipping through tour guides. "We're gonna go here and here and here and here."

"Where have you been so far?" Lee asked me.

"The Abyss."

"Where's that?"

They searched their guides.

"Don't bother looking."

"We want to see *everything*," said Joanna. "Where are you coming from?"

"Lots of places. I'm a bit of a traveler."

"Us too!"

"Finally I'm in the right place," I said. "Hey, let's go for a drink."

Joanna looked at Lee. They blushed.

"What?" I asked.

"We're not really drinkers."

Somehow I ended up in the one sober room with a dry mouth. The thumping bass from downstairs was driving me insane. I left the building alone.

—

IT WAS DARK in the streets and shops were already flickering off. I walked towards the light—whichever corner glowed brightest, wherever the voices were. Eventually I stumbled upon a cafe with young people outside, a cloud of smoke hovering above like one big hazy halo.

I sat down and read the menu, ordering a beer first. It was tall but not very good. Then came my chicken salad. I was hungry and shoveled it into my gut, sitting back as the fat American, watching Parisians pass by on the TV of life. The people seated next to me were travelers from Poland. They spoke English and glanced at me from time to time, but I didn't feel much like talking. I thought it more interesting to listen, although they said nothing interesting. I started to think about my bank account and whether or not I could afford the fancy food digesting in my intestines. It seemed that I worried about money wherever I went, and it was starting to sicken me. I wanted to barf up the entire meal and ask for a refund.

—

THE STREETS WERE even darker now and all the mysterious characters were out, dressed in black. So dark that you couldn't tell a person from their shadow.

Abruptly, out of nowhere, I bumped into a tall African man—about six-foot-six—who blocked my path to the hostel. He said something I didn't understand.

"Sorry, I don't speak French," I told him.

"GIVE ME ONE EURO!"

He was speaking English now.

"I don't have any change," I told him, digging through my pockets, only feeling a wad of twenties I had just extracted from the ATM.

"Where are you from?" he asked.

"America. Los Angeles."

"OHHH! Snoop Doggy Dog!" he said, moving in for a hug.

I backed off.

"GIVE ME ONE EURO!"

"Sorry, man. I don't have it."

Now he jolted forward as if he were going to pick me up by the ankles and shake everything from my pockets. I was walking backwards without realizing it.

"ONE EURO NOW!!"

His hand shot forward and then someone stepped in—a friend of his—much shorter, but with a clear voice and level head. He muttered something in French and pulled the brute away.

The Basilica shone atop the hill.

"Jesus," I said, wiping my forehead.

—

THE WEEK MOVED right along.

I woke up each morning at six o'clock, feeling the techno music below my bed. Sometimes I fell back to sleep, sometimes I didn't. Then I showered in a stall that was just big enough to fit myself and shampoo bottle. The water was rationed at ten second intervals and I shivered between spurts. Afterwards, I creaked my way downstairs into the kitchen where they served free breakfasts—croissants, bread, cereal. And then off to the nearest metro station.

One day I set my sights on the Père Lachaise Cemetery as I heard that Jim Morrison was buried there. I'd studied his musical career throughout the summer and wanted to pay my respects. And so I walked down the streets, passing through a market of fruit stands, vegetable stands, hat and scarf stands. Horns honking, registers registering, boomboxes blaring, salesmen staring. And yelling. Yelling as though guns were pressed to their backs—'Sell that head of cabbage, or it's your head!'

It was a bright day and warm for November. But once again map-less, I got lost and bounced from person to person asking directions. I came to enjoy this method better than using a map, as it forced me to mingle with the locals.

Usually I grabbed the first person I saw.

Today it was an old woman inching her way down the sidewalk. Her face was wrinkled with lines and I read the entire history of France on her face. She pointed me down a street, and then I got lost, and then I was pointed again by another old lady. Somehow I kept asking very old ladies where the cemetery was and began to feel awkward.

When I reached the cemetery, I passed through the main gates, under a high cement arch, and began hobbling up the cobblestone, eyes peeled for MORRISON.

"Where are you, Lizard King?"

Thousands of graves of different sizes. Some were small stones while others were tombs with roofs and front doors, usually covered in vines and cobwebs and crow shit. Crows perched everywhere. Black crows with shiny feathers, flapping loudly as they passed overhead. Flap flap flap. Just like in the movies. Nobody was around, save for those in the ground, and I felt strange energies swirling with the wind.

The City of Light!

Even on overcast days, matte surfaces reflected light as though it was their given right as the inanimate inhabitants of Paris.

I continued upwards.

A continuous climb through a maze of graves. Apparently this was a cemetery for prestigious people, yet I'd never heard of the majority of them. I didn't know painter from king from priest. I thought about the nature of fame as I walked around trying to pronounce names.

When I found Jim's grave, there was a crowd of tourists congregating in front of it. The gravesite was surrounded by a steel barricade, strewn with flower petals and folded up notes. Two framed photos of the musician stood atop the tombstone. I waited until the crowd cleared and observed in silence, thinking again about life and death. Then I thought of Helena—Jim was her favorite. And Helena's philosophy: "I look forward to death. I think it will be a peaceful thing."

I closed my eyes.

It was quite peaceful, I had to admit.

—

LATER THAT DAY I rode the train to the Latin Quarter, looking to offset the morbid morning with vibrancy. I heard the Quarter was where it was at. Immediately I came upon the Seine—the river that snaked through the city and caressed it with calm waters. And above the Seine, Notre Dame with its Gothic architecture needling the skies.

I wandered the Quarter, drifting through the alleys, past the shops and high apartments, leveled and shaved at the top by the blade of Parisian gods. There were crepes cooking nearby and I promptly purchased one.

Roses were shoved in my face. I smelled the roses, but had no one to give them to. I was thinking of people again. I wanted to give the world a rose. Street thieves and their roses, what were they thinking? Did they not realize the emotional stir-up they were causing?

On my way back to the hostel, I stopped at a convenience store for a cheap bottle of wine. The shop was bright and, like other bright places, slapped me in the face. Not only was I sober, but also hungry and looking for food.

It wasn't Paris' best. Aisles of crap.

I couldn't decide which crap I liked the best. Next to me was a middle-aged Mexican woman who looked as though she had something to say. I thought she might tell me the secret of the universe.

"*Dónde está el queso?*" she asked.

I took her to the dairy section.

"*Sí, sí! Gracias*!!"

Cheese. She wanted cheese.

It wasn't the secret of the universe, but something brilliant had happened. The absence of French language had enabled us to connect through my limited Spanish.

—

THE NEXT MORNING I was eager to get the hell out of the hostel. Joanna, the cute Asian, kept pestering me about The Louvre—"You *must* see The Louvre, the *Mona Lisa* is at The Louvre, you can't *not* see The Louvre." I couldn't resist her charming innocence nor her enthusiasm. I wanted to stick her in my pocket and pull her out when I felt a frown coming on.

Getting off at my stop for The Louvre, I immediately noticed that I was forced to walk through a shopping mall to reach the museum entrance. Advertisements hit me like spitballs, plastering my face with leather jackets, diamond studded wristwatches, smoothies.

It was Wednesday and the museum wasn't very crowded, which was good. Crowds bothered me. Too many people chattering, sniffling, coughing, sneezing, crying, sneering, cackling, smacking their lips. Hot bodies pressed against one another, bumping into each other—everyone annoying each other by simply existing. I loved people but preferred them in small doses, or to think of them collectively as one big smiley face.

So there I stood amid thousand-year old statues and sculptures—the sniffling gods of their time. Everything exposed as nature intended. Stone cocks frozen and breasts forever sagging. After greeting each bust, I walked upstairs to the Italian Renaissance section, towards the mythical Mona Lisa. The building's ceilings were stunning—epic murals and golden etchings. An ostentatious display of emotion. I came

208

upon rooms of paintings that were equally beautiful, albeit violent and oozing with drama. Tortured, tattered souls stabbed through eye sockets, impaled on spikes and kicked into choppy waters. Tourists stood by and smiled for pictures: thumbs-up and peace signs. I watched the happy people take photos in front of sad people and pondered the nature of humanity. I thought of flooded Zephyr and the suppressed amusement of tourists. Then I thought of sideshow freaks. And car crashes and rubber necks, tabloids, and 'Who broke up with who?'

More violence as I walked along.

Crying mothers reaching for something out of frame

Naked, bloody bodies

Red, shouting faces and despaired, upturned faces

Demons crawling through the apocalypse

When I reached the Mona Lisa, I fought a small crowd of people taking selfies in front of it, eventually making my way to the front.

There she sat, smirking at me.

It was nice to see a friendly face behind bulletproof glass.

—

WHEN I CHECKED OUT of the hostel the next morning, I headed straight for the laundromat. My next temporary home would be with a French couple I'd met on CouchSurfing. They were about to allow a strange foreigner into their home for a few days. Greeting them with a smelly bag of clothing was not going to work.

I got to the laundromat early. No one was around and I had trouble figuring out the washing machines. The buttons were labeled with icons, but even then they confused me—a couple of water droplets with a slash through it. What does that mean, no rain today? Traveling to countries you've never been, everything becomes a challenge. Anyhow, I sat on a bench reading a book, listening to the machine whir, then stop, then whir, then stop. My stomach grumbled. It was a mundane morning.

I looked at my sad backpack leaning against the wall. Wow, I thought. That's my life in there. How did I end up like this? Suddenly I was thinking about my days in Hollywood, high up in chic office spaces with trendy posters covering the walls and coffee machines around every corner. Harsh sunlight beating down on Aston Martins parked on the Boulevard. Everyone smiling like they had found the end of their own rainbows. And now the cold Parisian laundromat.

I loved it.

—

WHEN MY LAUNDRY was done, I raced across the street to the metro station where I was to meet with my new friends. I was hoping they were crazy—the good kind of crazy. The crazy that rips you from your bubble and rockets you into space. That's what we need: more rocket-people.

While waiting on a bench, sharing a baguette with my pigeon friends, I saw a colorful couple walking towards me— Dessie and Pierre. They both had bags slung around their shoulders with art supplies poking out. I waved to them and their faces lit up as they hurried over.

Pierre was tall like me, bearded and dressed in a jacket that looked like something a jock might've worn in the fifties. Dessie wore a blue patterned vest with black sleeves, skirt, pants. She had straight brown hair and circular glasses. Both in their late twenties.

"Nice to meet you," said Dessie. "You've got all your stuff?"

"Oui," I said, slapping my backpack.

"We'll go back to our place and drop off our bags, then find some fun."

"Let's find some fun."

We hurried underground and hopped a train across town. I had yet to take an afternoon train and didn't realize how crowded they became at this hour. Supposedly Line 13 was the worst. There it was, rocking across the tracks, faces flattened against glass; people cramming and jamming their way into mobility.

I couldn't believe it.

Dessie and Pierre looked at me—the entire station looked at me—and made sour faces. When we finally got on, Dessie asked if there was anything special I wanted to see in Paris.

"I want to see what isn't written in the guidebooks."

And so began our adventure as the Parisian-American trio. Like Rocco and Helena, D & P were enthusiastic. They bounced down the streets with me, stopping at random shops for baguettes, cheese, wine, then threw it all in their bottomless bag.

"We're going to make a big, big dinner tonight!" Dessie said, handing me the wine. "Homemade soup!"

"She loves to cook," said Pierre.

"I bet it's great."

"Orgasmic, bro."

Pierre loved to use the word bro. He was heavy into hip-hop culture and street art—evidenced at their apartment—an entire bookcase of graffiti picture books. Having always taken interest in urban art, I convinced D & P to show me the local flavor. Once we dropped off our bags and baguettes we hit the sidewalks, eventually stopping before a high concrete wall with spiked metal fence running across the top. It was jagged and dangerous-looking.

"We have to climb over that?" I asked.

"Yes! But worth it!" Dessie said.

"You wanted to see what wasn't in the guides, bro."

I looked up at it, then down at my poor leg that was finally starting to heal.

Fuck it. Let's go.

D & P went first, then me. I took my time, slowly pulling my leg over the black daggers and jumping onto the staircase below. We descended the stairs onto a set of old train tracks, which were covered in vegetation, including the walls bordering the tracks. The main reason for our visit was to bear witness to the decorated brick and stone, tagged with designs that twirled up to the streets, just as the smoky underworld would have it.

We traversed the tracks and came upon a monstrous face painted around a hole that had been smashed in the wall— cleverly rendering a gaping mouth. D & P stood inside of it, feigning terror while I snapped photos.

"These tracks were used to move products around Paris before the trucks took over," Pierre said.

"What are they used for now?"

"Nothing. They're just here. That's why you see all the street art. Nobody gives a fuck."

"Hey," I said, "What about the catacombs? I heard about tunnels of graves that run beneath the city."

"Yes! You can get to them from here!" he said, pointing ahead.

We kept walking and the sky darkened.

"Over here!" yelled Pierre. "This is one of the entry points!"

I crouched down with him and looked into a black hole three-by-three feet wide. He shined a flashlight into it.

"You have to crawl into that until it opens up into the tunnels."

It was littered with crushed Pepsi cans and rusty nails.

"I don't think so," I said.

—

DESSIE WAS a wonderful cook—a vegetarian cook. She made giant steaming bowls of spiced potato soup, which we sopped up with bread, all of us sharing the same baguette. Breaking bread, passing bread, dipping bread.

During the meal, Dessie jumped up and walked to a turntable, threw down an LP and suddenly we were in Africa. Reggae bumped throughout the room while we finished our soups, and then spliffs were presented for dessert. D & P passed the joint while I took small drags and looked around the living room.

It was an interesting place, their flat.

Everything crammed perfectly, efficient. The gas stove required lighting by flame, clothes were hang-dried, dishes washed by hand. The floorboards creaked all over and I was conscious of my footsteps in the late hours when D & P slept and I got up to use the bathroom or pour a glass of water. The walls were peeling in every room, and one day while taking a shower I swung around to wash my back and a whole page of paint came crashing down. They even had a lamp that fizzled on and off. You had to slap it to brighten it. Sometimes I got shocked. It was great.

—

THE NEXT DAY Dessie invited me to her studio. She worked during the nights as a clothing designer for her small business that she was passionately dedicated to. I hopped the 13 to the 3, got off at Arts et Métiers, and followed Dessie's directions to a street lined with nondescript buildings. I punched a code outside of the studio and the door opened with a buzz and a click. Then I walked through a cold corridor, crouched under a hobbit-sized door, and entered a courtyard with three smaller buildings.

In the first building sat a curly, short-haired blonde who glanced at me through the windows, hat in her hand. She was sewing. Hats on the walls, hats everywhere. In another stretch of windows were men hunched over computers, clicking away, puffing cigarettes. A fluorescent, slap-you-in-the-face kind of place. Then came the final building, windowless, with a big steel door.

I knocked.

"Saluuuuuut!" said Dessie, inviting me inside.

And the kiss greeting. And then me looking around her small studio, seeing all the frilly fabrics folded on shelves. Shiny sewing machines, spools, specialized tools. Everything you'd expect from one who is committed to their craft.

"Would you like to take a coffee?" she asked, pointing to a full pot.

I poured myself a cup and moseyed around while Dessie worked on a hooded sweatshirt.

Suddenly Pierre burst through the door with a toolbox in hand—"Salut!"

He slammed it down on the floor along with a six-pack, then began pulling tools out of it—hammers, sanders, pry bars.

"What's all that for?"

"Shoes," he said, pulling out a fake wooden foot and waving it at me. "I make shoes, bro."

"Wow, you guys are the real deal."

He turned on hip-hop music and went to work.

I stood around for a long time, downing beers, walking to buy more beers, passing around beers. Then I saw a camera sitting on one of the shelves—a digital Nikon with good lens. I began playing around with it, noticing that it had a video function, and before long I was pointing the lens at Dessie while she pedaled away at her machine. I swung the camera all over the place, capturing her in the moment; in her glorious enthusiasm. Pierre hammered and bobbed his head to beats. My shutter clicked. Machines whirred. We all swirled together as one collective, artistic spirit. I couldn't have been happier.

When we finished and cleaned up, I had a couple hours worth of footage as well as a nice buzz going from the drinks. There was noise coming from the courtyard and it seemed that everyone had finished working at the same time. The curly blonde hat-maker wandered into our studio and sat down with us. All I did was steal glances. She was a classic beauty—pale face with big, sensuous eyes and thin frame that she held with grace. An actress from a Humphrey

Bogart film. Whenever she opened her mouth, smoke spilled out in the shape of her body. I couldn't stand it anymore.

I turned to Dessie—

"You guys want to go out for dinner tonight? My treat."

"Sure! Do you like Ethiopian food?"

"We'll find out."

And so we hit the streets, half empty bottles in hand, stumbling about the night. The camera was slung around my neck and I fired at everything I saw. We took the long way to the restaurant, as Pierre wanted to show me a stretch of impressive street art. He slapped his own sticker designs on poles and signs as we walked along. Sometimes he found that his old ones had been ripped off, quickly re-plastering them. He pointed out his stickers all across the city.

"What's that over there?" he'd ask.

Sure enough it was him.

At the restaurant we sat down and awaited our Ethiopian meal, served traditionally as one large flatbread covered in various vegetables and meats that we all shared and ate from. Dessie remained faithful to her vegetarianism. She seemed right at home surrounded by all the African photos and tapestries—greens, yellows, reds. Her spirit was rooted in Africa and I thought of Helena, the Spanish mountain girl.

We ate and ate, famished from the long afternoon. It was spicy food soaked in sauces. Even the greens were hot and delicious. I considered rolling everything together and eating it like a burrito.

"I have some really great footage from the studio today," I told Dessie.

"Yeah?"

"Yeah. Could put together a promotional piece for your company if you'd like."

"I'd love that! How long will it take you?"

"About a week. Might have to grab some extra shots with better lighting. Would you mind if I stayed at your place until I finish?"

"Of course. Whatever you need."

25

I WAS SITTING on a deck with people I didn't know, drinking a drink I'd never had in a place I'd never been. I looked around. The trees were fluffy and green, which was strange considering that it was already late autumn. The people around me were mostly women. Beautiful, graceful women sipping cocktails alongside me. I noticed that we were very high up—a deck protruding off the side of a skyscraper with nothing but verdant vistas beneath us.

Suddenly we broke away from the building and began floating over the land like a hovercraft. Me and my cold drink and beautiful women just drifting through space. I couldn't believe it. I sprang from my chair and walked to the edge and peered down at the plush earth. It was so green that my eyes burned—a salad suitable for the belly of the soul. I was besieged with joy, I couldn't breathe, I cried. Behind me the women remained seated, content, like mothers.

Then it all went black.

I awoke and there we were, still on the deck. The women woke up, too.

"Did you—? Were we just flying over the—?"

They nodded.

"So we all had the same dream?"

They nodded.

"How fuckin' amazing was that!?"

Then it all went black.

Now I laid fully clothed on the futon in D & P's living room. My head pounded and my mouth was so dry that I could barely feel my tongue, nonetheless moisten my lips with it. I took a sip of water. It was like flipping a switch. I could taste again—the gooey morning-after flavor of an unclean mouth. Faint traces of Ethiopian spices and stale beer and hot breath.

There came a knock at the door.

Before I could reply, Pierre waltzed in.

"How you feeling, bro?"

"Ugh."

"Does your back hurt?" he asked.

"No, why?"

"You fell over last night while you were sitting in your chair. Your legs went straight up. All I saw were shoes."

"Sorry, man."

"It's okay. I just hoped you didn't get hurt."

"We'll see once I start walking around."

"Okay. Dessie is already at work and I have to go now, too. We have coffees and *pain au chocolat* in the kitchen for you."

The door slammed behind Pierre and I sat still for a few moments thinking about the dream and how good I felt in the dream, floating freely and happily with warm people around. And the fact that nobody was speaking even as we took flight. We were simply existing—loving each other without explanation. It seemed that, in the dream, this was normal. This is what people did. They sat, smiled, and floated. There was nothing to fear; nothing to question.

—

I HAD SPENT two weeks in Paris and was beginning to feel restless again—again! Prague, Berlin, Rome. Where to? It drove me nuts. What's worse is that when I met French locals or fellow travelers, they all told me to go elsewhere.

"You gotta see Amsterdam!"

In Amsterdam I was sure they'd tell me "You gotta see Paris!"

I remained at the old flat, sitting around in the mornings, editing video footage for Dessie and then running out the door at sunset to catch a train somewhere. The place felt like home for a while. I slept, bathed, cooked, cleaned, and sometimes just kicked back and stared at the wall, happy to have a heartbeat. I picked up the mail and pretended to read it—"Ah, a letter from so and so and something I can't pronounce." I waved to neighbors and nodded at whatever they said. I bought food at the store across the street and came to know the cashiers by name. I was practically settled.

—

ONE DAY I received invitation from Virgile to a party he was having that night—a video game tournament in which he promised booze, food, and plenty of kicks. I'd never been to a video game party and thought it could be fun, so I hopped on the train with a couple of six-packs, again observing the strange people and wondering about their lives when they got off the train—where they go, what they do in their spare time, what they think and dream about. Each person a world unto themselves.

At Virgile's place, I forgot the code for his building and was stuck outside with my two cases of beer. I stood staring up at the glowing fourth story window, listening to all the laughter. It was getting colder as winter neared, temperatures dipping into the low forties.

I waited for a long time until someone exited the building and then casually slid inside. Upstairs, I knocked on Virgile's door and he opened it.

"Hey, man! Glad you could make it!"

"And I brought some friends!" I said, holding up the six packs.

I hoisted them onto his kitchen table and walked into the living room where I ran into a wall of faces. Young, bright, swigging faces.

"This is my American friend, Johan!" yelled Virgile.

The room went silent.

"Salut," I said, giving a tiny wave.

Many waved back, very few spoke. I recognized no one except Mya. There she was with her hair tied up and big shiny doe eyes. Two chairs were set up in front of a small television and partygoers sat jamming away on the controllers, playing the fighting game *Soul Calibur*. Everyone in the room hooted and hollered when someone was nearly defeated or had just been defeated. It was like being in a sports bar.

Mya sat across from me and I tried to make conversation.

"So, how've you been?" I asked.

"Good. Studying."

"What are you studying?"

"Biochemistry."

"Do you like it?"

"Yes."

"Cool."

"Cool."

We sat across from each other, and between us, the language barrier.

Next to me was a Frenchman who did not look French. Dutch or Scandinavian maybe. But then again it was always hard to tell. In the twenty-first century, who was from where? The world is an airport. Anyhow, he spoke English quite well and once we got through the "Where are you from, what are you doing" questions, we delved into heavier stuff like happiness. I pulled out a magazine clipping from earlier in the day that showed the top twenty countries with 'highest happiness levels.' We mused on it for awhile, ruminating on the fact that neither France nor America had made the cut despite being economic powerhouses.

I went to the bathroom to take a leak and forgot where the light switch was. All throughout France it was the same. Switches were hardly ever in the same place or the same type. Some were toggle switches, some buttons, some automatic sensors. Sometimes I'd enter the bathroom, get locked in somehow—locked in the dark—and the only way out was to use the flashlight attached to my keychain to find the switch and take a successful piss.

When I escaped from the bathroom, I noticed a girl sitting against the wall, away from the pack, playing an acoustic guitar and singing American songs. She had short brown hair, olive complexion, and long legs that wrapped around the room. I sat across from her and bobbed my head, stealing glances between chords, absorbing her sounds, folksy and light. The good vibes eventually took us to the balcony where we rolled cigarettes and lit them, the clanking of weaponry muffled behind a glass door. We had carved ourselves a small slice of the city.

"You play nicely." I said.

"I'm still learning."

A moped buzzed past. All the buildings looked orange. Beautifully stale.

"Where are you from, what are you doing?" I asked.

"I'm from Versailles, and I was *supposed* to graduate from a university in Lyon last week. But the problem is that I failed my exams and have to stay an extra semester. My parents are really upset."

"You live with them?"

"Unfortunately."

We took slow, methodic drags and scavenged for stars. Her name was Aurélie.

"What are you studying?" I asked, thankful to be able to continue the conversation, only wishing I knew enough French to charm.

"Robotics."

"Wow. Is that something you've always been interested in?"

"Sort of. My parents think it could make a good career. Hey—I'm getting my motorcycle license!"

"Oh yeah?"

"Yeah, I love bikes."

I thought of the Badlands.

"Maybe we'll ride together one day, when I'm old with a long white beard and exams no longer matter."

We took a final drag and let the cigarettes drop, grabbing each other and kissing. Epic kisses that lasted like TV episodes, complete with twists and turns. I didn't know how long we were on the porch. All I remembered were handfuls of her body.

—

IT WAS NOON when I woke the next day. Virgile was still asleep, face down, snoring. Coffee table trashed with empty bottles and containers. I helped clean up, trying not to wake him as each Heineken clinked into the garbage bag. But just before leaving he awoke and handed me a pack of tobacco and rolling papers.

"Aurélie left these. She wants you to bring them to her."

He pronounced her name with a throaty "R" and I didn't recognize it.

"Who?"

"Aurélie? The girl you were . . ."

"Ah, oui!"

And so I dropped the sagging bag in the dumpster, grabbed a baguette, and dragged myself down the street, lagging from lack of sleep. But I was glad because I had Aurélie's info and her tobacco and was sure to see her again.

In the meantime I had work to do, as Dessie's video was still incomplete and I knew that I was pressing my luck with each day I stayed at her flat. Also, I'd already burned through half of my Camaro money and my bank account was starting to run dry—a fact that always kicked me in the ass. I saw the ol' Camaro in my mind and wondered where it was today. Hopefully warm in Shep's garage.

—

WHEN I GOT BACK to D & P's, I sat down and popped open my laptop—plugging away, cutting away, piecing together snippets of video and music. Sometime during all the movie magic I messaged Aurélie and asked when we could rendezvous. She told me to meet her in Versailles the next day; that she would show me around her hometown. We agreed and I continued working, and before long D & P came home—hovering over my shoulders—wanting to see the video. I played it for them and they seemed pleased.

We celebrated over a glass of wine and Dessie brought in a delicious meal of something or other. Everything she made was delicious. Could've been cardboard casserole for all I knew. We got to talking and I started telling D & P about all the creative ventures we could start in France, should I return in the future. Ideas were shooting from everywhere— each of us contributing, burning with possibility, creative ambassadors to one another. Finally one of the ideas had us all nodding our heads, and we kept nodding and couldn't stop nodding and decided that it was the one to develop.

The concept was based on street art—a collaborative event in which artists would work together on a single canvas. We began discussing logistics and visualizing the whole thing when Pierre stopped and shook his head, speaking in French to Dessie. Then they were both speaking French, getting louder and louder, pointing fingers and shouting.

"Guys, guys. What's wrong?"

"He's so negative!" said Dessie.

"I just think it would be a hard thing to organize," Pierre told me.

"We would have to plan and write a proposal first," I said.

"Yes, but I'm not sure people would want to pay to see this kind of thing. It might not make money."

"You have to give it a chance! You're so negative!" Dessie screamed, gathering dishes and storming away.

Pierre shrugged.

"It's a good *idea*, bro."

It wasn't the first time the night had ended like this. D & P had a volatile relationship and I never knew what to expect from moment to moment. It reminded me of my parents— growing up, stuck between bouts of spitting and hair pulling.

At times I felt like a child again.

The overgrown American child of a French couple younger than me. It was strange because when I looked at Pierre I did in fact see an old man. He had a boyish face, but it was hardened by cynicism, as though somebody told him early on that life was a struggle to the grave—a very serious thing with serious consequences. On the contrary, Dessie was a flower child with a Rastafarian spirit. A pit bull and dove stuck inside a cage—one flapping wings, the other barking. But they were beautiful together even when they argued. I only wished they could break free together.

Run for your lives, D & P!
Run for your souls!
Run to Africa!
Run to the sky!

—

THE NEXT DAY I left for Versailles to see Aurélie, departing on the big Line C train, which went further than the others. As soon as I jumped aboard there was a black guitarist playing blues music.

By God, Memphis had found me.

Now all I needed was Sage and a cigarette.

He was jamming behind a glass window, stained with fingerprints and unknown smears, splatters, splashes of matter, and nothing really mattered because soon we set off and all I thought about was Memphis-Paris guy and how the world was just one big puzzle that was complete as-is, despite pieces being all over.

I practiced the pronunciation of Aurélie's name while we rolled along past industry and construction trucks—Paris: Behind The Scenes.

Now I was hearing Zepplin's "Stairway to Heaven" from the guitar, watching the construction transform to suburbia. Blocky houses spaced randomly, and some color in the trees which reminded me that it was still autumn.

The short trip was already stirring the travel bug and I thought of taking bigger trains to faraway places. Maybe there was a train that wrapped around the whole world.

—

I GOT OFF in Versailles and saw Aurélie waving from across the station. She was jumping around excitedly, walking towards me, then running towards me, and when we met she grabbed my face and kissed it. She pulled away and I couldn't see anymore—my glasses were fogged up. They always fogged when we kissed.

"Well bonjour to you, too!"

"Come with me," she said. "My car is over here."

"First, is there a bathroom around? I've been holding it all the way here."

"Mhm, don't think so. Can you wait a little longer?"

"Sure."

We got inside her small Peugeot.

"So where are we going?" I asked.

"You'll see!"

We drove through the streets and I saw all sorts of interesting things, but couldn't stop thinking about my brimming bladder.

Aurélie smiled at me the whole way. I cringed one back at her.

We parked and I looked around for toilets. Nothing.

"How far to the place? I really have to pee."

"Not far. It's a lake, maybe ten minutes away."

The last thing I wanted to see was an expanse of calm water.

"Can we find a bathroom first?"

We walked into town and found a small cafe with men behind the counter who looked like washed up mobsters. Moping around, mad about something. Mad that we only ordered coffees so that I could relieve myself; mad that we were their only patrons. Mad just to be mad because anger somehow felt better or more comfortable than gladness.

Aurélie and I did not return to the lake, however. We just kept walking through the city, holding hands and kissing— her body heat fogging up my glasses and me stumbling because I couldn't see, and Aurélie laughing because I was stumbling, and the world spinning regardless of whether the mobsters were mad or we were laughing. She pointed out the Cathédrale Saint-Louis de Versailles, and we ducked inside the monument to warm our bones. The ceilings were high and seemed to rise forever, with chandeliers hung from long cords like fairies strung from heaven down to the pews. It was one big pretty cave of worship.

"Are you religious?" I asked Aurélie.

"I believe in everything," she said.

"What does that mean?"

"Just . . . everything."

Everything. Why not.

—

AURÉLIE CONTINUED to give me a tour of the city. It was a wealthy community with luxury cars and hotels. Not a street sign stained or bulb burned black. And then there was the famous Château de Versailles, a symbol of wealth itself. We peeked through the golden gates to observe the castle—low and wide, ornate, with points and trimmings dipped in gold. People mingled in front of it. Everyone seemed to be wearing black for one reason or another.

Dusk was upon us and the weather grew brisk as we kept walking through a nearby park lined with trees, perfectly spaced like the palms of LA. We huddled as we went along, stopping for hot teas, and then turned down a dark path where again I had to pee.

I was done with formalities. I walked into the woods and watered a few trees.

Now I was feeling happy with my hollow bladder, hopping along until Aurélie began telling me about her family. She told me about her depressed mother, spiteful brother, and spiteful brother's spiteful girlfriend. She told me about how nobody got along—even the grandmother made phone calls just to insult them. I thought of similar stories I'd heard about my relatives, recalling the shouts and bouts, and Francine and I from earlier in the year, and D & P arguing.

I was starting to get angry at people in general. At *people*. Because I kept hearing about people being bad to one another. Even in a town like Versailles where gold drips onto streets and dogs shit flower petals, people shat on each other.

And why?

"What do you think causes hatred?" I asked Aurélie.
"We're unable to let go of the past," she replied.
There it was again. Simple and easy.
"Hey!" she said, "Want to come with me to Lyon this weekend, to my school? It's my graduation. Even though I won't be graduating, I have lots of friends that will and they're expecting me to show. We'll take my car—a road trip."
"*Allons-y!*" I said, "Let's go!"
"I knew you'd say yes."
We kissed.
I waited for the fog to clear and strolled back to the car.

26

Dessie walked into the room with a lit match.

She was coming straight at me, extending her arm. Pierre appeared behind her. The flame neared closer and closer to my face. Then they began singing a familiar tune, albeit it in French—*"Joyyyyeux Anniversaire. . ."*

The ol' birthday song.

"Sorry we don't have any cake, bro."

"No problem," I said, blowing out the match before Dessie's hand melted.

It was my final night with D & P and I felt sad all of a sudden. We'd become quite the trio. They were everything I needed. Best friends. Tomorrow I would leave and they would continue living their lives, swimming in separate directions—new jobs, marriage, kids maybe; new hairstyles and pairs of shoes. Pierre would certainly have new shoes.

We popped a bottle of wine and hung around as usual.

"So where are you going now?" asked Dessie.

"Lyon, with a girl that I met at a party."

"French girl?" asked Pierre.

"Yes."

"Ooooooooohhhhhhhh!"

"French affair, bro. Everyone's got to have one."

—

The next morning I jogged to the metro station, already late to meet with Aurélie. Lo and behold, Line 13 was packed at nine a.m.—trains bulged with flesh and bone. I looked at my backpack and knew that boarding would be a physical impossibility. Instead, I decided to take a northbound train to another station that headed back south, where I could then connect to the big Line C. Aurélie would be left waiting an extra half hour.

We hummed along as usual. I tapped my feet, read, stared out the window. At one of the stops I watched a Turkish girl who sat on a bench, touching up her lashes in a pocket mirror. She seemed to be reassuring herself: You're beautiful. You're beautiful.

In Versailles, Aurélie greeted me from across the station and again nearly tackled me with her lips. I tossed my bag in her car, hopped inside, and off we went on our great adventure to Lyon.

—

I FELT COMFORTABLE on the road, watching the big rigs—same style as in America save for shortened cabs. Once we got away from the city, the land stretched far and wide with smooth rolling hills and I thought of Kansas. Again things were blurring together. People, land—everything blurs. At one point I told Aurélie to pull over so that I could drive.

"As long as you're careful," she warned. "I don't think this is legal!"

I got behind the wheel, put the shifter in first, and tore across the highway in the little Peugeot.

"Slow dowwwwwnnnn!" Aurélie yelled.

Yes, of course. One must be responsible while speeding as an uninsured, unlicensed foreigner. I set the cruise control and we began singing together—Willie Nelson's "On The Road Again" and Red Hot Chili Peppers. Blurring, blurring, blurring. It seemed that this was one big mass of land I'd already traveled, with women I'd already been with, and music from memories I'd already stored. But no! Slight tweaks made all the difference.

"Look up there!" exclaimed Aurélie.

I peered through the windshield to see a castle atop a hill. It looked old—cracked and weathered, yet held its structure nicely. Nothing but land around it. Land for miles. Land inviting us to live beyond it. Then Aurélie pulled out a camera and began snapping pictures of me, and after awhile

I wanted to chuck the damn thing out the window just to give a hitchhiker something to think about.

Soon we came upon Lyon and I couldn't wait to see what waited in the town. We stopped somewhere along the outskirts at our hotel (always cheaper in the outskirts), and wheeled our luggage inside the place—Aurélie doing most of the talking to the front desk clerk—"Oui, oui, oui." All the way up to the fourth floor, buzzing on the elevator, Aurélie with her hands under my shirt, and me with my hands on her ass.

There it was: ROOM 438

A dark little hole with bunk beds and a small window opening to a lovely view of construction sites. I went to put my stuff down and Aurélie grabbed me before it hit the floor. Onto the bed we landed, me on top of her, her shirt unbuttoning itself. I began removing more of her clothes, and my clothes, and because of winter there were so many clothes. Clothes everywhere, like a Macy's piñata exploded. Eventually we were skin pressed against skin. The room darkened as her epic, endless legs wrapped around me.

—

THE NEXT DAY was Aurélie's would-be graduation. We woke up hungry and she suggested "the perfect place to eat," hurrying me on a train to Old Town Lyon. As we zoomed across I thought about Colorado and my trip to Lamont with Valerie, and those French expats we saw standing in the doorways there, waving glossy art show flyers at us. I thought of Virgile and his Hendrix posters and LA pictures. As with the previous day, everything continued to blur and rearrange as if I were piecing together a puzzle. I recalled the Nigerian cabbie's words on that cold February morning and wondered if I was in control or standing waist deep in a larger hand.

In Old Town we walked around on cobblestone streets, down alleyways, across bridges, squinting at churches stuck on top of the hillside—the hills happy to have them there as though they were pleasant growths on nature's head.

"We should go up there!" Aurélie said.

But alas we were both hungry.

Down one of the alleys we found a *bouchon*—a restaurant specializing in meat dishes and cozy seat cushions. Sausage, pork, fish. We were famished. Sex organs satisfied and stomachs sad and crying.

I held Aurélie's hand and looked into her eyes. People were chattering about, but I couldn't hear anything in her eyes. I saw straight through to her soul and felt her seeing straight into mine.

"Tonight," she said, "my friends are having a party after graduation."

"Okay."

"You're welcome to join if you'd like."

"Of course. I'd love to."

"I have to warn you that my friends are crazy."

"How crazy are they?"

"Very."

"I think I can handle them."

How crazy could a group of engineers be? I imagined them drawing a slightly askew right triangle.

We went back to the hotel after dinner to get dressed for the party. I left our room to go downstairs for coffee, and when I returned, Aurélie was hiding beneath the bed sheets. When I peeled them back I saw that she was completely nude. I undressed, crawled under the covers to my favorite safe haven, pre-heated by Aurélie's body, and we went at it again. Until the construction trucks stopped beeping and the window disappeared.

—

WE RAN LATE to the party, dashing across campus while Aurélie pointed out buildings—her dorm, the sports hall, cafeteria. It was a nice looking campus. Fairly new with modern architecture, clean windows, and well-paved parking lots. In the common area we walked upstairs to the second floor and entered a long room with tables littered with cups, bottles, boxes. All the good resources had been depleted and Aurélie's friends began improvising drinks, squeezing leftover wine from bags and mixing cheap, ugly concoctions.

The room was occupied by students—nearly all graduates or post-graduates with the occasional freshman or sophomore sprinkled in. They were part of an engineering group, which seemed a co-ed fraternity. They organized like a fraternity, shouted like a fraternity, and drank like a fraternity.

A group of girls approached to greet Aurélie.

"Who's *this*?" asked a dark-skinned girl, looking at me.

"This is Johan from America," said Aurélie.

"Hi, Johan from America."

They walked off with Aurélie to chat and giggle, and glanced back at me while I lingered as the observant wallflower.

At some point the lights turned off and a projector flickered on. The crowd gathered around, hooting and hollering, puking into empty spaces, then continuing to hoot and holler. On screen were images of party scenes from past semesters—some kind of quiz, translated by Aurélie:

WHICH GUY KISSED THE MOST GUYS?

WHO'S PUKED THE MOST TIMES IN ONE NIGHT?

WHO DRAWS THE MOST REALISTIC PENIS ON SKIN?

The answer to all three questions was a student named Gerard who proceeded to hop onto the table and demonstrate his talents. He ripped off his shirt and began waving a baguette through the air like a Jedi.

"Are you okay?" Aurélie asked me.

"Of course! Go have fun!"

"I told you they were crazy . . ."

"Go have fun!"

I wandered around, and now I was feeling pretty good with my swirling stomach and the room swirling magic. It was a strange, young French magic.

"Who are you?" they all asked.

"Je suis Américan," I'd say.

"Who are you with?"

"Aurélie."

"Why are you here?"

"I wanted to visit Paris and I met Aurélie."

"Oooooooooohhhhhhhh!"

—

THE ENTIRE ROOM was drunk. I watched faces flash in the night. Dancing around shirtless, kissing, spilling beer, walking off and pissing.

Then they became tired, unexpectedly, like race cars that had simultaneously run out of gas. A mishmash of yawning youths. Yawning with half finished glasses of rum—fighting sleep, fighting death. Wondering what they're fighting for but still slugging away because why the hell not?

One exception to the yawning was KitKat.

That was his frat name at least.

He bounced off the walls like a ping-pong ball. No one could catch him. Skinny like a twig, gangly and quick, blond hair spiked like his soda drink. His face jutted from his skull in bony formations and he spoke as fast as he walked. He was one of the sophomores, barely twenty but already wanting to know the secrets of life.

"I like boys," he said, "and I wish everyone could accept that."

"Do you care if they don't?" I asked.

"It bothers me sometimes."

"Listen man, life is short and the world is small. Look around you. We're all specks on a speck. You have no reason to hide. You've got to be yourself."

He nodded knowingly, albeit nauseously—as though I had just told him to run through a brick wall, promising that he'd emerge unscathed if he trusted enough.

KitKat stuck around conversing with me and eventually others flocked over, attracted to our enthusiasm, or possibly curious as to how I got the kid to stand still for so long. One of them was a petite, pale-faced girl with long hair. She was one of the few who greeted me when I arrived with Aurélie. Her flirtatiousness had vanished. She now stared at me suspiciously.

"How's it going?" I asked.

"Okay," she said. "Hey . . . how old are you?"

"Just turned twenty-nine."

"Twenty-*nine*? You're old!"

"Time goes fast."

"For you."

She trotted off and I was left in shock. I had never been called old, nonetheless with such outright bluntness. All this time my age was hardly a thought. I knew I was getting older but never felt as though it were a problem. In fact, most of my idols were people decades older than me: poets, directors, musicians.

I looked forward to getting old, gathering experience along the way, learning and expanding. Although we may be children trapped in fleshy vehicles on the rollercoaster of life, we can choose whether or not to have fun on the ride or moan the whole way.

Still, I had been jostled.

I began looking around the room at the scampering students, heads bobbling on their necks, hearing their cackling, and soon my body grew rigid, abruptly, as though the girl's words had trickled down my spine and hardened each vertebrae.

—

AURÉLIE AND I left the party with KitKat. We were to follow him to his flat and stay the night. He was unruly. Skipping through streets, swinging around poles and tossing piles of leaves into the air like some lost maniac. We laughed, sometimes cringing when he ran straight into traffic without warning.

"KitKat! No, KitKat!"

Back at the flat, his craziness continued as he hugged everyone in the house—his poor roommates who were busy working on their computers—and then falling onto the creaky old floors and rolling around in himself.

"He belongs in a circus or something," I told Aurélie. "His enthusiasm is off the charts."

"He's like this even when he's not drunk," she said.

KitKat left the room and returned with a bottle of green liquid. He danced two feet in front of us, talking and sloshing, my eyes following the big waves as he fell onto us.

I saw myself in KitKat, from earlier in the year.
Moonshine. Kelsey.
Headlocks in the rain and mud-splattered Chucks.

I saw the Abyss from the outside for the first time, from a sober mind, and grasped the chaos of it all. KitKat was a suppressed spirit, finally yawning, drowning in great green gay dreams. I knew how he felt dancing around—he was alive as ever inside that fleshy vehicle. Maybe he was hanging from a rope in a leopard suit at Cirque du Soleil.

"You should go to bed, KitKat," Aurélie suggested.

The poor kid muttered something and walked off.

—

THE NEXT MORNING we left Lyon and drove back to Versailles. Aurélie's parents demanded that she return home before dark, and because she still lived under their roof, she also lived under their rules. Again we cruised the highway, singing our songs—"Sweet Home Alabama." Aurélie sang it, twang and all.

It was December now, but the sky was clear blue and the sun streamed through the car like summertime. I worried about winter, which seemed quite odd because earlier in the year I didn't want the season to end. Maybe it was a reminder of the Abyss—the fear of not knowing what came next in my life. Not knowing where I'd live, who I'd date, how I'd make money.

I began to realize that it wasn't winter I was worried about at all; rather, uncertainty. Not knowing what the future holds; whether or not it will be good. To that effect, I feared that I would never escape the Abyss, for life is always uncertain without promise of guarantee.

"Hey!" Aurélie interrupted, "What are you thinking about?"

"Nothing."

"You were thinking about something, you busy-minded American."

"I was thinking about what we were going to eat for dinner."

"I have a suggestion," she said. "How about you come home with me and eat with me and my parents?"

"We've barely been dating a week. Won't that be awkward?"

"No, they said they wanted to meet you."

"Alright."

And so we drove along with our songs, and I placed my hand on Aurélie's thigh, imagining that this was my life. Married, living in Paris, Aurélie my wife, driving home from our job together, going to pick up the kids.

It was easy to imagine and bizarre to compare with reality: two strangers from different lands drifting through the sands of time. It's the same feeling I had with Sage, sitting on the beach with our could-be children running across the shoreline. All the women and scenarios! The possibilities were endless! So many combinations of love and lovely things.

—

AURÉLIE'S PLACE WAS located in the suburbs. A clean neighborhood with small homes and square lawns. Squat chimneys blowing out their afternoon sighs. Her parents greeted us at the front door—mother tall with silver hair and father short with dark skin, reminding me of Greek people I knew. I wondered if he was Greek just as I wondered about everything.

They hurried us into the kitchen for dinner and we all sat down at the round table like meek, modern day knights, ready to feast on Aurélie's mother's home-cooked meal—a special quiche with something tasty on the side. Flan for desert.

During the meal we spoke of America and European culture, and language, teaching each other vocabulary and pronunciations, and me getting red-faced about the throaty R's.

"C'mon, just say it!" her father joked. "Pronounce my daughter's name!"

At some point he unfolded a map to show me France in its entirety, waving his finger around like Magellan.

The whole thing was surreal.

One month into my trip and I was already meeting the parents of my new love. Despite all the uncertainty, I felt as though I had everything I needed.

—

AFTER EATING, Aurélie and I went for a walk around a nearby reservoir. The water was astonishingly clear and I saw the entire sky in it, shattered only by swans and ducks. I

236

thought if I had to watch the sky shatter, I'd prefer it this way, via adorable animals.

We held hands and watched the glistening flow, taking awkward little steps because we knew it was all drawing to an end.

Where's the moment of weightlessness?

Lucky ducks and their constant sky. No wonder they looked so content.

"I've been checking my bank account, Aurélie."

"Yeah? You still have money?"

"It's getting low, and Christmas is around the corner, which means my family will be expecting me."

"So when are you leaving?"

Ah there it was!

"Well, I'd like to see more of Europe before I go. Amsterdam mainly. I've heard good things, and it's much cheaper to fly home from there."

"You would have *fun* in Amsterdam," she said.

"Think so?"

She smiled.

"I'll miss you," I said.

"Promise you'll see me before you go?"

We kissed.

And with that, she drove me back to the metro station where I hopped aboard the dark train and disappeared.

27

I STARED at six hundred dollars on my computer screen. The cost of a flight home. Back to Maryland, back to good ol' Moonshine and Lorenzo the smiling bartender. Back to the Abyss?

God, I prayed not.

But I saw it all unfolding in my brain.

I saw drinks being passed across the smooth table, sliding into my palm. I saw the county girls in their tight jeans. I smelled the grain of the walls, and I saw myself sitting at home with a bottle wondering what I'd do next. I did not want to return to that. I did not want to pay six hundred bucks for that.

I'll stay!

I'll marry Aurélie and we'll live off the land.

We'll live under the sea!

Alas, I thought of cobbler and Mom, and ornaments and trees. I bought the ticket. But not without also booking a train to Brussels, my next stop on the way up to Amsterdam.

—

SO THERE I WAS, back at the hostel again, gazing at the ceiling sometime after six a.m. when the techno music began. I was ready for my croissant and jam sandwich, stomach grumbling synchronously with the mopeds firing up outside.

Had a couple more days to enjoy Paris.

The first thing I did was visit the Eiffel Tower in daylight. I thought it strange that I'd only seen it at night. When I arrived in front of it that morning, standing under the steel beams, I noticed hoards of people waiting to ride the elevator to the top; fighting for places in line. Nah. Not gonna do that. Instead, I made my way to the end of Champ de Mars where I chose to sit down and watch the tourists.

Busses pulling up. People streaming out. Smirking and shifting in their coats, gazing upwards, fixing hair and preparing for pictures—a small corner of their souls redeemed.

A Japanese man with pink backpack snapped photos of a girl with furry coat and boots. She leapt into the air, large-rimmed glasses falling off her face.

I didn't quite get it.

Beautiful as the structure was, what amazed me more was a pigeon bobbing past.

Look at its little head and feet!

—

I CONTINUED ALONG with this way of thinking, riding the subway across town to Les Invalides, a cluster of buildings representing the military history of France. Walking its perimeter, I noticed an old man sitting on a bench. I could not see his face because his back was turned to me, but I immediately knew that he was homeless. Pigeons congregated while he rubbed his scruffy chin with crooked fingers.

Staring at nothing.

Just flesh and bone, like some avant-garde street exhibit.

All those cells moving around in that blood and those organs. All that commotion inside. Yet from the outside I wondered how he could go on like this. What did he think about? Where was he born? How will he die?

I roamed aimlessly, as I had done since arriving in the grand old land. I thought about movement—how I couldn't sit still. I was restless like the others in my family. Restless to go anywhere. Even if it was going in circles. I liked the feel of motion. The joints of knees, rubber of tires, sloshing of boats, whistle of planes. I wanted to rip up the roads of the world and wrap them around my body.

THE NEXT DAY I met up with curly Aurélie in Versailles. She was waiting for me as always, at the station with a kiss in queue. We set off together to an indoor ice rink. The plan was to meet up with Virgile and his friend Jean for a skating adventure. I hadn't been skating in years and figured I would have to learn all over again.

I strapped into my sharp shoes and wobbled onto the ice holding Aurélie's hand, while Virgile and Jean zipped past.

"Sorry, sorry," I told Aurélie, apologizing for my stumbles.

"Don't say sorry!" she replied.

"I feel like a child."

"That's the point! Just have fun!"

"Just have fun, huh?"

She stopped to kiss me.

"Yes, have fun. Why worry?"

"Listen," I said, "Why don't you skate ahead? I'll practice on my own and we can meet up in a few minutes."

"Yeah?"

"Absolutely."

She took off like a rocket.

I kept circling around, trying to suppress my inner critic.

You're horrible at this!

It was the same voice from the day I got ticketed for speeding, wound up lost, and from the nights I drank myself stupid. Or when I left Mom and her cobbler. All the things I couldn't forgive myself for sat on my conscience, piling and piling.

Aurélie was right—I shouldn't be sorry. What am I apologizing for anyway? Not skating like a superstar after ten years away from the rink? For the remainder of the afternoon I followed Aurélie's advice. I closed my eyes as we breezed along, holding hands, cracking jokes.

I tried to stay in the moment.

Didn't want it to end.

I thought that if I focused deeply enough, I could at least save the details for my deathbed.

—

IT WAS A QUIET DRIVE back to the train station, a melancholic mixture of sadness and memories. And as Aurélie and I held each other close, we promised that we would see each other again.

"I'll find you wherever you are," she whispered.

"Yeah?"

"I hope you're not creeped out by that or anything."

"No, it's fine. We all have a little creepy in us."

She laughed and hugged me—"I love you."

I hesitated, not quite knowing what to say. Could Aurélie possibly love me after two weeks? Did I love her? Had the word lost meaning all together? Surely I loved her. Love is simple. It's a feeling of deep affection.

"I love you too."

winter

28

THE TRAIN PULLED AWAY from Gare du Nord sometime around three p.m., and I looked outside the wide windows of the burgundy cabin as we began to pick up speed, passing industry and tattered suburbia. Faster and faster towards Brussels—the unknown land of Belgium that waited at the end of the rails.

Faster past farmland.

Goodbye for now, sweet Paris! Goodbye, Versailles!

I tried not to dwell on it because I knew that life was stretchable and I could always return. I looked over to see a cute blonde sitting next to me, biting her nails, and thought of the girl from the plane at the beginning of the year.

Could always return.

Soon the train was really going—flying! Felt unsafe almost. Rocking softly side to side, only to look out the window and see telephone poles flicker past like a camera shutter. Whole towns on display for mere seconds. I fell asleep to the rhythms of the land.

—

WHEN I CAME TO, it was dark and passengers were shuffling around, gathering possessions. For some reason I thought of school—the end of class. I slung my pack over my shoulders and walked to the local metro, which took me straight through to the heart of the city.

I moseyed across the canal while looking for my hostel, which was supposedly nearby inside of a renovated warehouse. For the life of me I couldn't find it. I wound up in a neighborhood full of Turkish residents and little markets that all looked the same. Canned goods, meats, random pieces of clothing hung from ceilings. The buildings were grungy and monochrome, and I could tell that this place was much different than the City of Light.

I caught the attention of an older gentleman with black hair. I had no clue how to speak to him, so I chose my default English-plus-miming act. He pointed me in the right direction and before long I came upon the brick hostel, which indeed looked like a warehouse except for a neon H attached to the front.

Inside the lobby I stood in line with the hunched backpackers. We were all dirty and looking for a shower. To my left I saw a bar with microbrews in the window, and became excited as I'd heard Belgium was a paradise for beer lovers. When it was my turn at the counter, I checked in with a clerk who wore a name badge indicating that she knew four languages. Felt a little jealous. Many Europeans were this way—they all knew a language or two. O how it must be growing up on such a diverse continent.

Soon I was entering my room, making my bed and acquainting with my home for the next couple of days. The room housed eight, and there were already three Australian girls occupying it. I would come to meet four others. Aussies everywhere. It was their summer and they were on a traveling rampage.

—

I IMMEDIATELY HIT the streets to savor the night, heading back across the canal to The Grand Place, swallowing and digesting the city along the way. My feet were sweaty inside my socks—scabs from scratching my ankle wounds. I started limping again and it seemed that I was back to square one.

Looking at the tall buildings, there was a distinct difference between Brussels and Paris. These were glassy-windowed buildings not pointing toward the sky, but flat like Baltimore, all with balconies. The people did not wear scarves; rather, heavy coats.

Scents in the air.

Smoke, meats, breads, raw city stench.

A man with big wide eyes stared at children on a carousel while munching on a plate of shrimp.

I suddenly felt weak at the knees and pined for food.

Before long, I stumbled upon a stretch of road with a bustling Christmas market. Cabin-shacks covered in fake snow, bulbs blinking red and green. The whole street alive with festivities. And inside one of the shacks: a small bar specializing in shots of Jager.

It wasn't food, but nourishment nonetheless.

"One shot, please" I told the bartender, a cute brunette from somewhere in the western hemisphere. She was tall and tan, and when she handed me my Jager, I downed it with visions of her dancing in my head.

Then I switched to beer and watched city folk pass by the shack on a Wednesday that felt like Saturday.

"How long has this festival been going on?" I asked the bartender.

"A few weeks."

"Really?"

"Uh-huh."

"You guys love the holidays around here, don't you?"

"We do!"

I had nothing else to say, so I left, continuing to wander and observe. Everyone celebrated with steamy waffles in their hands. I ate one and it tasted like a carnival. Sweet and doughy.

—

THE FOLLOWING DAY I woke up, looked over, and noticed a scruffy-faced Australian in the nearby bunk, Aaron. He mentioned that he was going on a hostel-sponsored tour of the city and invited me to join. We hit the lobby around noon and filed out with a group forty-strong.

Along with Aaron, I met two other Aussies, Chris and Taylor. Chris had a goatee and freckles. Taylor was tall—a basketball player with pale skin who hardly spoke. We were soon greeted by Jasper, the tour guide, a short Flemish guy in his early thirties with insatiable enthusiasm. He was like a wind-up toy that was constantly cranked.

"Despite the fact that Belgium has developed into a multicultural country, I am an ORIGINAL!" he yelled. "I am pure-blooded Flemish, my grandfather fought in World War II, and today I will show you the fighting face of Brussels!"

He had lightning in his eyes and thunder in his voice—the spirit of a lost warrior looking for battle, channeling his energy through crowds of drooling faces. I envisioned him atop a horse galloping towards the forests of Luxembourg just as I envisioned KitKat at Cirque du Soleil.

The Aussies and I laughed. We were in for a good tour.

It was a brutally cold day, worsened by the wind, and Jasper kept huddling us together to tell stories of the city I barely came to know. I was astounded to hear of its rich history, dating back a thousand years with Medieval and Gothic architecture still intact. In fact, while at The Grand Place, Jasper told us that the town square has been so well preserved that, in glancing around, we were seeing an exact picture of how it appeared during the seventeenth century.

The tour continued past street art murals that were just as popular in Belgium as in France; past Mannequin Pis, the famed fountain constructed around the statue of a peeing toddler; all the way to the Cathedral of St. Michael and St. Gudula. Again my neck bent upward at the ceilings and kaleidoscopic windows. Jasper showed us an area where bodies of the wealthy had been buried in underground tombs hundreds of years ago and still remained.

"Hence the term stinking rich," he said with a smirk.

Then he fell into a trance, fixated on the engravings of the tomb. "I remember . . . my father used to bring me here when I was a kid and made me decipher the Latin. I knew Latin by the time I was twelve. He was a professor, you know? I'm so grateful that he did that."

Only a few of us heard him. He seemed to be talking to himself.

After we left the church we went for lunch at a nearby pub. It appeared to be Jasper's usual drinking spot, and I found it funny that he brought such a mixed group of tourists there. The bartenders were young Irishmen with Irish mouths and Jasper batted insults back and forth with them. "You fucking Irish perverts!" He even adopted an Irish accent when he did this. I thought of Mackenzie, the morphing medusa of Colorado. Jasper was the chameleon of Brussels.

The Aussies and I stuck together, cramming sandwiches down our throats by the time Jasper pointed to the clock.

Back outside, between landmarks, he carried on in his cathartic rambling—

"You guys play any instruments? No? I played violin thirteen years. That's what I wanted to do with my life. Like Vivaldi. No matter how hard I tried, I couldn't reach that level. My father was a pianist."

We stopped at La Monnaie, a popular opera house, huddling under its columns. Jasper had a special affinity for the place, presenting a "six minutes exactly" historical speech.

I didn't hear a word he said.

Everything muted and I stood there watching his hands fly around, wrinkles twitching at the sides of his eyes. His face turned red and his hair seemed to stand on end.

By God, he's going to burst a blood vessel!

Like the Paris bum and pigeons, I wondered more about the miracle of Jasper than the opera house. What sustains all that energy?

". . . And that's why La Monnaie is so critical to our cultural preservation. Time!"

"Six minutes," someone hollered.

"WOOHOO! Still got it."

—

IT WAS LATE in the afternoon now and Aaron whispered to me about going on a pub-crawl in the evening. I nodded and turned my attention to Jasper who had clustered us together for the tour finale, situated in front of a panoramic view of Brussels—the entire city on display as a visual feast.

We sat on the stairs while Jasper took center stage . . .

"You know, most people see Belgium as a stopping point between Paris and Amsterdam. They figure 'Why not? I'll stay a day or two, check out Brussels.' And they call it boring. But Brussels is anything but boring! We are a country small in size but large in pride. My grandfather fought in World War II as a general for the army, defending us at the frontlines when German forces were closing in. He was captured and tortured in a POW camp for five years before getting picked up by American troops. He was then sent home where he shared a single orange with his family for Christmas dinner."

He was starting to tear up. We all were.

"I have a degree in architecture," he said. "I'm an architect. I can do anything I want. I choose this job because I love my country."

We applauded and handed him tips. Everyone dispersed.

The Aussies and I tagged along as Jasper walked to get a burger. He counted the cash, folded it, and tucked it into his front pocket, conceding that he was required to forfeit half to his boss.

"It's a damn shame," he said, lighting up a cigarette.

—

AS PLANNED, I met up with the Aussie trio later that night. We navigated the ancient city in search of a pub-crawl event. After an hour of circling to no avail, we stumbled upon a jazz club that looked quite interesting, and entered. I had a Rochefort Trappist beer that nearly knocked me off my feet—heavy and sweet—and the guys all had a swig and agreed that it was one of the most complex brews they'd ever tasted.

There was no jazz music to be heard, but plenty of cover bands playing their poor hearts out. I began to think of Jasper again and wondered whether he ever left that burger joint or if he just dissolved into thin air—pieces of his spirit dividing into each of us. I looked at the happy Aussies and mysterious land outside and took a mental snapshot of the whole night, just as I had my ice skating adventure, and again realized that nothing is permanent. We're constantly pasting in the scrapbook of life.

Off we went to the next bar, swaying through the bizarre street people. Reincarnations of carnivorous cavemen in the Belgium before Belgium was Belgium; when there was only soft soil for battered feet and souls were just as lost as the Jaspers of today.

Our chosen pub was epic with two thousand brews on tap. The menu read like The Bible, and the back of the bar was snaked with tubing that fed into a collection of kegs. The building had two floors and they were sticky all over. Bathroom saturated with urine. Even the walls dripped. Downstairs, a hair metal band riffed on jagged guitars while people pushed their way through the crowd—the whole room filled to capacity with breathing, peeing beings.

We had a good time.

—

"I NEED TO PURCHASE this bottle of water," I told the red-haired receptionist in the morning.

"*Purchase?*" she chuckled.

I was still drunk.

"Too many strong Belgian beers last night."

"That'll do it."

"Yes, I should have *purchased* this last night."

"That's what they all say."

Back upstairs in the dorm, Aaron was just waking up. He was disoriented, reaching for the clock, reaching for his head.

"Bloody hell, mate. Your skull throbbing too?"

"Like a gong."

"Good night though, ay?"

"Jasper was right. Brussels isn't boring."

"So what are your travel plans from here?" he asked.

"Boarding a train to Amsterdam in a few hours."

He smiled like Aurélie. "You'll have fun. Just came from there myself. Stoned out of my fucking mind the entire time. I'm still coughing."

—

AS I STOOD on the platform waiting for my train that afternoon, I thought about Aaron's words and wondered about the land of Amsterdam. I wondered if it might be the ultimate Abyss—a place where I would find a thousand KitKats. A place where I might lose myself all together.

Perhaps it would be a final test.

Anyhow, there was no time to think about it as the train rapidly approached, squeeeeeealing to a stop. I heaved my pack into the overhead luggage compartment and nodded goodbye to the country from beyond its crusty perimeter.

Similar to Paris, I noticed all the behind-the-scenes footage as we pushed north. Stained walls and back alleys with busty women dancing behind glass like mechanical mannequins. I would move while they stayed.

Directly in front of me sat three women dressed in all black, mid-fifties. They seemed to be friends, beaming with red faces, giddy with laughter as though they shared a great secret of society. One of them had a bag of peppermints and kept passing it around. I was beginning to fall asleep when the bag was handed to me.

"It'll wake you up," said the smiling lady.

She pointed to a logo on the packaging—Queen Wilhelmina of the Netherlands.

"It's old," she said.

"The brand or the candy?" I asked.

They broke out in laughter.

The train slowed down through the cities and occasionally I woke up to catch signs displaying our whereabouts: ANTWERP, KAPELLEN. Or catching sight of the small villages in between with silhouetted steeples and black roofs. The women carried on laughing and joking in Dutch, and I no longer questioned it: This was exactly where I was supposed to be.

29

THEN I WAS ON A BOAT.

I planned to take the ferry across the river to Northern Amsterdam to meet yet another kind soul I had found on the internet—a guy named Igor.

It was night.

The water was dark and my pack weighed on my neck. The air had a brisk Atlantic bite, not unlike the nights of my native east coast, and I knew that I had come that much closer to Maryland. We bobbed across the river. Me and all the bleary-eyed locals sniffling into tissues and breathing heat into their hands. O what madness waited on the other side? What was I in for now? When would it all stop, and did I want it to stop? As the ferry neared the land, I saw a bright-bulbed sign floating on a buoy:

A PLACE BEYOND BELIEF

—

WHEN WE DOCKED, I hopped off the boat and immediately saw Igor waiting for me. He was sitting on his bicycle—very tall, skinny, donning a thick jacket and beanie, with a thick accent that reminded me of a Russian I once met in LA on a much warmer night.

As we walked, we made obligatory small talk all the way to his apartment, which was actually a shipping container converted into a living space. An entire housing complex of stacked containers. I couldn't believe it.

"Dutch efficiency!" I blurted.

Igor laughed and we walked upstairs into the small studio. As we entered, he removed his hat and hair went everywhere. He must have been six-six counting the hair. Anyhow, the studio was a long rectangle just as I expected and the furniture simple and minimal. I was happy to drop my pack and sit down. Igor stood at the stove, preparing an omelet, humming a tune.

Soon we were both seated and eating.

I thought Igor looked like a young Bob Dylan, pure and unblemished, with that crazy hair. All he needed was a pair of dark shades and unlit cigarette. While it was too dark for sunglasses and he wasn't a smoker, Igor did have a guitar, which he could play quite well. Even better than his playing was his singing, and after we finished our meal he proceeded to demonstrate his talents. I applauded and suggested that he start doing live shows at cafes and such.

"I don't think I'm good enough for that yet," he replied.

I sighed.

"Let's go for a drink!"

We strode into the night past the colorful containers— orange, red, white, blue—stacked like Lego blocks with windows cut out on the ends. Then onward past graffiti walls and warehouses. One of them was booming with bass and we went inside to find a skate park with crowds of tattooed teens. Ramps built all throughout, wheels rumbling, faces shouting. Igor looked around, surprised—"I didn't even know this place was here."

Further and further we walked, approaching an abandoned military campsite by a deserted dock. In the distance, out in the water, we noticed a floating shack covered with string lights, blinking like a dumb attempt at SOS.

"What is it?" I asked.

"Art," said Igor.

Before long we reached a building shaped like an airplane hangar, except it was transparent like a greenhouse, and from the outside we could see all the colors from spinning house lights. Upon entering, I bought Igor a beer and meandered around the place, digging the irony of its new age, rustic design. We found a seat upstairs, where a party was underway. It was a strange party. An older crowd, most of them sitting cross-legged on leather couches. Some played pool. Igor and I talked and tried to blend in, although it wasn't working too well, as the crowd was quite distinguished, dressed in kitschy costumes and listening to nineties eurodance.

Igor and I managed to strike up conversation with a dimpled, long-haired gentleman. He looked like the manager of a semi-successful rock band, and also like someone who emerged from a fairy tale wearing lederhosen—town baker or blacksmith perhaps. Tonight he would tell us that he was just a guy celebrating his friend's birthday.

We stuck around and had another beer.

"Pretty risky of you to go hopping around Europe, staying with strangers, don't you think?" asked Igor.

"It all comes down to trust versus fear," I replied.

"What if I were a serial killer or something?"

"What if *I* were?"

"You've got a point, my friend."

"The way I see it," I told him, "if you can't trust, you live in fear. And what kind of life is that?"

"I like the way you think."

"Likewise."

". . ."

"You're not a serial killer are you?"

We shared a good laugh, as Igor and I trusted each other and understood the value of trust, and furthermore shared the barista brotherhood. He worked at a local coffee shop where we'd spend plenty of time at over the next few days. Igor knew about all of the good cafes, even the ones that served more than coffee.

"But I have to tell you," he said, "despite having grown up here, I'm not really into pot."

And so we stuck to coffee and good conversation, which was good enough for me.

—

THE VERY NEXT DAY Igor and I jumped the ferry to downtown. He led me to the center of all the madness and now it was my chance to explore as I had always done. Meanwhile he would go off to serve coffees and lattes, and flip cups in his hands and smile at customers.

I set off through town by foot, trying not to get run over by the bikes, which had their own traffic lanes. Bicycles everywhere. Bikes entangled in bikes, wrapped around poles with rusty chains, and whizzing past with friendly or not-so-friendly chimes. Everyone cranking away with their weed breath exhaust fumes.

Looking around, as with Brussels and Paris, I immediately noticed the differences. Undoubtedly modern and chic, Amsterdam was more streamlined than any of the cities I had seen or ever seen. Architecture of rhyme and reason; well-lit streets and clearly outlined corridors. Lovers in boats strolling down canals, full of fancy men with fancy haircuts drinking wine as they skimmed across.

Love and bicycles and boats.
Hints of strange love in the light northern air.
Everybody loving something, smiling about something.

Cologne, Cheetos, beers, and pot wafting next to waffle stands—I breathed it in and laughed it through my mouth. Two women arm in arm, black and blonde, and neon red above on a white and gold hotel—lights and the nightfall nearing on a Saturday. Cobblestone streets took me to more lights and smells, and suddenly I thought A'dam was the City of Smells, as it were the smells that led me.

Igor told me to buy a map, but as with Paris I did not.

And the pesky voice no longer pestered me because I trusted my two feet and the smells of cinnamon, spiced sausages, and the trapped smoke of stoner jackets.

Then the bicycle bells rang alongside the church bells, which reminded everyone of their sins, only to get drowned out by thumping bass from the speakers of the universe. Or the quacking of ducks who reminded us that we're all human.

Red-headed transvestites on bikes with heavy makeup and high cheekbones, pedaling high toward the sky, which was just around the corner from the Red Light District where they would undoubtedly spend their night behind the scratched glass I would soon come to see.

Bald-headed, bearded plumber on scooter. Neon orange shoelaces. Cannabis culture emblazoned on t-shirts in the windows of sex shops displaying rubber dildos and plastic penises, an alley away from all the Christmas cheer.

Suddenly somebody's whistling. Somebody's happy, somebody's high. Somebody's just trying to get by.

—

"THERE'S A REALLY NICE church in the red light district," Igor told me the night before.

I laughed.

"You're serious," I said.

"Yes!"

And now I stood before it in all its cracked holiness.

Behind me were the aforementioned women encased in steamy glass with their hot breaths and strips of clothing. Thick, Turkish, dark-skinned souls beckoning with their pointer fingers—"Come hither!" A fat man passed by one of them and lifted up his shirt, already drunk, mocking with his own skin show. Beauty behind it all—somehow, somewhere—and still the church bells rang the songs of Christmas and life itself.

Everyone was curious about the Red Light District as if it were some kind of tourist attraction. But what exactly were people coming to see? This was certainly a city of order and respect, but there was an underlying sense of the Abyss. A quiet sense, as though people understood the nature of it and how to control it. They were willingly and knowingly entering the darkness; intentionally making peace with their demons.

Dancing with their demons!

But not allowing themselves to be held captive.

I thought about this while venturing into one of the local cannabis cafes to see what the hype was all about. Sure enough it was quite the scene, complete with wooden tables and low lighting, which cast shadows under heavy eyelids. There was a coffee bar to my left serving actual coffee—strange coffee that tasted more like hot chocolate, half-filled with whipped cream so that when you drank it you immediately grew a white mustache. And to my right, all the people sitting and smoking at the tables, and looking at me from another planet. In the back of the room was the bar where you ordered the sticky stuff—indica or sativa strains—each with clever names and accompanied rolling papers.

"Hey mate, come join us!" I heard from one of the tables.

I looked over to see a pudgy white guy with short haircut. His face was like a child's, perpetually jolly, with two beady eyes pinched between pillowy cheeks.

"Name's Greg," he said. "I'm from Canada, and these are some friends I met tonight."

Two hands extended.

One attached to a gangly Aussie with bushy beard and scraggly hair, Leonard, and the other to a pale South African girl of British descent, Marie. She had black hair and freckles concealed under foundation.

A blunt was immediately passed to me as I sat down. I took a big hit and felt the smoke fill my lungs, holding it there, then releasing it into the light.

"You're smoking an indica-sativa blend," said Greg. "Very nice crystal texture with about eighteen percent THC content. Smell it? Sweet odor and citrusy taste across the palate."

"You're like a marijuana connoisseur," I said.

"Well, what do _you_ taste?" asked Leonard.

I took another drag.

"I'm detecting hints of. . ."

Everyone leaned forward.

". . . pot."

We all laughed and continued passing until we generated a healthy high. I'm not sure what was discussed after that. All I remember was Marie and her eyes.

I was deeply attracted to her.

And as we spoke I felt my mouth functioning on its own, speaking words on its own. Brain on autopilot while my soul stole glances. She was of another era. A cosmic gypsy. I didn't know how she came to sit in front of me and I did not recognize her accent. It was a mix of British, Italian, and Romanian.

I knew that I could have smoked more and saw more, but did not want to push my luck, as I had promised to meet Igor later that night in order to obtain a bicycle that he was helping me rent.

"Let's go for a walk!" Greg hollered.

"A short one," I replied.

"Wish I could join, but I've got to be going now," said Leonard.

Marie shook her head—"Me too. Sorry."

Off they went. Babies, jobs, relationships, new houses, couches, joys, and politics. Along with everyone else and my beautiful Laredo girl in Texas, these people would live worlds unto their own—disconnected and reconnected. The entire planet a series of flapping cords beaming electric love.

—

GREG AND I took off for nowhere, street bound, with hopes that we would learn something new about the madness or simply share a solid laugh. Along the way we bumped into a strange unkempt fellow walking with his mother. Greg noticed that the guy wore a Toronto Blue Jays hat.

"Hey, look at that! A fellow Jays fan. You from Canada?"

"Sure am," said the man.

"Ya? Whereabouts?"

"Manitoba. How about yourself?"

"Saskatchewan. Small world, eh? What brings you all the way out here?"

"Well, we live here now, my mother and I. Just wanted to get out of Canada for awhile. Different way of life n' all."

As with Marie, the man had a peculiar accent—part British, part something. The mother kept quiet and nodded, expressionless.

"Okay, well it was good talkin' to ya!" Greg said.

And then we were off again.

"What did you make of them?" I asked.

"Odd folks weren't they? Definitely Canadian, but with a hint of European hick."

"So now you're a connoisseur of culture, too?"

—

LATER THAT NIGHT I met Igor outside the bicycle rental shop. My high lingered and all I wanted to do was lie down and sleep. We picked out a decent bike with good frame and tires for three euros per day, a rate usually reserved for locals.

"Ever rode on the back of a bicycle before?" Igor asked.

"Nope."

"Well, you're going to have to. My place is a few kilometers away. No use walking when we have a bike."

Igor got a head start pedaling while I jogged alongside and jumped on, barely landing my ass on the flat grate; Igor wobbling and powering forward. I steadied myself by grabbing hold of his jacket, fearing I might plummet two feet to my death.

Despite the discomfort, it was a peaceful ride.

I watched the ground move beneath my feet and all the dark buildings along the way. Occasionally we came across a bridge and Igor had to really crank. I felt like a helpless child and chuckled at the fact. There was nothing I could do to assist him, and besides he didn't seem to want help. A graffiti message caught my eye as we rode:

DON'T COUNT THE DAYS
MAKE THE DAYS COUNT

30

THERE'S NOTHING I LOVED more than being a strange man in a strange land. There's nothing I loved more than ruffling a few feathers within, getting under the skin, playing the keys of the internal organs and capturing neurons as they soared across the universe of my mind.

This is exactly what I set out to do on my final day in Europe. I would take an intentional trip to the Abyss in order to dig deeper than ever before.

But first, I had a bike to ride.

Igor and I rode off together, now on two bikes instead of one, thankfully. It was an overcast day, but the clouds were thin enough so that we didn't notice. Occasionally a ray would poke through and slap me in the face. We pedaled off in our respective lanes and rang our bells to the soundtrack of life.

"I know of a cool place, follow me!" Igor shouted, hanging a sharp left.

Mopeds, scooters, and even cars zipped past as we rode. It was pure Amsterdam: organized chaos.

We came upon a neighborhood much quieter than the others, crossing a bridge to find brick apartment buildings along the canal—blood red shutters flung open at the sides of balconies. It was all very upscale with Audis parked carefully along curbs and heels clacking across cobblestone.

Igor and I pulled up to a metal fence and walked onto a dirt lot that seemed a joke in the ritzy surroundings. There was a small barn from which an older woman emerged—hair dry as hay, chicken in her arms.

"Can we enter?" asked Igor.

"Go right ahead!"

We walked through the barn, and on the other side was a petting zoo. By now I didn't know what to expect and prepared for the animals to start talking. There were chickens, lamas, pigs, rabbits, and a dog that chased them all. And two seven-year-old kids chasing the dog. Igor immediately picked up a rabbit, which didn't move a muscle. The only way I could tell it was alive was by looking at its black eyes and tiny teeth.

"Do you want to hold him?" Igor asked.

I picked up the rabbit and soon knew he was alive for another reason—a warm wetness seeping through my coat. But I tried not to mind because, after all, it felt nice to hold something so close—the instantaneous, unconditional love rarely witnessed between humans. Or maybe it was my own love that I felt, reflected in the poor creature along with the perception that such beauty is possible.

Out of nowhere, a lama approached and blew my mind. It stood alone from the pack—black with heavy, half-closed eyelids. Its jaw moved in loops, comically, characteristic of a fool lost for manners. It seemed to be speaking to me: *We are the same, you and I. Enjoy your big brain, but don't let it deceive you.*

After we met our cuddle quota, Igor and I walked our bikes down to the canal and observed the boats docked nearby. One was yellow and shaped like a submarine, and we mused at the idea of turning it into a Beatles-themed coffee shop.

"It was brought here from Paris," Igor said. "Used to be a strip club. I heard there's a pole and everything."

We sat and listened to the water, and then it was time to say goodbye. I wouldn't see Igor anymore. He was leaving town for a few days and left me the keys to his place.

We really did trust each other.

—

I CONTINUED RIDING in the direction of Nieuwmarkt, to where the Christmas market was underway similar to Brussels, with cabins covered in fake snow and shopkeepers bellowing hellos. Candy treats, packaged sweets, handbags and grab bags of lotions and smelly potions—what'll you have?

The world. They're selling the world.

And sure enough I bought a piece of it to take home to my family, as I didn't want to return empty handed.

In a t-shirt store, I asked for help from one of the clerks because I couldn't decide on a size or design for Bella. The clerk was Polish—blonde and skinny with long breasts, which led my eyes down and then back up to her sad face. It was strange because she looked sad but spoke happy.

"You live in Amsterdam?" I asked.

"Yes, for three years now."

"And what did you come for?"

"Opportunity. New way of life."

"And you?" she asked.

"This and that. I'm a bit of a traveler."

She smirked and picked out a shirt for me—gray with bright colored bicycle.

"What are you doing tonight?" she asked.

"That's what I'm trying to figure out."

"You like to smoke?"

"I came for the opportunities just like you," I smiled.

"I know the perfect place! Lots of Polish women there. Unlike the other places where you'll find cheap blunts and drunk men dancing on tables."

She wrote down the address of a cafe called Lost in Smoke. I figured if I'd find myself anywhere it would be there.

—

BAG IN HAND, feeling like a cheap Santa Claus, I hit the strip of Nieuwmarkt and turned down an alley, away from the lights—the flashing lights that played softly on the ground in front of me as I walked, fading until I saw only stone. And then they appeared again, and I looked up and saw the screaming cafe.

For a moment I hesitated.

The place was dark inside with crimson lighting and, sure enough, Polish women behind the bar. It wasn't very busy, save for one lone man about my age sitting Indian-style on a carpeted space, two older men at the bar rolling cigarettes, and a few Italians congregating in the corner. Light electronic music played.

I sat down and ordered a beer and joint, but the woman behind the bar explained that they did not sell marijuana because it was against the law to sell both marijuana and alcohol in the same establishment.

"But you can walk across the street and buy something to smoke, then bring it back?"

She posed it as a question, but there was no question about it. That's what I'd do. Minutes later I returned and looked around for a cozy spot to blaze up. In the back of the place there was an area with couches, and on the couches were a couple of British guys, both with buzz cuts. I sat down there and began to smoke.

"What are you fellas doing in Amsterdam?" I asked.

"You're lookin' at it," said the larger of the two.

"Just here to smoke?"

"Yeup."

"You're committed."

"Let me ask you . . . how many of these do you think we smoke a day, bloke?"

"I don't know. Couple?"

They looked at each other and laughed.

"Seven skunk joints, with ease."

"Impressive," I replied. "What do you think the future holds for avid smokers like yourselves? Think pot will get legalized in London so you don't have to keep making the journey?"

"Pssht. Twenty years maybe."

"Yeah, if we're still alive," chimed his friend.

I was astonished to hear this because they were no older than twenty. I thought about our generation and the coming generation and wondered if we were all just a bunch of cynics looking for the next kick.

—

EVENTUALLY MY five-minute friends got up to leave and I was left alone in the cushy space. This bothered me, so I moseyed back through the bar near the entrance where the cross-legged guy sat.

"Mind if I sit with you?"

"Go right ahead," he said. "Name's Zed. From Toronto, but originally Poland."

"Hence why you're here."

"Exactly. Could I have a swig of your beer?" asked Zed.

"Only if you'll smoke with me."

We drank beer and passed joints and kept on just as I had with my British friends, and once again I felt like I was getting high with the whole planet.

"How old are you?" asked Zed.

"Twenty-nine, and you?"

"Cool. Same."

He looked like me and I felt like I was facing a mirror. The entire world, the entire mass of the year and all its happenings reciprocated between two individuals.

"What do you do for a living?" I asked.

He blew out a big puff of smoke.

"Advertising. You?"

"I just kind of wander and write about what I see."

Zed smiled. He told me about all the perks he got at his job. The difference between a four thousand dollar, first class plane ride and a four hundred dollar coach seat—that is, that there really wasn't a difference. And the way he felt about advertising. The way he felt about modern society. It was all truth, and the more we smoked, the more truth came out.

"Johan," said Zed, "this place is about to close. We should head across the street to another bar."

By now I felt woozy from the weed and knew that I was close to my limit. Zed wasn't phased.

The next bar was like an alternate dimension—brighter and dingier. Zed bought two joints and some extra pot and rolling papers, and we sat down on a couple of stools with a shiny round table between us. Again the lighter ticked and lit the spliff, and I hit the cliff but did not fall off. Instead we passed back and forth like a game of Russian roulette to see who would drop first, and as we did, we dug deeper into the dense earth of existence.

"Do you ever think about *the path*, Zed?"

He nodded.

"You know what I mean?"

He nodded.

"There's something else," I said. "Something more to all of this. And you hit a point—a fork—where you can choose to seek it or ignore it."

He seemed to know what I was talking about because he kept nodding. Mostly he kept smoking and passing, and before long I was forgetting my words but knew that I HAD A POINT! That there was a point to the whole year. To this relentless spiral. To fear and trust, etc.

Head swirling and limbs rubber, I stopped Zed.

"I think your tolerance is way higher than mine, bud. How often do you smoke?"

"Every day."

We kept at it.

Cloudy mouths, clear brains, desert lips. The world on the tips of our tongues, spit through our lungs, adrift in the fluorescent sun. "I don't know about you but my heart's racing," Zed finally said.

And with that, we exchanged information and went separate ways.

—

I LEFT THE BAR and stumbled into the quiet street not knowing what time it was. There was an Italian pizza joint next to the bar, and as I passed I heard the baker in the window—

"HelLllloooOoooOoo!"

It was the clearest voice I'd ever heard. It sizzled like the grease he cooked with, like a studio recording fed through the speakers of his mouth. The ground bounced me right along, each stone a springboard singing crunchy songs beneath my soles.

Soon I came upon a crosswalk at a main intersection.
I stood there for a while, watching the signs blink.

WALK. DO NOT WALK.
WALK. DO NOT WALK.

Things got complicated.
At one point they blinked simultaneously—WALK *and* DO NOT WALK, red *and* green, and I was confused.

'Twas the season after all.

I started across only to hear the sound of engines.
To my left, blinding high beams barreling ahead.
I ran as fast as I could, and in my mind I saw myself running, as though I were watching the movie of my life.
"Oh shit, oh shit, oh shit!" I yelled.
An Asian man on the sidewalk looked at me, also yelling—"OH SHIT!!!"

WHHHHHHHOOOOOOOOOSSSSSHHHHH

I didn't know if I was dead or alive.

I saw my own dumb death—getting smashed by a truck for being stoned. Stoned and smashed, what a way to go!

Despite my uncertainties, I continued to look for my bus back to Igor's place. Except I couldn't find it. There was a vast plaza of bus platforms and I didn't know which to be on. I was lost, begging locals on benches for a hint of where I should be, but nobody knew where I should be—a purgatory of sorts. And I thought, 'What if this is hell? A place where the only torture is being stuck and lonely?'

No one knew where I should be.

I was trying my best to ask proper questions, but all the bus drivers smirked without saying a word. At one point I came across a driver who mesmerized me because, like Zed, we seemed to share the same face. Yet again I was reminded that all human beings are one in the same. I couldn't shake this idea because I kept seeing the same traits in people— their appearance, their eyes, and spirits—features recurring in varying combinations like a puzzle rearranged, except you can pick out the pieces you've seen before. It's weird. We are beautifully weird.

Finally, while wandering round and round, I met people who were willing to help me—a German couple who led me to a map and even routed me to the correct station. But then I realized that I didn't have enough money for the bus fare.

The man muttered something in German and handed me a two-euro piece. I gazed upon it as though it were a blood diamond.

"Wow. Good Karma to you guys, man! Good Karma!!"

He rolled his eyes and walked off with his girlfriend.

It dawned on me. The guy thinks I'm a bum.

I looked down at my finger-less gloves and saw the shiny coin in my cloth hand. Then I remembered limping around Paris.

But I didn't feel like a bum. Just looked like one.

Anyhow, I adjusted my scarf and found my way to the correct station. And as I stood there breathing the black air, I suddenly felt eyes upon me. There were men standing around, of all ages and ethnicities, watching me with slow-blinking eyes. Some had women at their sides, and the women had the same faces as the men.

"What is this?" I mumbled.

"Sorry?" one of them asked.

"No, I'm sorry."

"Sorry?" asked another.

"No, *I'm* sorry."

"Don't be sorry. What are you sorry for?" they asked in unison.

It was the pot, I thought.

Then the bus approached, squealing to a halt. And when the driver belched out a laugh, I knew that I was at the wrong station again.

"This bus runs to Belgium!" he said, smiling with twinkly brown teeth.

Round and round. A child on a constant carousel, minus the music. Looking for a parent or a familiar face (but not too familiar), or a big red stop button.

Fuck it.

Freeze me in Amsterdam. Just kill my brain so that I don't know that I'm doing the same thing over and over. So that I can't remember what I'm missing out on.

Across the plaza, I saw another platform with lots of people bunched together. I walked over to stand with them. There was a woman next to me wearing a black coat, her back to me—black hair flowing past her knees. It was long and I saw a microscopic-me climbing it.

She turned around. "Hi."

"Hey."

"Are you lost?" she asked.

I was speechless, focusing on her features.

"Laredo girl?"

"What?"

But she looked like her!

"Where are you from?" I asked.

"Well, I work at the Victoria Hotel," she said. "But I'm originally from Italy."

"Why are you here in Amsterdam?" I asked.

"Different way of life."

She rolled a cigarette and tucked it between her lips.

By God. An Italian Laredo girl with the positive energy of Valerie and Aurélie rolled into the cigarette of herself; burning with Sage's posture and Francine's warmth and Helena's galaxy.

It started to rain.

She pulled up her hood and it made her even more beautiful because it drew my focus to her eyes, which seemed to blink slowly, and I wasn't sure whether it was my high or if she was beating her heart at me.

"So why are *you* in Amsterdam?" she asked.

"For moments like this."

"Standing in the rain waiting for a bus?"

"Yep."

"I like this, too," she said, spinning through the water with outstretched arms. She moved her fingers around and I watched them dance in the light. Closer and closer she came towards me, laughing as though this were the only thing ever worth laughing about. And then she just stood there in silence like an exhibit at a human soul museum.

Without a single thought, I kissed her.

Her lips were cold and wet, but it all quickly warmed, and as I wrapped my arms around this woman's body I felt like I had known her my entire life.

On the surface, I didn't even know her name.

Didn't know her age, whether she had a boyfriend, or husband, or children. Her favorite color, music, vacation spot. Whether she wore glasses before bed or had any tattoos or odd birthmarks. The way that she liked her eggs, or whether she was allergic to eggs, or whether she preferred them white, brown, or organic and cage-free. Whether or not she had a good childhood. Whether she had ambitions. Whether she painted, dreamed, stared at the stars like Paulette. Whether she flirted with other guys every night at this same stop, rain or shine.

None of it mattered.

I knew that she was full of love.

Air brakes hissed. A bus in front of us.

"That's my ride," she said, handing me the remainder of her soggy cigarette. "I think yours is the next."

And off she went, taking the universe with her, leaving me to wonder if I'd ever find it again. I smiled because I knew I would.

It's everywhere after all.

about the author

Steve Nahaj's work is based on his travels, which include exploring the US via semi-truck and mingling with bohemians in Paris. The follow-up prequel to this debut is called *Other Lives for the Desert*. Steve has also written a series of poetry chapbooks titled *Substantial*. He lives in Berlin, Germany with his wife and a large monstera plant named Fran.

connect

Social: @nahajguy
Website: runawaypoets.com

acknowledgments

I owe immense gratitude to a number of people for helping me put ink to page. To start, my loving family. Mom and Dad, for your support that has manifested in so many ways. Kelly, for our late night living room talks that ignited inspiration. Brea, for keeping me young. John, for keeping me fiery. All of my barista brethren in the Rocky Mountains, serving world class espresso and wisdom. The Spoken Word and Paris Lit Up communities, for giving me the unconditional opportunity to perform with full passion. Narelle A. Sheehan, for your brilliant creative coaching. Susanne, thank you for always being there, and for being the first to lay eyes on this text. Matt Appleby, for your edits. And to friends, readers, and everyone everywhere: Enthusiasm. Here and now and forever. Is my wish for you.

www.ingramcontent.com/pod-product-compliance
Lightning Source LLC
Chambersburg PA
CBHW052034240626
47153CB00006B/2074